Praise for
Sweet Justice

"I loved this one. Ms. Jeffries always gives her readers a look into a world of the rich and famous. Just when I had a question about why something was happening or not, her dialog and narration would satisfy my need."

—Carole O'Neal, Author

"Reading and totally immersed in this wonderful work of art. As always, Ms. Jeffries' novels are fascinating, and I am able to read for pure enjoyment!"

—Barb Ryan, Author

"Once again, Ann Jeffries has hit a home run with *Sweet Justice*. Her characters are so down to earth with their feelings and commitments yet they live in a world of privilege most of us will never know. If only the real world could copy this book what a great place it would be. I like how she updated anyone who hasn't read some of her other books so they know what is happening. She doesn't make it too complicated but inputs the necessary facts to make this a stand-alone book."

—Rebecca Bridges, Author

Copyright © 2018 by Ann Jeffries
www.annjeffries.net
annjeffriesauthor@gmail.com
All rights reserved
Printed and Bound in the United States of America

Published and Distributed By
New View Literature
820 67th Avenue N, #7603
Myrtle Beach, South Carolina 29572
annjeffries@newviewliterature.com
www.newviewliterature.com

Cover and Interior design: TWA Solutions
ISBN: 978-1-941603-05-5 Print
ISBN: 978-1-941603-67-3 eBook
Library of Congress Control Number: 2014947433

First printing December 2018

For inquiries, contact the publisher.

ANN JEFFRIES

Sweet Justice

Book Three in the Chi-Town Girls Trilogy

Another Family Reunion Novel
In The Wisdom of the
Ancestors Series
— Book 15 —

ACKNOWLEDGMENTS

The Creator

The Ancestors

Jenetha Hollis, Editor

Jessica Tilles, Book Designer, TWA Solutions

The Carolina Forest Authors' Group

The Carolina Forest Library, Horry County, SC

Faithful family, friends, and fans

The struggle for literary perfection continues and
shall never cease.

I remain faithfully yours,

Ann Jeffries

The Justice Family

Miguel

Juan

Keenen

Tyson

Diaz

Bouchard "Butch"

Constantina "Tina"

Redman "Big Red" Justice
m.
Marguerite Alonza Dela Vega

Reverend Ellis Justice
m.
Anna Lettie Outlaw

Rafael Alonzo Dela Vega
m.
Alicia Diaz Vazquez

. . . but you are so

Quaint no pun

Could still

Stay legal

And do sweet justice

Drdamiang

Prologue

He remembered . . .

She busted into the club like she owned the joint.

Heads quickly turned and murmurs rose amid building enthusiastically-lively applause. Newspaper photographers and other reporters scurried ahead of her frantically snapping pictures, shouting questions while her security team cleared the way.

She ignored it all.

Her entrance was an academy-award performance in and of itself. Restaurant patrons quickly got to their feet in roof-raising adulation and admiration like hundreds of geese rising from a lake, noisily squawking and honking, wings loudly beating the air. One would have thought she was giving out thousand-dollar bills for all the attention focused on her. Yet, no one could deny she looked like a cool million, freshly minted in her money-green, shimmering sheath.

Initially, he thought all of the hoopla was over the very popular male matinee idol and heartthrob, Miguel Menendez-Gaza. He had just won best male actor for his role in the latest film her company, Sweet Justice, produced, and he was her escort for the evening. However, the crowd quickly disabused him of that notion when they started chanting "Sweet Justice" in a rhythmic rendition of the title song from the soundtrack of her movie. The blockbuster film won a slew of other awards, too. The music was scored and sung by the top artist of the year, Matt Kennedy, and accompanied by singing sensation, Loretta. They were both award winners that evening. Even the club's jazz combo altered its itinerary to accompany the crowd. Mr. Movie Magic was grinning at her like he was auditioning for a toothpaste ad, but he was truly outclassed by the vision at his side, Ms. Constantina Anna Alonza Justice.

1

Nicholas "Nico" Collins laid aside the glossy eight-by-ten picture of Constantina Justice, leaned back into the rich, thick folds of his comfortable ergonomic, conference-room chair, steepled his long, strong fingers, and refocused his attention on his production vice president's commentary. The man had been going on now for about ten minutes and Nico's thoughts had wandered back to the night, nearly eighteen months ago in Los Angeles.

He was in town for business meetings with several different ad agency executives and representatives. The agency he was with that night, the third and last one he was scheduled to meet with, really wanted his company, NICO Communications, as a client. Much the same as the other companies had done, the advertising agency's president and other top executives laid out the red carpet for him and his team at an exclusive, LA nightclub and restaurant, complete with two women who possessed incredible physical... attributes. Nico, his Chief of Operations, Phil Reed, and his in-house legal counsel, Zackary "Zack" Cooper, were wined and dined sufficiently all week and were discussing proposed ad campaigns when they were interrupted by Constantina Justice's arrival with her entourage trailing her. The boisterous applause and adulation were so loud and raucous they had eclipsed everyone's ability to talk over the din.

He had noticed Constantina Justice and even momentarily appreciated what a beauty and fine figure of a woman she was, but nearly spread eagle in the round, plush, sofa-like booth, his attention had been diverted by the sultry, dark-eyed charmer on his right, whose long, lithe fingers were creeping up his thigh and dangerously close to his manhood. The woman definitely was in contention for a starring role as his wife-for-a-night interlude, but so was the light chocolate vision of loveliness on his left who was strumming his ear with her own breathless song.

Funny how he couldn't remember either of those women's names now, considering the fact he had spent eight hours of erotic intimacy with them both that night, but Constantina Justice he remembered vividly and in great detail. Something about her radiated power, confidence, and sensuality all at the same time. Generally, he preferred his women more on the body-by-Fischer, brain-by-Mattel side. With such women, there were no complications. No strings attached. Ships that passed in the night, and he liked it that way. Still, a woman, like Constantina Justice, was an entirely different matter. She was no flavor of the moment.

She was dangerous with a capital D.

To his way of thinking, Constantina Justice was high energy, high profile, high society, and high maintenance all the way. No, if he was going to have to convince her to move her production company, popular television and radio talk shows to his new satellite-delivered network, it was going to take a bit of work. It might be simpler to do a takeover and be done with it. He would buy Sweet Justice Production instead of taking time to entice her to move to his network. Regardless, he intended to get his way; he always did. The question was whether he was up to the task right now. He was extremely busy and had a lot of deals in various stages of completion. Yet, he had never shrunk from any challenge whether it was on the gridiron, in the boardroom or bedroom. Still, Constantina Justice created a new playing field. From all accounts, she was just like him. His equal in every respect.

That's what made her even more dangerous . . . and intriguing.

"Nico, I've done everything I can to convince Ms. Justice's people to let me talk directly with her, but nothing seems to work. They protect her like she's the Hope Diamond. I hate to admit it, boss, but, after six months of trying to reach her, I've come up empty," Jerrod Duncan whined, mopping his brow, and flushed with exasperation. "You may have to step in personally. I don't know how else to get to her."

Nico considered Jerrod as one of the best negotiators in the business. He was as tenacious as a Rottweiler. Over the last eight years, every contract Jerrod went after for NICO Enterprises International, he had gotten, but this potential contract with Sweet Justice Production to join Nico's new, satellite-distributed, broadcast and cable television network, had the man stymied.

That night, eighteen months ago, instead of hiring the ad agency, he bought the top two of three in hostile takeovers, fired the presidents and most of the senior officers, overhauled their operations, and combined the companies as one of many subsidiaries under NICO Enterprises. Impressed and inspired by Nico's heads-will-roll approach, the remaining personnel had his advertising arm bringing in new business at a steady and impressive rate.

Perhaps he could do the same thing with Sweet Justice Productions. After all, how hard could it be to pull several production companies together to create programming for his new satellite and transponder?

He earned the title "Corporate Raider" and owed no one an apology for his avarice. He gobbled up all forms of communication entities: newspapers, magazines, radio and television stations, and internet platforms. He could buy a few more production companies to combine with Sweet Justice and shape it into what he wanted.

Still, Nico picked up the glossy picture again and studied the headshot of Constantina Justice. That sensuous grin on her full lips, the mystery in her sultry eyes, the high cheekbones under a supple-looking, sun-kissed brown skin, a narrow nose, and loose, lazy, curly dark auburn hair feathered and layered around her oval face and onto her neck and shoulders all seemed to combine to say *I dare you*.

Nico tore his eyes away from her mesmerizing ones in the photograph and looked toward his head talent agent. "What do you think, Gail? Is it worth me personally taking my time to go after Sweet Justice Productions?"

Gail Simons' grin was almost feral. She took off her designer eyeglasses and pinned him with a silently, sultry gaze. "She's good, I'll admit. Her Q rating topped all of the other talk show hosts in twenty-six of the forty major television markets we researched. Number two and climbing in the remaining markets. Her Nobel Peace Prize for the exposé on the plight of women in Third World countries was well deserved and the Academy Award for her movie docudrama adaptation just busted all records. She's got name recognition and wide audience appeal, which, I might add, includes most age groups. She's a megastar. That's somewhat of a surprise because her television show, Sweet Justice, doesn't cover high-profile court cases. Rather, she turns her investigative teams loose to find little known domestic and foreign cases where justice might be denied were it not for the publicity she brings to the international or domestic courtroom arena. That approach appeals across the board in all ethnic groups and socioeconomic strata as well. Because she deals on a grass-roots level, she's seen as a female, twenty-first-century, legendary Ed Bradley. She gets results without making a spectacle of herself or the court cases."

"Do I hear a but, Gail?"

"Nico, she's no day at the beach. Tina Justice is tough, tenacious, and smart. She rolls up her sleeves and digs in with both hands. She kicks butt and takes no prisoners. She did that exposé on the plight of women and young girls in African countries personally and it earned her the highest Presidential Award, the Medal of Freedom, for meritorious contribution to world peace. She turned the tide of world opinion and earned a Nobel Prize in the process along with a Congressional Gold Medal. Add to that," she clicked off each point with her fingers, "that she's A-political, publicly squeaky clean, intensely loyal to her family and friends, and a fiercely private person. She's also an experienced lawyer who isn't a bottom feeder. That is to say, she got hers the hard way: she earned it. Is she worth it?" she absently shrugged. "You tell me. The question is how badly do you want this new network of yours to instantly reach into the high ratings and compete with other established networks? With Constantina Justice and her television and radio conglomerate on board, it's a no-brainer. She's Academy proof and money in the bank."

"We should also mention we're not the only game in town going after her," Colton Adams, Nico's business vice president added. "Some of our major competition for her show comes from the ranks of the established network conglomerates: ABC, CBS, NBC, MSNBC, CNN, etc. At least six or seven other networks are trying to get to her, including the BBC."

"Not to overlook the fact her show is currently carried on the largest television and radio network in broadcasting today. No one knows the terms and condition of her current contract except it will expire this year," Gail interjected. "The number one network has the highest rated shows and Ms. Justice's show tops the list. They're not about to let Sweet Justice Productions get away from them without a helluva fight.

"Yeah. Right," Zackary Taylor, Nico's in-house chief legal counsel, snorted. "If Tina wants out, she will eat them alive. I should know. We dated a few times when I was with the law firm Alexander, Carter, Chandler, *et. al.* Two of her best buds, Cheryl Lawrence, Peter Brock, and I worked together at the firm before I came on board here. They set me and Tina up on a date a couple of times." He leaned back in his chair, thoughtfully stroking his chin. "I can attest to the fact there is no way to predict what Tina Justice will do, boss, except whatever the hell she wants."

"What other options do we have to fill that two-hour time slot, Tyrone?" Nico asked. He wasn't convinced Sweet Justice Production was worth his time or the apparent trouble it would take to woo Constantina Justice into switching networks.

"Several. Since NICO Communications will be the first, satellite-delivered, all-digital, interactive, video network we've got producers and production companies beating down our doors to get onto the launch of the new satellite transponders and channels. Some are good, some are better than others, but for the prime-time slot, Sweet Justice would sweep the ratings. As Gail said, she's money in the bank."

Nico turned to his accountant. "All right, Pensy, speaking of money, if I go after Sweet Justice Productions, how much is this going to cost?"

Roman Pansy squinted through his coke-bottle thick glasses at the figures on the page before him. He passed a sheet of paper to Nico, his hand shaking a bit. "It's all there, Nico," he croaked as if the dollar amounts were about to raise up from the page and attack him.

Although it was a considerable package amount, including stock options, bonuses, and other perks, Nico didn't flinch when he saw the bottom line. He was accustomed to big numbers and this was bigger than usual. Never doing anything in half measures, Nico went top shelf with any deal he cut or brokered. Something he had learned from his father, Jock Collins, among other things.

Nico had grown up with never more than two dimes to rub together at any time. His father never married his mother and she died when he was born. The man had made an art out of finding ways not to work. From the moment Nico had drawn his first breath, Jock Collins, had found a way to use him in his con games. Jock played the role of the bereaved husband with a small child to raise alone. Women had eaten it up and swallowed his line of bull right along with it. He and his father had lived in more women's homes than Nico could remember. As soon as Jock settled in with a new woman, he was already looking for the next goodbye. He would rely on the kindness of strangers until the next woman came along with a little bit more to offer. The next woman always had more.

Top shelf.

Big for his age, Nico was fifteen when the first of his father's lovers took him to her bed behind his philandering father's back. She was nearly twenty years his senior. Soon the woman had put his father out, but kept Nico around calling him her "nephew" in public. However, what she did with him at night in the privacy of the bedroom would have been considered illegal in forty-nine out of fifty states. He could write his own **Fifty Shades of Grey** book. The woman, Lana Norton, a widow and wealthy, would take the starring role as the dominatrix. Still, she saw to his every need and put him in a local private school. Sadly, it was the first fairly stable home Nico experienced.

Later, Nico won a football scholarship to play at a Big Ten university. When he graduated from college, he was drafted in the first round to play in the NFL where he made a fortune. Always a good student in the bedroom and the classroom, he had taken full advantage of his education, both academic and social. During the offseason, he had gotten his MBA and started investing his money in lucrative businesses and brokering deals for friends and acquaintances he had made while in the game. At the top of his football career, eight years ago, he had quit the profession and started his own company, NICO Enterprises International (NICO-EI).

He still brokered big deals, becoming somewhat of a boy wonder, and grew wealthier in the process. Nico Enterprises International was a conglomerate; a partnership with many professional male and female sports figures and athletes, but NICO Communications, a new satellite-delivered broadcasting/cablecasting network, was Nico's alone. The company owned the satellite and would sell or lease its more than one hundred transponders to other entities. Nico would use a few of the transponders to launch his own television networks and shows. However, for that, he needed to create his own production company. That's why he zeroed in on Sweet Justice Productions because, from all indications, it was the best in the business.

Women had used Nico's body and he had used theirs, as a result, he never grew close to any one woman, not even Lana. Now it didn't matter that he had never felt love from a woman. He could have any woman he wanted for the asking and usually did. No woman had ever told him no in the bedroom or in the boardroom. The fact Constantina Justice had said no to offers to even talk about moving her show to his new digital satellite had him intrigued. Intelligence reports indicated NICO Communications was offering more money for her production company and shows than any other competitor and with greater exposure, both nationally and internationally. Why she was refusing to even consider his offer was a wonder. Yet, he never let such things stand in his way.

He put an end to his meeting and walked into his private office. A man stood looking out of the picture-sized windows talking quietly on a cell phone. He turned when Nico entered.

Nico regarded the tall, striking man who resembled the actor Sendhil Ramamurthy from the shows Heroes and

Covert Affairs. This man held some of the top secrets in the world in his unhackable databases. Slade Richardson had begun his intelligence career after five years as a US Navy SEAL. He was recruited into a super-secret organization that didn't have the benefit of initials but had the authority to operate worldwide granted by the G8. Nico had met Slade, quite by accident, more than fifteen years earlier in a country where they shouldn't have been and would have been killed if their identities had been discovered. They helped each other out fighting back to back with bare knuckles and Taekwondo. Since that time, they rarely saw each other but were a phone call away if one or the other needed a favor. Nico had called Slade to find personal information on Tina Justice.

Slade ended his call and extended his hand for a shake.

"Slade," Nico said, accepting his hand.

"How are you, good buddy?"

"Makin' it. You?"

"Like you. Makin' the donuts."

"You saw the meeting?"

"I did. Is that Gail Simons legal?"

Nico laughed. "She's older than she looks."

"Married or otherwise engaged?"

"Not married, but the rest," he shrugged. "I don't have a clue."

"I'll figure it out."

"Speaking of impossible quests, what can you tell me I don't already know about Tina Justice?"

"If you're thinking hostile takeover . . ."

"I am," Nico said nodding.

"Forget about it. Constantina Justice is single, the seventh child, and only daughter of Redmond and Marguerite

Justice. Redmond is known as Big Red in the refuse and recycling collection industries and in the trucking and roll-off businesses. He has fleets of trash collection trucks and exclusive contracts with many corporate offices to collect and destroy sensitive documents. They also serve condo and apartment complexes, hospitals with medical waste and colleges and universities. The company uses much of the non-toxic refuse as a part of his recycling business. They lease dump trucks, cement trucks, and other heavy rolling equipment to builders and leases his roll-offs to collect construction debris. There is a product recycle store he owns on the south side of the city that does a brisk business. They specialize in deconstructing old homes before the wrecking ball is brought in. One of his sons, the oldest one, Miguel, runs that operation. Most of what he collects ends up as asphalt for highways or concrete for high-rise office buildings. His trucks are well known in Illinois, Ohio, and Indiana. They make a statement. You can't miss them. They're not gas powered and they're bright red in color.

"Big Red fought off remnants of the old Chicago mobs, but he didn't do it alone. Like his daughter, he's the seventh child of his parents, Ellis and Anna Lettie Outlaw Justice. Reverend Ellis Justice is the senior minister of the largest and most influential church in Chicago. Redmond's brothers are no slackers either. One of them, the oldest, is the current Chicago Police Commissioner and he came up through the ranks.

"Justice, Inc. may appear to be a small business by some standards, but my report outlines the bios of the rest of the Justice clan. They are legion, private, and protective.

"Tina's mother, Marguerite Alonza Dela Vega Justice, descends from Spanish royalty. Marguerite came to America from Argentina at age seventeen to study nursing, much to her parents' dismay. Marguerite's father is Raphael Dela Vega, a direct descendant of Spain and royalty. Currently, he is an Argentinian Ambassador. His wife, Marguerite's mother, is Alicia Diaz Vazquez Dela Vega. She was the daughter of a prominent businessman in Argentina. She was featured in a beauty contest at the age of fourteen. Raphael was twenty and asked for her hand in marriage on the spot. Four years later they married.

"Nevertheless, on her first day of class in Chicago and unfamiliar with the streets, Marguerite plowed into the rear of one of Redmond's big, red trucks. It happened to be his first truck and he was driving it that day. According to Justice family folklore, he took one look at the little Argentinian spitfire and was her husband in less than a year. Seven children later, Tina was born. Marguerite is a Registered Nurse who does home-care visits administering medicine to those who can't get out to a doctor's office or clinic. The Dela Vega family is also large, influential in both Spain and Argentina, and connected in ways not discussed openly.

"Although the Justice family could afford to live anywhere they chose, Constantina and her six older brothers grew up on the south side of Chicago with all of the benefits at their disposal. They learned street survival skills right along with proper decorum in private schools. Their parents have a close-knit community of friends; all Southsiders. Tina's BFFs are Federal Court Justice Kristen Catherine Bryant and her husband Thomas Ashton Marshal, III, Esq.; Kristen's two brothers, Clarence, Jr. and George Bryant, both sports and entertainment lawyers, and her father, Illinois State Supreme Court Judge Clarence Bryant, Sr."

"I know George Bryant. We were in the NFL together."

"Then you may know Tina's other BFFs, Cheryl Lawrence, and her husband, Peter Brock; also both very highly sought-after attorneys. Cheryl's an only child and her parents are the syndicated columnists and television personalities, Farrow Lawrence and Helen Kendall Lawrence. Peter's parents are Peter and Cassia Brock, Senior. The elder Brock owns a chain of neighborhood laundry and dry cleaning establishments which also serve restaurants and hospitals throughout Illinois.

"The elder Justice, Bryant, Brock, and Laurence families have been a tightly-knit cluster of friends since they were in college together. All twelve of the Justice, Bryant, Brock and Laurence children were raised together on the same South-Side Chicago street, mostly by Cassia Brock, who was the only stay at home mother. They are extremely protective of each other. They play fair, but they don't *play* if you get my meaning. They, too, are extremely well connected.

"Beyond Tina's life-long friends and immediate families, she's very close to Supreme Court Justice Vivian Alexander Montgomery, one of the wealthiest women in the world. Her husband is former basketball icon Chuck Montgomery, now an expert, emergency room physician. Vivian and Tina were in undergrad at Spelman together with their pal Dr. Savannah Logan Flack. Savannah's husband is the US United Nations Ambassador Nathan Flack, Esq. Dr. Logan-Flack is also the sister of former Ambassador Jefferson Logan who is married to one of the Hawkins's family heiresses, Dakota Sinclair, aka LaiLoni Skai Hawkins. LaiLoni's younger sister, JaiHonnah is a world-renowned architect and civil and structural engineer who is married to former basketball icon J. Roderick Baylor, also known as JRock. Both JaiHonnah and LaiLoni are Tina's pals and were at Spelman with Tina, Cheryl, Kristen, Savannah, and Vivian. They are all still very close. Roderick and JaiHonnah head one of the largest companies in the world, BlackHawk Global, on behalf of her father, Ambassador Jake Hawkins.

"As I said, Tina Justice has got an impressive, but a tightly-knit band of family and friends. If you attempted a takeover, you could lose everything.

"In her own right, Tina Justice is very wealthy and extremely intelligent. Beyond her family and friends, she has enviable connections on every conceivable level. If you decide to approach her, you'd better bring your A-game and be determined to win, because there is little if anything she needs or wants she can't have for the asking . . . or taking. Your head on a silver platter included."

Slade didn't mention he had a few ways to reach Tina Justice through her inner circle. His best friend from childhood, Thomas Ashton Marshall, III, Esquire, and Vivian Alexander Montgomery used his investigation and security company exclusively. Thomas, being the husband of Tina's BFF, Judge Kristen Catherine Bryant Marshall. Even back in his clandestine days, Vivian's first husband, basketball great, Derrick Jackson, had been an outlier; a member of the super-secret organization, The Nursery. Derrick died unexpectedly of a heart condition and his incredible multibillion-dollar estate transferred to his young wife, Vivian. Derrick and Ashton invested in Richardson Investigations and Security as silent partners, giving him the venture capital he needed to start his business on a firm, financial basis. He was also in business with Vivian's older brother, Kenneth Alexander, head of the telecommunications company, CompuCorrect Global and her younger brother Gregory Alexander, the basketball phenom turned Wall Street tycoon with his own brokerage NYC house, CTI. He and Vivian were close friends through several connections.

There were connections within connections he would never divulge even to his friend Nico. Still, Nico was a man who knew how and where to get what he needed. He would find out on his own what he needed to know and value it more rather than have it spoon fed to him.

Nico again picked up the glossy picture of Tina Justice. Her frozen image didn't do her justice, but the expression on her face screamed *I dare you.*

He was no fool. It was abundantly clear he could not go the overt hostile takeover route. He recognized that it was too risky. Rather, he would have to go after her the old fashioned way: up front and personal. Still, based on what he had learned so far, he would take the dare.

2

"Give me a friggin' break, Claude!" Constantina Justice flared as she marched back and forth in her well-appointed office at the Sweet Justice Productions' studio with hands on her impressive hips, glaring at her publicist. "I don't have time for this foolishness!"

"Tina, baby..." Claude tried to cajole her, splaying his hands in supplication.

Tina skidded to a stop. "Don't 'Tina, baby,' me, Claude Hopper! I've told you more than a few times I do not want my privacy invaded!"

"They just want to do one of those homes-of-the-rich-and-famous exposés, Tina. One hour maybe two and they'll be in and out of your Sheridan Avenue estate in no time. I promise," he said crossing his heart with a hope to die sign. "I didn't even mention your other homes."

A perfectly shaped eyebrow raised, her arms going akimbo. "What word did you not understand, Claude? No or no?" she said through clenched teeth.

Claude sighed, shaking his head. "You spent all of that money rehabilitating and remodeling that old mansion and those grounds into a showplace, but you won't let the media in to see what you've done to the place that's now listed on the National Registry of Historic Homes. It's one of the top one hundred largest remaining single-family homes in the United States that hasn't been converted into a hotel. All the media can do is the flyovers and you've even put a halt to that."

She merely stared at him.

"All right, Tina," he breathed out in frustration. He had been at it for fifteen minutes. Claude sensed Tina's patience ran out fourteen minutes earlier. "No at-home interview . . ."

A knock on the door and Bruce Joyner, Tina's executive assistant, stuck his head in. "Tina, you have thirty minutes before you have to be on set and four important calls waiting."

"Take messages, Bruce, and tell the program director I'm on my way down to hair and makeup . . ."

"Uh, Tina, one of the calls is from the president and CEO of NICO Communications. He's been trying to reach you for two weeks. He wants an appointment . . ."

"NICO?" she said, her gaze swinging from Bruce to Claude. If looks could kill, he'd be dead. "I told you I'm not interested in meeting with them, Claude. Why are they still calling?"

Claude blanched under her penetrating glare. "Tina, they want to make you a deal you simply shouldn't refuse to hear."

Hands on hips again, she glared at Claude and her voice dropped dangerously low. "Handle it, Claude. I don't know why you brought their deal to me in the first place. That's not your role with Sweet Justice Productions. Still, I'm not taking a meeting with them or moving my show to their network. Is that understood?"

His hands flew up in supplication again trying to placate what he recognized as her rapidly flagging patience with him.

"They sought me out because of our relationship. What do you want me to tell them, Tina?" he whined. "It's a very good offer. Stock options, unlimited budget, perks that boggle the mind. The press and news media are eating this up. According to all indications, NICO is going to be on top in no time. It's a new, high-energy, high-class, satellite-distributed, broadcasting and cablecasting interactive network and it's going to be . . ."

Tina casually leaned her butt against her hand-carved, African mahogany-wood desk, crossed her ankles, folded her arms under her breasts, and then glared at him. "You know, Claude," she began conversationally at length, "we've worked very well together over the past five years. I'm sure when your contract with me comes up for consideration in a few months . . ." she let the implications hang while she smiled viciously. "As my publicist, since you need direction on what to say to Nico Com, tell them you'll be making a career-ending decision with Sweet Justice Productions if they call me again."

Claude swallowed hard. Sweat popped on his bibulous nose. "All right, all right," he said to Tina, frustrated. Tina didn't make idle threats. Then to Bruce, he said, "I'll handle the call."

"Fine," Tina said, grabbing her notes for today's show. She marched out of her office suite into a very busy hallway.

"Women!" Claude fumed after making sure Tina was out of the door before he cursed a blue streak and flipping her the bird. If it wasn't for the fact Tina Justice was his biggest client and he had big money riding on this deal, he'd walk out on her the way he had his last three wives. That was a close one, though, he thought as he nervously wiped his brow. Generally, he could manipulate women at will as he had done to the newspapers and tabloids, but not with Tina. She could scale him like a fish with a look or slice and dice him like a Ginza Master. He was her publicist and that was all she was going to allow him to be. Well, Claude had other ideas, he mused taking on false courage as he straightened his tie and stiffened his shoulders. He sat in Tina's chair, propped his feet up on her desk, and reached for the telephone. He was a man, after all, and no woman had ever gotten the better of Claude Hopper!

Beside and slightly ahead of Tina was Chicago native BoBo Carter, a man standing six feet, ten inches tall and two hundred and forty-five pounds of molten masculinity who led the way down the crowded hallway. A chest a yard wide, a black, shiny, bald head, and two small gold loops in his left earlobe, he was black on black in black with a T-shirt that silently screamed, **MOVE** in bright white letters. Everyone did. No one crossed BoBo Carter and lived to brag about it. If the sight of those muscles covering every inch of his body didn't impress, the scowl on his face did.

People nodded and smiled at Tina as she traversed the hallway taking three steps to each one of BoBo's just to keep up with him. She'd seen the wary look on the faces of many people who came within sight of BoBo. He looked like Mr. Clean in Black with not a smile anywhere in the vicinity of his face. What people didn't know and she would never reveal, was that BoBo's bell had been rung too many times on the football field. As a result, he had been taken advantage of and robbed of his football earnings to the point where he was nearly broke. He had gotten into a skirmish outside a bar and his former teammate, George Bryant, an attorney, came to his rescue in court. Since then, the Justice family and friends looked after BoBo and his welfare.

BoBo, without a word, opened the door to the studio's make-up room, checked to ensure no intruder was inside, and then stepped aside to let Tina enter. Rayne Pepper, a svelte, six-foot Black man with angelic good looks, silky black hair, smiled broadly as they entered. Only then did BoBo's dour expression change into one of pure lust. Rayne winked at BoBo, and he returned the gesture forming a soundless puckered-lips kiss.

"Would you two cut it out." Tina exhaled. "You act like newlyweds."

One hand on his narrow, nearly nonexistent hips, Rayne arched a fine eyebrow. "Tsk, tsk. My, we are really testy today, aren't we, hon?"

Tina rolled her eyes to the ceiling. "Rayne, don't start with me today. I'm in no mood."

"Well, Tina, darling, if you had a man," he grinned at BoBo, "like my lover, you wouldn't come in here with your face all cracked up looking like an African-influenced Picasso painting on Prozac. You know it takes more muscles to frown than it does to smile. Your frown muscles are working overtime, chile. I haven't seen a smile on your face since you dumped what's-his-name, the one with the big . . ."

"Rayne . . ." she warned in a low, menacing tone.

Rayne's mouth opened and then snapped closed. He rolled his eyes and flitted his hand breezily in the air. "All right, darling, let's see whether I can work any magic on this otherwise lovely face of yours today." With that, he started to work.

Tina permitted herself a few moments to relax while Rayne worked on her face and hair. Her relationship with Claude Hopper was becoming more worrisome and problematic than beneficial. After five years he should know her privacy was tantamount to the search for the Holy Grail in her life. Lately, Claude had been encouraging her to do more public appearances which she felt weren't necessary or in her best interest. This new stunt . . . and how she felt about it . . . letting some tabloid do an at-home interview with the *real* Tina Justice was the latest in a long line of unacceptable public relations displays. How she spent her private time was no one's business but her own.

After her hair, face, and wardrobe sittings were completed, Tina entered the ice-cold studio set and took her position standing before a colorful world map under the hot studio lights. The theme song for the show started as the floor director counted down and then cued Tina. She looked into the red eye beside the camera lens and smiled.

"Justice delayed, is justice denied," she began, "but sweet justice will not be put aside. Greetings, I'm Tina Justice and welcome to today's investigative reports on the American legal system and world events . . ." On cue, shifting to camera two, she continued with the show as trouble spots of little renown were highlighted on the map.

3

Nico was dog tired and royally pissed when he wheeled the rented Lexus SUV up into the cul-de-sac where Sweet Justice Productions' studio and offices were housed. The four-story building was all smoked glass and mirrors on the outside with its own front courtyard, nicely landscaped with trees, shrubbery and flowers, and cobblestone road and driveway. He couldn't appreciate the beauty of his surroundings in his present state of mind.

After being told by one of Constantina Justice's minions, Claude Hopper, he would have to "sweeten the pot" to get Tina's attention, because his bid for her show was far below what other networks were offering, Nico had his leased Adventurer Executive Airline jet readied and flew from New York City to Chicago that very same day. Instead of landing at O'Hare International Airport, which had been stacked up for hours, he had wisely chosen to land at Chicago's Midway Airport. After picking up his rental car and setting the GPS system directions to Sweet Justice's offices outside of Chicago, he had driven in heavy downtown traffic and then clogged highways. Why the building was located so far outside of the city he didn't know, but after getting lost three times, he was having anything but sweet thoughts about Ms. Constantina Justice.

As he finally approached the building, the headlights of his car reflected on two passengers in an oncoming black Ferrari F355. As the car passed by him, he got a quick glimpse of the woman seated behind the wheel and noticed the tag read: **TINA**. Quickly swinging his car around, Nico followed, intending to overtake the sleek, black Ferrari with its tinted windows and have a long overdue face-to-face discussion with the elusive Ms. Justice. As luck would have it, the Ferrari reached the highway headed back into town before he could catch up. All Nico could do was follow and that too was difficult. If Constantina Justice was driving the car, she did it like she did everything else, masterfully.

"BoBo," Tina said again glancing at her rear-view mirror. "I think we're being followed."

BoBo checked his side-view mirror and then turned as much of his bulky body as his plush bucket seat would permit in the little two-seater car. "Where?" he asked.

Tina kept her eyes on the road and then quickly glanced at her mirror again. "The silver Lexus SUV. It's about two cars back on the right. I noticed it back at the office."

Tina took a deep, steadying breath. Her hate mail recently had begun to worry her. There were the usual assortments of kooks and crazies, but a few didn't seem to fall into those categories. They were more sinister in content and tone. More than one intruder was caught trying to break into the grounds of her estate, others at the studio. As a result, security had been tightened, but Tina was not feeling very secure. She had turned her cameras on cases where there were criminal elements on both sides of the law. Rapists, murders, child molesters, wife beaters, even organized crime types on the one side of the spectrum, and rogue cops, crooked politicians, and lynch-mentality judicial systems on the other. Recently she had won a Nobel Peace Prize for her work on the plight of women in Third World counties. There were nations that continued to oppress the women treating them as if they were chattel. She was banned from entering certain countries and she was aware some of the threats came from elements practicing Sharia Law. Her career garnered a lot of friends, but it had also made her a number of enemies as well both domestically and abroad.

"I got it," BoBo said picking up a cell phone from its perch between them. He dialed one number. "Yeah, this Bo. We got a tail. Handle it," was all he said.

The tone of his voice gave Tina a chill. "BoBo, I don't want anyone hurt. It could just be some fan looking for an autograph."

BoBo nodded his head as if he was keeping time with the music on the radio. He cut his eyes at her and kept on nodding. "They don't start no mess, won't be no mess," his Darth Vader-like baritone voice rumbled while still bobbing his head.

Tina kept glancing in the rear-view mirror as she continued through downtown Chicago. Finally, she pulled into a courtyard surrounded by identical, tall, concrete buildings. She and BoBo got out of the car and walked into the dark hallway of one of the buildings and scaled several steps. BoBo seemed to be around her on every side. In the dark, she could feel the presence of others. Soon the dim light cast shadows on the staircase walls. Hooded forms passed by her as silently as ants crossing the desert and headed toward the door she had just entered. No one said a word as they passed. BoBo didn't even acknowledge they were there. He continued to guide her down a long, dingy, narrow hallway. It smelled of someone's fried fish, collard greens, and mac and cheese dinner. When they turned a corner at the end of the hall, another long hallway of similar description rolled out before them and smelled of other, more unpleasant scents. Finally, they entered a door and immediately the room came alive.

"Hey, Tina, you running late tonight," a tall, thin man said and smiled.

"Hey, JC." She returned his greeting, smiled, then nodded to the other ten or twelve people sitting in the room patiently awaiting her arrival. "How many tonight?" she asked.

JC laughed showing perfectly even white teeth in his handsome milk-chocolate face. "Not as many as last time," he smiled and winked, mischievously, "but then again, it's early."

Tina nodded at the handsome man she had known for many years. His hair was still dark as well as the hairs in his mustache, eyebrows, and long eyelashes. For a man of fifty-something, he had a sensuality and smoothly-toned body that still turned women's heads. He was a charmer and a flirt with his bedroom dark eyes, but he had managed the low-income apartment complex with ease and aplomb.

"Well, let's get started. Who's first?" Tina asked looking around the room.

JC nodded to Mr. Rustin, an elderly man, whose bent torso showed every bit of his seventy-five years. "He's having trouble with them Social Security people again. Said they want to cut his disability check some more because he works part-time stuffin' those discount envelopes for pocket change. He don't make nearly enough to keep body and soul together now," he said and shook his head in sympathy.

Tina moved toward the elderly man, leaned over him, and smiled broadly. "Mr. Rustin, let's go into the office and figure out how to kick some Social Security butt."

The old man's grey-rimmed irises danced. "Now you talkin', Ms. Tina. Just let them bureau-rats try and mess with us," he said, laughing as he grunted and shuffled to get to his feet. "We'll show em, won't we?" he grunted with the effort to rise. It took three tries, but finally, Mr. Rustin rocked forward enough to gain his feet. He was a proud man, a former school teacher, who wouldn't take a handout and was hard-pressed to ask anyone for help.

Tina's smile broadened as she offered her bent arm to the man to make him feel as if he was her escort. "You bet we will, Mr. Rustin." Linking arms together, they slowly walked into another room and closed the door.

Nico pulled into a parking space next to the Ferrari he had been tailing for miles. As he turned off his engine, he scanned the area, his eyebrows bunching. This couldn't be where Constantina Justice lived, he thought, looking around the desolate, dilapidated area. Some of the windows in the austere high-rise building were boarded up. There wasn't a tree or even a blade of grass anywhere in sight. Rats as big as cats scurried around a huge, red dumpster with JUSTICE stenciled in black on the side. Peering at the door through which he had seen a woman and mountain of a man enter, Nico thought maybe he had been following the wrong person. Then again, although the sleek, black Ferrari seemed incongruent with the run-down conditions, the Illinois tags did read **TINA**.

The prudent thing to do would be to go to her office on Monday early, but that meant he'd waste the weekend. He had entirely too much on his plate to waste his time this way.

Not spotting another soul in his vicinity, Nico cautiously got out of his rental car, locked it, and started walking toward the building doorway. Three huge cats scurried across his path toward the dumpster and the war with the rats was on. The light was so dim he could barely see where to walk. No street lamps illuminated the exterior and only what had to be a forty-watt bulb was in the ceiling down a long narrow hallway. He gingerly stepped into the surrounding abyss and his sixth sense immediately said danger abounded. Before he could retreat, he was grabbed from behind around his neck, his arms pinned back, and a powerful blow connected with his midsection.

"Who you?" a gruff, faceless, hooded shadow barked at him.

Nico couldn't breathe, let alone talk. Finally, the wind that had been knocked out of him began to return. Coughing he tried to answer, but before he could speak, another blow again knocked the wind out of him.

"Look, black, I said, who you?"

Ire immediately rose, Nico pushed back hard and fast slamming the attacker behind him into the wall, then using him as leverage to lift his feet and kick up into the groin of the attacker in front of him. Before he could wrench himself away, a blow landed with power to the side of his head, and then all faded to black.

4

Tina was mentally and physically exhausted. She had been up and out since five in the morning. It was nearly midnight when she finished interviewing and assisting people as they worked through their problems. She came to the projects once and sometimes twice a month or more often if it was an emergency to offer her legal skills to those who could never have afforded an attorney to help them through their crisis. It was rewarding work because, in most cases, she was able to make a difference. Everyone got their concerns heard and knew she would do whatever humanly possible to help. Usually, it only took a phone call from her to right a wrong or make the wheels of government move in the right direction. However, many of the ones she helped didn't even have a phone to begin with. That's why she came to them.

Often her celebrity brought swift attention to most issues. When the problem required a personal appearance or a court pleading, she had a Rolodex app full of attorneys who she could call on to handle the matters *pro bono*. Sometimes it was as simple as getting the city government to send retirement checks to the right street address or as difficult as getting child care payments out of a recalcitrant parent. The toughest cases often involved helping to get a son's or father's penitentiary sentence reduced or an appeal heard in a higher court.

Tonight, she had seen fifteen people or families who didn't have phones and their problems had run the gamut. One man had cried because he couldn't find a clinic willing to help his wife kick her prescription drug habit. Tomorrow morning, she would have to get up early again to start working on tonight's collection of problems. Before she left her office tomorrow, she expected she would have a favorable solution for each and every one of the clients she had seen. That she set the bar high for herself was of no surprise to anyone.

Stretching her neck from side to side to loosen her tight muscles, Tina closed her eyes, expelled a deep breath, and leaned back in her chair. Moments later, a knock at the door brought her to an upright, sitting position. She thought she was finished for the night, but perhaps she was wrong, she considered as JC stuck his head in. He smiled and swaggered into the room carrying two paper cups of black coffee.

"You done good, Ms. Tina." He smiled handing one cup to her while sipping at the other.

Tina took the offered cup, sipped it, and smiled tiredly. "Thanks, JC. How many more do we have?"

"The Ramirez family was the last for tonight."

"Good." She took another sip. Then glancing up at JC, who had taken a seat across from her, she asked. "How are things with you?"

He shrugged absently. "Fair ta' middlin', I guess."

Tina chuckled. "You always say that, JC. Nothing ever seems to get you down."

He chuckled, too. "Well, I wouldn't say that exactly. A pretty woman can always get me ta' lie down," he flirted.

"So, I hear, JC." She grinned over the rim of the cup. "You've got all the women around here trying to tie you down. When are you gonna let someone take care of you permanently? I hear Ms. Marcus is trying hard."

"'Bout the time you let some young buck tie you down," he said laughing.

"Tying me down is one thing, keeping me down is an entirely different matter," she parried.

JC shook his head. "That'll be the day, Ms. Tina. When some man can keep hold of you for two minutes at a time, I'll know it's time for Armageddon."

"True that." Tina laughed as she rose from her seat and stretched. She downed the rest of her coffee and tossed the cup in the trash can by the desk. "Where's BoBo?" she asked absently.

JC nodded toward the door. "Sleep on the couch. He said ta' wake him when you was ready ta' go."

"I'm ready as soon as I gather these cases."

JC waited until she had put everything in a tote bag, then stood head down, hands in his pockets, shuffling his feet against the old, worn linoleum floor. Tina noticed the nervous gesture in the man. He was a gregarious fifty-something-year-old man who never failed to have a twinkle in his eyes or a devilish grin on his face. There was something he was reluctant to talk about, she sensed. With a little patience, Tina knew she could get the man to talk. The question was did she have the energy to listen? In less than a heartbeat, she decided to make the time. JC never asked her for help for himself. He was always looking out for the welfare of those near-indigent people who lived in the buildings he managed. Tina knew if something was bothering him, she'd do what she could to help.

Shifting a hip onto the corner of the worn, grey metal desk, Tina folded her arms across her chest and waited. JC, still scuffing his booted foot on the cracked linoleum, looked up when he sensed Tina was watching him.

"Heard Big Red was across the pond," JC said to his chest.

The statement momentarily surprised Tina. Big Red was the nickname people in their community called her father, Redmond Justice. Across the pond referred to the Atlantic Ocean. Her father had been in several African cities where poor sanitary conditions and refuse removal were directly linked to deadly diseases for both the animal and human populations. The World Health Organization (WHO) and US Ambassador Jake Hawkins asked her father to come to a conference in Africa to discuss what measures should be taken to stem the tide of disease. Ambassador Hawkins was the father of her friends JaiHonnah Hawkins Baylor and LaiLoni Hawkins Logan.

Big Red stood as tall as BoBo Carter and probably as strong. He had grown up the youngest of seven sons to Reverend Ellis and Anna Lettie Outlaw Justice, Tina's paternal grandparents. Redmond had started in his early teens working summer jobs on dump trucks that collected and deposited the city's waste. Later, he had bought his own dump truck and started a small hauling business. The first day he took his new refuse recycling truck on the streets as a private contractor, a young nursing student, who spoke very little English, had plowed into the back of his truck. Less than a year later, Redmond married the Argentinean nursing student, Marguerite Alonza Dela Vega in both a Catholic and a non-denominational ceremony. Before Marguerite earned her nursing certificate, she was already the mother of two sons with another on the way. The boys kept coming like stair steps, but Marguerite was determined to have a daughter. Tina was the seventh child and the only girl born to Redmond and Marguerite, a fact her six older brothers never let her forget. Tina was the jewel in Big Red's crown. Though he loved his boys fiercely, Big Red cherished his only daughter, Constantina.

Marguerite Justice also loved and cherished her only daughter, but she was as strict with Tina as she was with her sons. A slip of a woman who stood barely five-foot-two and a trim hundred-five pounds, she was the undisputed ruler of the Justice household. Even her husband, Redmond's six ten, two-hundred-plus pounds didn't intimidate Marguerite. Rather, no one in the household of rambunctious children wanted those flashing black eyes and Argentinean quick temper trained on them. When Marguerite reverted to her mother tongue, everyone, including Redmond, took notice and, usually, took cover. Marguerite only demurred to her father and mother, Tina's maternal grandparents.

Raphael and Alicia Alonza Dela Vega could trace their family heritage back to the Spanish invasion and were still considered Spanish royalty even now. Although Raphael was an Argentinean ambassador and confidant to the President of the country, he had once been the bane of his aristocratic family's existence.

At twenty he had seen a young, teenage dancer and beauty contestant on a float at Mardi Gras. He had followed her float through the crowded parade of revelers just to watch her as she danced. At the end of the parade, once he had gotten close enough to reach out and touch her, her father had stepped in front of him and ordered Raphael to stay away from his fourteen-year-old daughter.

It had taken four years of battling with her parents and his, but he had to have her. They married on her eighteenth birthday. She was a virgin on their wedding night with no experience with men. Raphael didn't care. Once he had Alicia, he never looked at another woman. After six children and forty years of marriage, she was still his lover and best friend.

Their youngest daughter, Marguerite, married the American, Redmond Justice, and now had seven children of her own. Like his daughter, Marguerite, Raphael's only granddaughter, Constantina, was his pride and joy.

JC had met Redmond years earlier on the streets on the south side of Chicago. JC, never one for getting his hands dirty had become a part-time dispatcher at Redmond's trucking company's business office. It wasn't unusual for JC to ask about Redmond, but Tina was concerned about JC's apparent apprehension about getting to the point.

"Dad will be home by the weekend," Tina said still waiting for JC to talk.

"Y'all having y'all's football party?" JC asked, finally raising his head.

"Yeah." Tina grinned. "The game is on Sunday. You coming this year, JC?"

JC shrugged. "Naw, y'all's thing is for y'all's family. Besides, I gotta' keep an eye on things 'round here."

Tina shook her head. "JC, first of all, we consider you family. Second, even if we didn't, the weekend always includes our friends, and, finally, we've got the Greene Team to police the buildings and grounds here. That's why we and Admiral

Stacy Greene-Alexander created them so they could protect the residents. You can't be everywhere at the same time, JC. The Greene Team is doing a good job. As soon as the government sells these properties to the residents, you'll have your hands full overseeing the renovations with Baylor and Baylor Design and Developers. You could afford to spend a few hours with me and the boys, couldn't you?"

JC grinned. "You and the boys are one thing, Miz. Tina, but your mamma been trying too hard to hitch me up."

It was an old excuse, but one that wore thin many years ago. While it was true Tina's mother, Marguerite, had been trying to get JC interested in some of her unmarried female friends, JC had been like a scared jackrabbit, running in zigzagging patterns to the nearest rabbit hole until the danger passed. While JC enjoyed the ladies, he didn't have marriage on his mind, but Marguerite did . . . and she was on a mission.

"Well, you try explaining it to my mother tomorrow, JC. She'll be here bright and early with the medical team for the monthly medical examinations." Tina chuckled at the incredulous expression on JC's face.

"Thought she'd be gittin' things ready for the weekend 'stead of pokin' and prodin' at folks' bodies," he grumbled. "Her mother and father are coming to town, ain't they?"

"Marguerite Justice has a houseful, yes, but Grandma Alicia and Grandma Anna Lettie don't allow youngins' in their kitchen, so mama's free to finish her home-visit rounds."

"Your pretty girlfriends comin' this year?" JC asked with a grin and a twinkle in his eyes.

Tina smiled smugly, "Yeah, Cheryl and Kristen Catherine wouldn't miss football weekend . . . and neither would their husbands, Peter and Thomas."

"Why them pretty little girls wanna go get themselves hitched up is a pure mystery ta' me," JC mused with a frown. Then looking into Tina's eyes, he asked, "You ain't thinkin', on getting' hitched to that Ronald fella, are ya'?"

"Bite your tongue, JC. Now tell me the real reason you're looking for my father."

JC eyed her carefully. "Can't put much past you, Tina, can I?"

"You can keep trying, JC, but remember, I'm Marguerite's daughter and Alicia's and Anna Lettie's granddaughter."

" 'Nough said," JC grumbled. "It's about that show you did. The one on convictions in organized crime."

"What about it? Why do you need to talk with my father and not me?"

"Word on the street is them mob people didn't like what you said about the feds not convicting enough of them wise guys who be bringing them damn drugs in."

"I wasn't making it up, JC. Drug traffic crosses into the states every day and the government hasn't been as successful in getting the people responsible. They arrest the little street dealers, but not enough of the kingpins. I still don't understand what this has to do with Dad."

"Them mob types are looking 'ta make some trouble. Maybe take it out on your daddy's business. You know, in union troubles."

That thought did have a chilling effect on Tina. She knew her father had not only the tough road most men in business had but also the constant intrusion of those who wanted to take away the success her father's businesses enjoyed. Most of these had been overt operations, and her father had persevered, but what JC was referring to was covert.

Something that wasn't legal as much as it was sinister. People who would go to any length to continue their nefarious operations. That was part of the reason her family insisted she have a bodyguard twenty-four-seven. Now her concern centered on whether her parents, grandparents or brothers might be in imminent physical danger.

She would have to talk with her Uncle Ned Justice, her father's eldest brother, and the Chicago Police Commissioner. Like the fictional family on the TV show Blue Bloods, the Justice family had five family members actively involved in law enforcement.

"Just tell Big Red I need 'ta talk wit-im," JC said as he picked up Tina's tote bag full of cases and then carried it leading her into the outer office. Bobo's loud snores nearly crushed the air. When JC approached the sleeping man, he stood well back away from him.

"Bo! Hey, Bo!" he called. *"Wake up, man!"*

BoBo got to his feet as if someone had yelled fire. He looked around wildly until the sleep began to lose its grip on him. Then pinning his friend Tina through bleary eyes, he said. "You ready 'ta roll?"

Tina smiled. "Yeah, and since you've been sleeping while I was working, you can drive."

BoBo's head began nodding. "You got it. Let's roll."

Tina said goodnight to JC and followed BoBo down the hallway. As they walked through the door to the exterior of the building, she remembered someone had followed them there. Tina was seated on the passenger side and BoBo behind the wheel when she asked, "What happened to the person following us?"

BoBo pressed the button and the Ferrari engine roared to life. "What person?"

Tina's eyes narrowed. "Wasn't someone following us?"

"Something must have changed his mind."

"Bo?" she asked pointedly.

BoBo knew that tone, but he wasn't about to elaborate. Tina knew BoBo had taken care of whoever it was. The matter was closed. She leaned back in her seat and closed her eyes. Before they were out of the parking lot, she was sound asleep.

5

Nico's body ached in places he didn't know existed. Nothing, during the many years he played high school, college or professional football, compared with the pain. His head pounded and his body refused to move faster than molasses moving uphill in the winter. When he awoke, he found himself sitting in the car facing Lake Michigan. For more than thirty minutes he had been trying to get his bearings. He had been mugged all right, but nothing had been taken. Whoever those hoodlums were, they had worked him over good, but other than aches from head to toe everything else was intact. His wallet was on the seat of the car with his credit cards and cash still in it and the car seemed untouched. Someone was sending him a message though, but he felt like killing the messenger.

He pressed the button starting the engine and pulled the car out onto nearly deserted Lakeshore Drive. In minutes, he was pulling up to one of the McCoy Group's five-star hotels. He hadn't completed his mission and couldn't have flown back to New York tonight if his life depended on it. Instead, he registered in the hotel for the night and then walked into the hotel bar.

The plush lobby bar was nearly deserted. Only a few people were still there. Nico took a seat on a tall stool at the granite-topped bar and ordered a double Stoli. The bartender had barely sat the drink in front of him before he downed it in one gulp, grimaced, and ordered another. As the alcohol began to dull the pain, Nico began to mellow out. He hadn't accomplished what he had come to Chicago to do, but he wasn't about to leave before he did. Tomorrow he would track down Ms. Constantina Justice, but tonight he needed rest.

He sensed that wasn't going to happen when he noticed a dark, scorching hot woman had been eyeing him for nearly fifteen minutes. When she picked up her drink and sauntered up to him, there was no question what she wanted.

"Hello, handsome," she breathed the words.

A lopsided grin curved his mouth. "Have we met?"

"Only in my dreams," she cooed.

"What do your dreams tell you?"

"That's it's going to be a very interesting night," she smiled sexily, eyeing his body. "A very interesting night. Your suite or mine?"

"You're staying here?"

"Yes, Suite 1144."

Nico nodded. He was accustomed to being picked up by women and this one seemed to have a little class about her. He learned from her that she was a hospital administrator and the hotel was filled with a nurses' convention. This woman looked like she could offer aid and comfort. Downing the rest of his second drink, he started to rise and turn away from the bar when a voice calling his name stopped him and his evening's companion.

"Nico!" the voice thundered.

Nico would know that voice anywhere. He grinned and shook his head as a mountain of a man moved toward him.

"Scout, how you doing, man?" Nico greeted his friend.

"Scout? Man, I haven't heard that since we rocked the gridiron," George Bryant grinned giving Nico a brother's handshake and bumping shoulders.

Nico winced in pain, and George noticed.

"Hey, man, what happened to you?"

"Somebody thought I was still running touchdowns and tried to take me out," he said trying to recover.

George eyed the beauty at Nico's side. "Now if this pretty lady wanted you to lay down, all she had to do was ask."

Nico had nearly forgotten about the woman, but he had noticed two gorgeous women were clinging like Saran Wrap to George.

"What's this? One woman still not enough for you, Scout?" Nico grinned nodding to George's companions.

"I'm pacing myself," he grinned back. "Look, what up with you for tonight?"

"My friend and I were heading upstairs to get better acquainted."

"Crush that. The night's young, son. You and your friend come on and hang out at my place not far from here on Lake Shore Drive. We got a party going on. Some of my bar association friends had a conference at the hotel tonight. We ran into women from this nurses' convention and, we, you know?" George said and grinned.

Nico did know and, already three sheets to the wind, it didn't take George any time to convince him and his companion to join them. The party was on and on and on.

6

"Hey, Tina Rabbit, get up and answer the damn phone!" a voice burrowed through Tina's deep sleep.

Tina fought for consciousness and glanced at the clock on her nightstand. It was nearly ten o'clock on Sunday morning and she was still tired. A string of expletives crossed her lips as she reached for the phone.

"*Bouchard* Justice, God don't like ugly!" she growled at the youngest one of her six brothers. "She ain't too fond of pretty either. Go away and leave me alone!"

Bouchard "Butch" Justice, the sixth son of Redmond and Marguerite Justice, roared with laughter. He enjoyed teasing his only sister as did all of her other brothers. She was the baby of the family and although they teased her relentlessly, they loved and protected her with passion.

"Get up, Tina Rabbit," he persisted, calling her by her childhood nickname. "Mass at 12:00 o'clock noon and the games at one. Remember, I owe you a butt kicking."

"Not in this lifetime, *Bou-chard*," she mockingly tossed back drawling out his name. "Grab your butt, brotherman, because that's the only one that's going to get kicked today."

"Yeah, we'll see about that, Tina Rabbit. *Mamacita* says you'll forfeit the game if you're five minutes late for mass."

Marguerite Justice would do it, too, Tina pouted. She was an Argentinean woman with hot-blooded traits. When she spoke, everyone listened including her husband, Redmond, who stood six-feet-ten inches to her petite five-feet-two-inch frame.

"*Mamasita* at the house yet?" Tina grumbled running her hands through her long, shaggy cut hair.

"She's on her way with the grands, uncles, and aunts. See ya' in church," he said, laughing and then hung up.

Tina hung up the phone and covered her face with both hands. Peering at the clock again, she knew she should get up, but she still wasn't ready to leave the warmth of her bed. She fell back against the thick cushion of pillows and pulled the cover up over her head again. She was getting into a comfortable position and drifting back into sleep when a thick arm reach around her waist and pulled her spoon fashion into a tight embrace.

"Who was that, baby?" Ronald Forman asked in a thick, sleepy voice.

"My brother, Bouchard," Tina mumbled into her pillow.

"What did he want?"

Tina mumbled something incoherent and burrowed deeper into the pillows. Ronald's big, soft hands began to plunder her body. Tina rolled her eyes ignoring his attempts at foreplay. Although he wasn't a bad lover, he didn't set her world on fire anymore. He was handsome, attentive, and well-built, but, for him, she felt no passion, no lust. Yet she succumbed to his ardent pleas, rocked his world, and then left the comfort of her bed to shower and dress while he slept.

Tina was sitting at the breakfast bar reading several Sunday newspapers on her iPad and having coffee and juice when Ronald came out of the bathroom, showered and dressed for the day. Bending, he kissed her on the neck.

"How about some breakfast, baby?" he crooned into her ear.

"Sure, help yourself. Nothing for me though," she said absently turning the page of the iPad. "I don't want to play on a full stomach. Slows me down, but you go ahead."

"No, I mean, aren't you going to cook?"

"No," she said as if he had asked a foolish question.

Ronald huffed in exasperation. "Tina, a man likes to be pampered by his woman sometime, you know?"

Tina's head swiveled in Ronald's direction. She studied him like he had grown a head out of the side of his neck. "Do tell. Well, Mr. Forman, I suggest you find yourself a woman…"

Ronald threw up his hands in annoyance. "Look, I don't want another woman. I want you, Tina."

"No way," she said around an unladylike snort and then went back to reading her newspaper.

"Damn, you're hard on a man! What is it with you, Tina? I'm in love with you. Can't you see that? What does it take to get that fact through to you?"

Putting her iPad aside, Tina looked directly into his eyes. "Ronald, we've had this discussion before. I'm not now nor will I ever be in love with you. You want something more permanent than an occasional roll in the sack, I'm not your woman. No hard feelings, but I wish you the best."

Nonplussed from Tina's directness, Ronald slammed out of the house banging the door as he left. Tina barely registered his childish behavior as she resumed reading the newspaper. She was finishing her second cup of coffee, a bagel, and orange juice and had finished speedreading four newspapers cover-to-cover when Ronald returned. He said nothing as he poured coffee for himself and sat across from her at the breakfast bar.

"Feeling better?" she asked laying the iPad aside again.

"No," he grumbled, "but I did have breakfast with your family at the mansion."

Tina piled her hair on top of her head, put on a baseball cap backward and smiled at Ronald. "Good, then you'll feel even better after church." She turned and headed out of the door. Ronald followed grumbling as they crossed the expansive lawn toward a domed, glass-enclosed sanctuary.

Tina dipped her finger in the holy water, crossed herself, and walked up the short aisle to take her seat. Her family and close friends were already assembled in the sanctuary that held only twenty, long, wooden pews. Kneeling, she was deep in prayer when the young, handsome minister, one of her uncles, began the service.

7

Nico roused himself from a deep sleep. Needing to go to the bathroom in the worst possible way, he untangled himself from the myriad of bare butts, arms, and legs flung carelessly about him in the king-sized bed. Naked as the day he was born, he wobbled on strong, firm, but unsteady legs, blindly reaching the en suite bathroom off a spare bedroom. He moaned pleasurably as he took care of his needs. *What a hell of a two-day party that had been. Party? Humph, it had been an orgy from the beginning.* Clothes had started disappearing shortly after the liquor started flowing on Thursday night, Friday morning, and the beer and liquor kept flowing through food feasts, fun, and frivolity. Vaguely he realized it had to be sometime on Sunday. His body still ached from the beating he took on Thursday, but now after pleasuring and being pleasured by several women at different times, his thirty-eight years were beginning to tell on him.

Shaking his head wearily, he turned on the shower and stepped in. Twenty minutes later, with a towel wrapped around his waist, he padded barefoot to the kitchen. His buddy, George, sat at a high-top table with his head bowed over his stacked arms.

"You still breathing?" Nico asked reaching for a cup and then pouring coffee."

"Ask me that a year from now," George mumbled. "Man, that was some crazy shit."

"Yeah, you got that right. When was the last time you hung out like that?"

"I don't even want to remember. I was still in my twenties," George moaned lifting his head from the table and palming his face. "Nurses will kill a brother."

"Yeah, you're right about that, too. They know every muscle in your body and how to make it work," Nico snorted.

"Yeah," George gave Nico a tired, but wicked grin. Then as his eyes focused, concern crossed his face. "Man, someone really tuned you up. Don't you need to see a doctor?"

Nico looked at the black-and-blue condition of his upper body and shook his head. "As I said before, nothing important. What time is it anyway?"

"Man, are you sure? You look like someone gave you more than just a beat down."

"I'll be fine. What time?"

"Daytime, I think," George said rubbing his eyes with the heels of his hands. Then he peered at the clock on the microwave oven. "Damn, I'm late."

"Late? Late for what?"

"Church. I was supposed to visit friends today."

"Somebody special?"

"Yeah. Family and friends. My sister, Kristen Catherine, her husband, Thomas Ashton Marshall, and their children,

Tommy, Eddie, and Lydia Martine, are in town. My father, Clarence Senior, too, with his new wife, Sheila Marshall. My brother, Clarence Junior and this new lady he's seeing, fashion model, Shannon."

"Your brother, he played basketball?"

"Yeah, NBA for five years. He and I have a sports and entertainment practice together now. We represent American athletes for contract negotiations. He took a mini-vacation with Shannon. She had a photo shoot in Mexico. He's mixing business with pleasure and talking with some up-and-coming Mexican baseball players. He and Shannon should be back today."

"Look, man, I'm going to get on up outta here so you can get moving. I was only in town to do some business. I was supposed to be back in New York Thursday night. Now I'll have to suit up for a Monday meeting"

"Business? I read about the upcoming launch of your satellite. What were you working on in Chicago?"

"I've been trying to talk with Constantina Justice about moving her television show to my new network on my satellite and getting nowhere fast . . ."

"Tina? Man, why didn't you say something before?"

"You know her, I've heard."

"Know her? Man, we grew up together. She and my sister, Kristen, are BFFs." George looked at the clock again.

"Wait a minute. Your sister is *Judge* K. Catherine Bryant?" he asked stunned.

"Uh, yeah," he said grinning.

"Why didn't you ever introduce me to her before she married?"

George snorted a laugh. "I didn't want to have a kill a good friend. Come on, let's get some exercise."

Nico looked at him quizzically. "Huh? What the hell do you call what we've been doing for the past forty-eight hours?"

George loaned Nico a Howard University sweat suit, tennis shoes, socks, and, in no time, they were whizzing up Sheridan Road. Nico, sacked out in the passenger seat of George's Jaguar, thought they were on their way to a gym to work out, but that thought quickly changed when George pulled to a high-arched, iron gate manned by two burly guards. George waved at the guards and was immediately granted entrance to the Sheridan Road estate on Chicago's North Shore. He hadn't told Nico where they were going or who they were going to see, but Nico was feeling uncomfortable dressed in borrowed sweats when he saw the English castle with its turrets and balconies that could have been the prototype for Downton Abbey. A number of expensive cars were parked on the grass near an eight-car garage. When they got out of the car, instead of heading to the front door of the castle, George took the long walk around the side of the house toward the back. Nico followed, still feeling the effects of the beating he had taken and of the two-day party, but more than curious about where George was taking him.

Nico expected almost anything except what he saw as they rounded the building. In an expansive yard, that bordered on a panoramic view of Lake Michigan, and what had to be nearly forty acres of land, were about thirty people, both male and female, in the midst of a touch football game. Nico stared at the sight without blinking. There were more people sitting on the sidelines with little children at their feet whooping and hollering with each play. Inside a toasty-warm looking, glass-enclosed area under the terrace were even more people. Very attractive women also sat on the sidelines, some holding babies in their arms, but Nico's eyes had scanned the collection on the playing field and lit on one woman wearing a burgundy and gold Redskins' baseball cap turned backward on her head and shouting plays to her team members who all wore burgundy and gold T-shirts. The opposing team wore blue and silver gray reminiscent of the Dallas Cowboys. There wasn't anyone wearing the Chicago Bears' colors.

Nico couldn't see the woman's face, her back toward him, but he admired her form. She was quarterbacking her team and doing a helluva good job at it. Her T-shirt was full of sweat and provocatively molded to her body. What a body she had, too. Hour-glass shape with a high, nicely rounded bottom that begged to be fondled. Strong, shapely legs that could wrap around a man with precision and crack his ribs like walnuts. Nothing he had experienced came close to the sight of this woman on the lawn playing full-throttle touch football.

Even as George introduced Nico to his toddler niece, the cute and captivating, Lydia Martine, his nephews, Tommy and Eddie Marshall; his father Judge Clarence Bryant, Sr.; his stepmother, Sheila Duckworth Bryant; and others sitting on the sidelines where heaters pumped out warmth into the chilly air, Nico couldn't keep his eyes off the quarterback for the burgundy-and-gold team. His overworked and, until that moment, flaccid phallus sprung to life and rose to the sight of this woman. She had a symmetry of motion, a fluidity that caught and held his attention. Regardless of whom she was or whom she was with, Nico wanted to know her . . . intimately.

A whistle blew sharply drawing Nico's attention to a petite woman wearing a referee's black-and-white shirt and black slacks. The woman signaled a timeout and the players began to walk off the field. Nico's eyes searched the crowd for the quarterback on the burgundy team. Finding her walking toward the sidelines, her head was bent, fist on her impressive hips, and what he could see of a scowl on her face. He had to blink twice when recognition dawned. The scowl didn't hide her beauty. It was Constantina Justice.

8

Tina's chest was heaving up and down trying to get the wind back into her lungs when she spotted a man on the sidelines appraising her from head to toe. Handsome wasn't the word she would have used for this Mandingo warrior. Drop-dead gorgeous came to mind. Feet apart, arms folded, every muscle in his too perfect body bulged under the Howard University sweat suit . . . every muscle. He looked vaguely familiar the closer she drew to him, but she knew if she had ever met this man before, she would have remembered. He was truly unforgettable. Dark, curly hair, thick eyebrows, long eyelashes and a mustache that would make Billy Dee Williams jealous. Their eyes locked and held as she bent to accept a towel from six-year-old Tommy Marshall and let him wipe the sweat from her face and upper body. She grabbed and kissed him all over his face making him giggle, twist and turn trying to get away until she let him go. Draping the towel around her neck, she stood, looked the stranger up from the bottom finally reaching the devilish, shit-eating grin on his perfect face.

"See something you want?" she asked the tall, tan, and all-too-handsome man. His sensuous appraisal of her body was making her sweat and sending tingling sensations up her spine.

Nico's eyes crawled slowly from her feet up the voluptuous body to a stunningly beautiful face that held a challenge. *I dare you* was written there, and despite his weakened condition, he was up to the task.

"We're going to be good together. Real good," he said taking her in again. He'd never believe a glossy print of her again. Even covered with sweat, a little dirt, and unadorned with enhancements of any type, she was a knockout. The raw, light-brown sugar standing before him, appraising him in the same way he was appraising her, had his blood warming on this cold Chicago day. He could visualize her sweating like that in hot, wet ecstasy beneath him, on top of him, with him firmly planted inside her.

He was bold, she'd give him that and much more if she wasn't careful. He looked like a man who could deliver on his statement. The problem was, she sensed she would enjoy him a little too much. He was potent even at two feet away.

"Constantina Justice. Nicholas Collins," George said by way of introductions.

Nico extended his hand. Tina didn't.

"Collins as in NICO Communications Network?" she asked, her brows furrowed.

"The same," Nico said withdrawing his hand. "I've been trying to reach you for a few months."

"Didn't they teach you anything at that Big Ten Wisconsin School you attended? After the first month, it should have dawned on you I didn't want to see you."

Nico was not to be denied. He took a bold step forward until they were nearly standing toe to toe. "What can I say? I'm a slow learner, but a quick study. I'm willing to be taught a number of new things," he said his voice dropping an octave. She has beautiful eyes he noticed. Sort of wine colored. Smooth, supple-looking skin. Perfection in the raw.

Tina didn't like that she had to look up into his hypnotic, ebony eyes or watch as that devilishly lazy grin grew lopsided over his pearl-white, even teeth. That mustache was a killer to any woman with a heartbeat. His kissable mouth was at eye level and she had trouble drawing her attention away from it. Absently she wondered how it would feel pressed against... *Wait a damn minute! What was she thinking? This man had invaded her home like he owned the joint.* She had to put him in his place.

Saddling up to him, closing the gap until their bodies touched, indolent eyes climbed up to meet his. "I don't teach. If you haven't got it coming in, pal, you won't get it going out. Playtime is over and school is out. You're dismissed."

With that, she turned to walk back onto the playing field. Nico watched her walk away and felt his body flush with a new-found excitement. No woman had ever told him no once. This woman had said no twice, but she wouldn't say no to him a third time. This was a completely new experience, and, oddly, he liked it. Never having to chase a woman because of his fame or fortune gave him easy access to any woman he wanted. However, Constantina Justice, the maven of Sweet Justice, was a temptress and no easy conquest. She was tough, all right, but he had a feeling, with the right ministration, she would soften into a delectable delicacy. His taste buds were watering at the thought.

"Man, you must have a death wish," George said, laughing. "Tina usually doesn't get her back up. She's slow to anger, but when you get her there, duck. She comes out swinging."

"I've been so informed," Nico said, still grinning and watching Tina. "I'm going to enjoy the challenge."

George shook his head in sympathy. "Nico, you don't know Tina. She ain't, and I do mean ain't, no round-the-way girl."

"I know. That's what makes her even more intriguing."

"Well, my friend, don't say that I didn't warn you. Come on, let's get some food and watch the game."

Tina's clothes should have been on fire from the laser-like intensity Nicholas Collins was focusing on her while he ate. Her attention wasn't totally on the game as a result. When BoBo crouched down and hiked the ball between his legs to her, she wasn't ready. The burgundy team lost three yards. On the very next play, Tina concentrated on calling the play, smoothly received the football, and back peddled looking for her receivers to streak down the right side. Bouchard zigzagged in then out as the ball hit him in the numbers. Bobbling the ball for a second, he finally clutched it to his chest only to be tagged before he could gain the necessary yards for a first down.

Tina's eyes dangerously glinted and her forehead furrowed as she watched her brother trot back to the huddle with a smug grin on his face.

"That's two, Bouchard," Tina hissed as she and her team huddled to discuss the next play.

"Yeah, yeah," he teased. "Next time don't rush the play."

Hunched over with her hands gripping her knees she cut

her eyes at Bouchard. "Next time remember the play," she fussed.

"Are you two children going to hiss at each other or play football?" Keenen, a Chicago Police Detective and third in the line of Justice brothers, asked. "Call the play, Tina Rabbit."

"Take it down the middle, Tina," BoBo interjected. "Fake it. They won't be lookin' for it. I'll take you in."

Tina grinned at BoBo and then winked. "It's me and you, kid. Now, on three, I wanna see nothing but daylight and real estate."

The burgundy team came out of the huddle, lined up and set as Tina called the cadence. The play unfolded masterfully. Tina faked the handoff to her brother, Tyson, cradled the ball, and then followed BoBo's wide body. Sidestepping one tag from her friend, Charon Madden, and then another from Percy Thomas, another friend, she was almost home free for a touchdown when BoBo twisted in the wrong direction and his bulky body went down hard.

Nico stood, too transfixed to sit and amazed at the level of concentration and determination on Tina's face. This wasn't just a fun romp on a crisp Sunday afternoon. Rather, this was high drama. She was quick and agile on her feet with a strong right arm. He could barely anticipate what she was going to do next. Even after so many years of playing football, the excitement had never ebbed for him. As he watched the burgundy team scramble for every yard, he itched to get into the game. Although he had chosen to leave the gridiron at the height of his professional career, sitting on the sidelines was still tough for him. Yet, watching Tina Justice was almost as pleasurable as being in the game himself.

Her long, strong thighs and legs seemed to start at her neck. A tight, voluptuous torso seemed more suited to long, leisurely Sunday afternoons in bed wrapped around him in hot, wet sex. Her nicely rounded, high bottom would fit nicely in his broad hands and long fingers, he thought, as he watched her brothers give her derriere a familiar pat for a good play. Though it was cold, her T-shirt matted to her upper body around full breasts, the nipples pouting provocatively.

George's masculine suffering groan brought Nico back from his intimate thoughts. Without turning his head, Nico said, "Yeah, man, I know just what you're thinking."

George chuckled. "Not quite, my man. I'm checking that super phine sister in the navy-blue shorts."

Nico shifted his eyes in time to see the object of George's attention pull her blue T-shirt up to wipe the sweat from her face and neck. She had a concaved stomach and killer abs. His gaze flickered only momentarily toward the woman before again landing on Tina. He fervently wished Tina would lift her T-shirt, but she swiped her moist face against the sleeve of her shirt or wristbands instead. He could visualize her straddling his lap, riding him buried deep inside her and both of them slick with sweat.

"Man, from the expression on your face, I can imagine what you're thinking, but you can forget about it. Tina will make you beg for mercy."

"You speaking from experience?" Nico asked.

"Not likely. Tina's like a little sister to me. My brother Clarence Junior and I represent her entertainment conglomerate for contracts with her in-house talent. I've known her all her life. Tina started breaking hearts when she grew out of her training bra at thirteen and she hasn't stopped yet. My sister, Kristen, my brother, and I grew up across the street from her and her six brothers. Kristen, Tina, and Cheryl Lawrence went to Spelman together with Vivian Alexander Montgomery. Then they all went to different law schools. Brotherman over there," he said nodding to Ronald Forman, "with the grey eyes is her current flavor of the season. If I know Tina, and believe me I do, the season is about to change."

"Who is he?" Nico asked, more closely regarding Ronald. He hadn't been in Slade's report as had been the others. He was able to put names and faces together from Slade's report and George's introductions.

"Ronald Forman, originally out of Dallas, Texas. Big time executive with the network that carries Tina's show. He's stationed here in Chicago. We hung out together one night a couple of weeks ago while Tina was away on location in Africa. Forman was crying in his beer about Tina cutting him back on a personal level."

"A man's got to know his limitations," Nico said confidently. Although Forman was what he was sure some women would call handsome; a pretty boy, he was clearly out of his element with Tina Justice. One of the things that had made Nico so successful when he played professional football was learning to gauge his competition, then learning their shortcomings and taking pleasure in mentally outwitting his opponents. He did in-depth research on anyone he played against or with. He would know his enemy and not be caught unaware. Forman wasn't going to be a problem, but Ms. Constantina Justice was.

George eyed him with skepticism. "Limitations? This from a man who has been buck wild all of his life? A rather licentious social life that's publicized with dizzying regularity."

It was true he had succumbed to his baser nature most of his life. He had a good teacher—Lana Norton. At fifteen he was just beginning to learn what his body could do. By sixteen, there had been nothing his body hadn't done—many times over.

As he briefly surveyed the families gathered and bundled up enjoying the game, he noticed a closeness between them and wondered whether any of them had been subjected to the type of sexual abuse he had experienced. He doubted it. There seemed to be a complete devotion within this tightly-knit group of family and friends. Exactly what his investigator had turned up. It was a new experience for him to witness. He certainly hadn't felt devotion to anything or anyone or received it in return either. He had nothing to complain about though. He lived the way he wanted. He always got what he wanted. He owed no one an apology for his lifestyle or his success. The fact there was no one who cared whether he lived or died occasionally wrenched him to his soul, but he dealt with the life fate had dealt him. It was what it was.

Nico was about to respond to George's thumbnail appraisal of his life when a whistle was blown and all play on the field ceased. Being assisted from the field by two of Tina's brothers was BoBo Carter. Nico remembered the bone crusher from their days of pro football, but he had no idea what had happened to the man until now. He had played against Carter and they had never been friends, particularly since BoBo could never get his hands on Nico when Nico was a running back. That fact had incensed BoBo, to say the least. He wasn't the only one. Rather, BoBo was among a long and distinguished list of bone crushers who had missed their opportunity with Nico. A fact Nico would eternally be grateful for. Back in their hay days, BoBo Carter had to weigh in at over three-hundred pounds of bone and muscle. To see him limping off the field of play had a sobering effect, even in this less than tension-filled game.

"Let's get him in the house so I can take a look at his knee," Juan Justice said as they passed Nico and George.

"Ain't nothin' ta worry 'bout, right, Doc?" BoBo asked though he grimaced in pain.

"I'm sure you're right, BoBo, but I take every opportunity to practice my craft."

"Yeah, since he got his license to practice medicine from the Chicago Sears Tower, he's been on a tear," Miguel Justice teased his younger brother.

BoBo looked skeptically at Juan. "Thought you went to John Hopkins, Juan."

Juan laughed. "Yeah, there, too."

Tina watched them as they went into the house, a scowl covering her face. Looking around she sized up her options for replacements. It was a motley crew that stood on the sidelines. A few wouldn't make eye contact fearing she would choose them. She didn't want to do it, but her eyes landed on George Bryant and Nicholas Collins. She groaned and shook her head. She had to make this play or they'd have to turn over the ball. She needed to keep the momentum going, but without BoBo and Juan that was going to be tough.

To make things worse, Ronald had a Cheshire-cat grin on his face. He was the quarterback for the blue team when on offense and he was ready to clean her clock after the way their tiff had gone earlier that morning. He wanted to put her in her place and he had no mercy. He didn't think women should play a "manly" sport. She'd already beat him at handball, tennis, racquetball, and a little one-on-one basketball. Well, she'd just have to show him again there wasn't anything a woman couldn't do, except stand up and pee.

She surveyed her potential replacements again. Well, at least they had both played the game before. George had played defensive back in college and in the pros. He was good on his feet, but she needed a center. Nico had a stellar career as a running back and he was about two inches taller and twenty pounds heavier than George, but she didn't know whether she could play that close to him and keep her mind on the game. From the grins on their smug faces, they knew they were her only real alternatives. *What the hell?* she thought.

"Yo, G Money," Tina called out to George and by association, Nicholas. "You slackers want a little exercise?"

"Money?" Nico asked looking at George as they slipped on numbered burgundy-and-gold T-shirts, started across the playing field, and approached Tina.

"Yeah," George laughed. "Tina started calling me G Money when I got my first job delivering newspapers when I was fourteen. Then my sister would con me into taking her, Cheryl, and Tina out to the movies every Saturday afternoon at my expense. I'm getting back a fraction of what I was often forced to spend on those three girls. Now, in addition to her talent contracts, I handle some of her labor relation affairs. It's all about the almighty green." He turned his head and continued walking toward her. "Come on, Tina Rabbit, let me and my buddy save your bacon for you," George teased, swinging an arm around her shoulders and guiding her back to the center of the field of play.

"Keep your mind on the game, George, and not on Greta's backfield," she said once they huddled. "Collins, you've got center. Can you handle that?"

"That and more," he said and grinned at her.

She rolled her eyes and laid out the play. When they broke and lined up, Tina slid her hands between Nico's muscular thighs. The brother was definitely carrying some heavy luggage, she absently thought as she called the cadence. He snapped the ball with perfect precision, held off all advances for a count of ten while she scrabbled for a receiver. She let fly a perfect short pass which connected with George. She yanked the air with her fist and said, "*Yes!*" demonstratively when the play worked and gained the necessary yardage for a first down. Her grin widened at Ronald's scowl.

"Not bad, Tina Rabbit," Nico said patting her on her rump after the play.

She returned the gesture and grinned, "You've got good, uh, hands," she said before sauntering back to the huddle.

Nonplussed, Nico slanted a look at her and then grinned. Considering where *her* hands had been, he doubted whether his hands were what she thought were good.

Nico was enjoying the game, but even more than the play, he enjoyed Tina, her brothers, and friends. It amazed him that this female captain of industry, who was as popular and nearly as wealthy as Bill Gates or Warren Buffet was totally guileless. She was having fun with sweat and dirt covering her body on a cold, fall day. So were the other women and men playing on both teams.

Playing a physical sport with women on the team was a new experience for him. The women were beautiful, every shade from vanilla wafer to mocha chocolate and everything in between. Although they played with vigor, they didn't lose their sensuality. That was also a new experience. The women he knew never would have let themselves be seen with so much as a hair out of place or without a face armored with makeup. However, here was the incomparable Constantina Justice with grungy tennis shoes, cutoff sweats over biker shorts, her football idol's, Doug Williams', faded No. 17 Redskins quarterback jersey, a baseball cap with Super Bowl XXII emblazoned on the brim, and turned backward on her head, swiping sweat from her face with her sleeve, having fun.

Go figure.

During the next time out, Nico leaned a shoulder against one of the solid, brick-and-block posts holding up the upper terrace and watched Tina as she guzzled a quart of spring water. She was in the midst of her friends and brothers involved in a very animated conversation. She had little Lydia Martine on her hip as she talked and periodically stole kisses from the three-year-old's cheeks to the toddler's delight. He gleaned from her sparkling eyes and the high-fives she exchanged with the group, that and her brother, Bouchard, had some type of bet going.

This woman wasn't still for two moments simultaneously. Rather, she was like nothing Nico had ever seen. Her energy and enthusiasm couldn't be conquered or suppressed. She had a guileless sensuality of a teenager and a body to match. There was no doubt she was all woman. She wasn't by any means thin, but nicely rounded in all the right places with supple-looking skin over very well-toned muscle.

Nico remembered seeing a film clip of her in a charity celebrity pro-am tennis tournament; with friends at basketball great Derrick Jackson's ski resort sluicing down one of the challenging ski runs; shooting rapids in the Grand Gorge with Vivian Alexander Montgomery; and surfing off Malibu with Astronaut Tate Kennedy and his wife, attorney and lobbyist, Capri McAllister. In contrast, other film clips showed her waltzing at the White House; shooting craps at a high-end casino in Monte Carlo; and being presented to the King and Queen of England at a formal dress ball.

In just the few hours he had spent in her company, it was obvious to Nico she was no ordinary woman. What she had accomplished in her thirty-something years was nothing less than awe-inspiring. Five feature-length films to her credit, all of which garnered a slew of awards, critical, and popular acclaim, and she was appearing to have more fun than the law allowed playing touch football.

"Incredible, is she not?" a silky, accented voice asked.

Nico turned in the direction of the voice and stared at one of the most regal profiles he had ever seen. He pushed off the column and stood erect. For some insane reason, this woman's presence made him want to bow down in reverence. When the woman turned her head and smiled up at him, a lump grew in Nico's throat. She was clearly an older woman, but still very beautiful.

"Ma'am?"

The woman tilted her head toward the group he had been watching. "Constantina," she said with a decidedly pronounced accent and a beguiling smile. "I said she is incredible; would not you agree? Yes?"

"Uh, yes," he warily agreed. He suddenly didn't know what to do with his hands. She must have sensed his uneasiness when she extended her hand.

"Alicia Diaz Vazquez Dela Vega," she said, smiling brightly, "and you are Nicholas Collins," she pronounced with a heavy accent which sounded like cultured Spanish to his ears.

"Yes, but how did you know . . .?"

"Ah," she breathed the sound, a purr in her throat. "Your name? This is simple to answer. Yes? I asked George," she chuckled, her voice husky and smooth.

Nico couldn't quite take his eyes from the dark hypnotic ones staring back at him, perhaps in amusement. They seemed so much like Constantina's hypnotic eyes. Of course, there should be some resemblance. This was Tina's maternal grandmother; though she didn't look like a woman over forty. She had raven-black hair pulled away from her gamine face into a severe bun at the nape of her long neck, precise curls flattened in front of her perfect ears, a narrow nose, and cherubic mouth. She had a light, golden, skin tone, the color of honey, offset by long, dark eyelashes and eyebrows. A slim build from what he could see in the very flattering royal blue, Ultrasuede slacks and matching fitted jacket with navy-blue piping intricately woven into what resembled an Aztec design on the collar and cuffs.

"You stand off from the others and watch. This is your first time here, I think. You are trying to figure out who they are, yes?"

"I, uh, don't . . . I know George. We played in the NFL together."

"Ah, yes, yes, he tells me this. You are still not comfortable. You will sit with me during supper and I will tell you. Yes?"

The whistle blew and the game resumed. He pardoned himself, ducking his head and trotted back onto the field of play. Yet, he looked back over his shoulder to the woman who looked more like an aristocratic Madonna than any image he had ever seen.

The game went on for another hour with the burgundy and gold team the victor by a touchdown scored by Nicholas.

***

After the game, George took Nico into what looked like a men's high-end haberdashery where they selected clothes and shoes to wear after they showered. Every conceivable amenity was provided for including underwear and socks.

"I don't get it," said Nico. "Tina keeps brand new men's clothes for all occasions?"

"Designers send things to her in the hope she will support or endorse their products. She stores the stuff here and gives it away to anyone who wants or needs it. She doesn't want anyone to believe her support can be bought. This will all clear out by Thanksgiving and Christmas and be replaced when the next fashion season starts."

He had to think about that as he selected shoes, socks, a pair of slacks, a shirt, and a sweater to wear after his shower. It appeared he was to be included in the day's activities with the Justice family and friends after all.

This had never happened to him before. He had never been invited into anyone's home for any occasion except when he was in his teens and some woman wanted him for sex. He had no friends to speak of; never had. The acquaintances he made, like George or Slade, were people he might see at odd times, but never anything planned. Although he was adept at the social graces and could handle himself in any crowd, he was usually alone and pretty much a loner.

Once dressed, he followed George into a huge recreation hall where assorted games were underway. Flat screens were mounted and offering up various sports, like football, soccer, Lacrosse, etc. from arenas worldwide. Some people sat watching the televisions or involved in the lively games in the salon, like poker, backgammon, chess, ping-pong, pool or checkers.

"Come over here, young man," Reverent Ellis Justice, Tina's paternal grandfather, hailed, as Nico strolled around looking at the gallery of pictures of family events on the walls.

"Sir?" Nico said.

"Come. Sit. Do you play?"

"Some," he said, but didn't mention he often played in high-stakes games in casinos around the globe.

"Good. Good. Sit and put some skin in the game."

He did, acknowledging the other men and women at the table. He was about to pull cash from his wallet when a tray of chips was placed before him.

"So, you're the guy who played football," said the Reverend while dealing cards. "Now you're launching a new television network."

"Yes, sir, on a new interstellar satellite with one hundred transponders," he said and picked up the hand he had been dealt.

"My Anna Lettie tells me you want our Tina to consider switching to your network."

He hesitated a moment not sure of whether he should have this conversation. "I, uh, do, yes." Yet, understanding the necessity to be forthcoming and, more importantly, honest.

"Mmmm," the Reverend hummed in his throat as his eyes continued to evaluate the cards in his hands.

Nico felt a presence at his knee and looked down into the small, upturned face of little Lydia Martine Marshall, George's toddler niece, staring up at him. She had deep dimples, pretty, big brown eyes, and a profusion of curly hair surrounding her cherubic little face. Others spoke to her, but she put her arms up toward him grinning. "Up," she said. "Go up."

He had never had contact with children and wasn't sure what to do. He didn't notice others discretely watching as he lifted her onto his lap. She snuggled into his embrace, stuck her thumb in her mouth, and promptly went to sleep. She smelled of all that was young, fresh, and sweet. He felt a little bereft when a while later Ashton Marshall gently retrieved his daughter to put her down for a nap. Little Lydia's mother, Judge Kristen Catherine Marshall, continued beating the pants off the poker players at the table with steely-eyed concentration. He was glad they were only playing with chips.

As they played, other players dropped in or out until many of the women and most of the men had participated in the game. During the entire time questions of him had been casually dropped into the various conversations. As she cleared the balls on the pool table with deadly accuracy, Peter Brock's mother, Cassia, regaled and teased them about the early days of their youth when she taught them to shoot pool. She would label this innocent looking woman a pool shark of the highest order.

The same thing occurred while he shot pool with other family members and friends. At a certain point, he realized he was being interrogated with the finesse of a Svengali. Yet, not once had Tina, her mother or either grandmother been in the room.

Tina sat at the long work island in the huge professional kitchen captured by her mother and both grandmothers being put to one kitchen task after the other. She was not a homemaker by choice, but her female family members intended she would learn something about the culinary arts. She could complain her six older brothers were not subjected to this treatment, but, of course, they were. Each and every one of the seven Justice offspring knew how to put together basic meals. Bouchard had enjoyed the lessons and was now a Le Cordon Bleu-trained chef of all things. She, however, had dodged every attempt to domesticate her. Still, she was no further along in her efforts to stay out of the kitchen than she was when she was a kid too short to see the table top.

She could, but didn't have the interest or inclination to cook. After all, she could always go to her parents' or grandparents' home in the Jackson Park community on Chicago's Southside neighborhood any day and have a great meal. After all, she didn't live that far from them in her Gold Coast neighborhood. They had the same view of Lake Michigan. Her mother and paternal grandmother cooked big meals and always had leftovers she and her brothers survived on. At times, she might stay with her parents and her grandparents at their home in the old neighborhood instead of her Gold Coast high-rise penthouse on Lake Shore Drive or this estate on Sheridan Road. She was an expert on the fabulous cuisines and restaurants along the Magnificent Mile where her brother's restaurant was located.

Any of her brothers and uncles might, and often did, end up at their homestead, too, with their families and friends. There was always a crowd in the senior Justices' households. Almost everyone still lived in the old neighborhood of Highland-Jackson Park area between Hyde Park and South Shore. Her grandmother, Anna Lettie and mother, Marguerite, got along like old friends and combined their talents in the kitchen so her siblings and uncles gravitated to the homestead every Sunday after church and several times during the week.

Of course, there were plenty of restaurants near her home in Chicago's Gold Coast to eat really good food, including her brother's restaurant, Bouchard's Place, on The Magnificent Mile and she had a condo in the middle of restaurant row. Even if she had the inclination to cook, she rarely had time to do so. Her schedule was so jam-packed except for those occasions when family events were planned, like their annual football game, the upcoming basketball game always scheduled to be held the day after Thanksgiving; and baseball game on April Fool's Day. These gatherings, in addition to other holidays, she cherished spending time with her family and close family friends at Point of View, her Sheridan Road mansion and estate.

As she sat sequestered, peeling potatoes, she itched to join her family and friends in the rec room. However, her mother and grandmothers only had to shift their gazes on her before she reached for another potato to peel. She sensed she was in trouble but wasn't clear on what infraction she was about to be scolded for. She stayed silent and awaited her fate. However, she didn't have long to wait.

"So, he comes to find you and you refuse to meet him? To even shake his hand?" Marguerite Justice asked her daughter.

"*Mamacita*, it is business," Tina said, a sigh in her voice. "This is family time."

"You think I do not know business?"

"I didn't mean it that way."

"You were raised to be rude, were you?" her mother continued.

"Of course not. You and dad raised us to be respectful of others."

"Did Cassia or Helen teach you to reject a person sight unseen?" Referring to her friends' mothers, Cassia Brock, a homemaker who raised her son, Peter, and the offspring of her friends, and Helen Kendall Lawrence, a world renowned investigative journalist. They were as much responsible for the raising of the Bryant, Justice, Brock, and Lawrence children as anyone.

"No, *Mamasita.*"

"Then you will see this young man and hear him out."

"Yes, *Mamasita,*" Tina sighed, aware there was no other option open to her.

She knew when her mother was not pleased with her behavior. This was one of those times. This was her punishment; being forced to perform menial kitchen duties and denied time spent with her friends. She reached for another potato to peel and resigned herself to listen to Nicholas Collins' proposal. However, she would peel the skin off George Bryant as efficiently as she peeled the potato in her hand, for bringing Nicholas Collins into her life.

9

It was something he thought about quite a bit as the Justice family and friends celebration continued through dinner with constant and often ridiculously hilarious suggestions for child care, baby names, and fatherly duties. It was odd for him to fully realize now, when he was finally wealthy enough to have his own, that he had never known the fullness of family.

Even more, he had never known the joy or the problems of having uncles, aunts, grandparents or siblings involved in every aspect of his life. As far as he knew, his paternal and maternal grandparents, whoever they had been, were deceased. To his knowledge, he had no aunts, uncles or cousins. His father left Chesapeake Beach, Maryland, more than twenty-two years ago for parts unknown and never looked back. Family was a thing Nico never had or knew anything about. He had not until now suddenly sensed the lack.

George pulled him into a conversation with Tina's brothers: Miguel Justice, the oldest, who was Vice President of the Justice family businesses; Dr. Juan Justice, a physician and surgeon with a booming private practice and privileges at every hospital in the city and suburbs; Keenen Justice, a Chicago Police Detective; Tyson Justice, a CIA operative; Diaz Justice, a Coast Guard Captain; and Bouchard Justice, a chef with his own popular Chicago restaurant.

He met each of Tina's uncles on her father's side of her family, the eldest of whom, Ned Justice, was the current Chicago Police Commissioner. Both sets of her grandparents were at the long dinner table set in a dining hall that could only be described as Gothic. Even the children were interwoven at the table beautifully dressed and set with gleaming fine china, crystal, and polished heavy silverware. At either end of the table, the grandparents sat as in a place of honor two abreast with everyone else arranged on either side. Only one seat was vacant next to Tina's mother at the center of a table long enough to be considered a bowling alley and just as highly polished. Intricately designed colorful fall flowers and lit, scented candles adorned all the way up and down the center of a very long crocheted table runner.

However, just after everyone settled from visiting various stations containing the steam tables of food, Redmond Justice entered the dining hall. It seemed ritualistic, but he went to his wife first for a warm welcome, before approaching his parents, his in-laws, his brothers, then his sons and his daughter, Tina, who sat on his left side. He hailed his close friends, the Brocks, Bryants, Lawrences, and their families and friends before he filled his plate and took a seat between his wife and daughter.

Though there were questions and conversations about Big Red's trip to Africa, Nico felt he was the topic of conversation between Tina's parents. At one point, Redmond looked down the table toward him seated to the left of Tina's grandmother Alicia. Before the food was blessed, she singled him out. It didn't feel like when women sought him out for sex. Though Alicia was a beautiful woman, she had to be in her late sixties or early seventies. She kept him next to her as she was one of the first through the buffet line following her husband carrying on a spirited conversation about Argentina.

He had last been in her country earlier that year for business and a few days during Mardi Gras. She shared that she had danced in the parade as a young girl and met the man who would become her husband there. His attention was balanced between her conversation and the staggering array of foods on the buffet stations. Intoxicating scents and aromas waffled through the air as lines formed on rounded sides of the hot and cold buffets. A soup and salad bar was crowded while a dessert bar sat beautifully arranged and awaiting its opportunity to serve. Drinks were at another station, but fine red or white wines of their choosing were generously served to the adults at the table.

Conversation was lively during the meal even as many dinner companions got up for multiple trips to the buffets. By the end of the meal several hours later, Nico was stuffed but could put names and backstories to the faces of the people who were closest to Tina. Among them were her best friends Cheryl Lawrence Brock, her husband, Peter Brock, and Kristen Catherine "KC" Bryant Marshall. There was a close comradery between Tina and KC Bryant's brothers George and Clarence, too. It was clearly a tightly knit group which included Tina's brothers. Through his own subtle probe, he learned all eleven offspring of the Justices, Brocks, Bryants, and Lawrences were raised together primarily by Mrs. Cassia

Brock and were all tighter than siblings in the womb. Those who were married with children were continuing the tradition by raising their children together.

By early evening he had spoken with each and everyone except Tina's father. That omission was cured when the men rose to clear the table and buffets, putting away leftovers, and proceeding to clean the dining hall and kitchen. The men made it an event with assembly-line precision. Nico rolled up his sleeves and found himself and Tina's father rinsing plates before stacking them in an industrial-sized dishwasher. Once the task was complete with all surfaces and floors spotless, the men retired to a smoking lounge with an array of fat Cuban cigars and port. The women were apparently relaxing in another part of the mansion. That's when Redmond took advantage of the comforting atmosphere to raise his questions.

"We haven't been introduced, but as you may have gathered, I'm Tina's father, Redmond Justice."

"Yes, sir," Nico answered accepting the hand extended in his direction.

"I understand you've been trying to reach my daughter without much success about a business deal."

"I have, yes. However, I believe I should have this conversation with her."

Redmond nodded thoughtfully while drawing smoke from his cigar. The smoke filtered out into the air slowly but was quickly swept up into ceiling exhaust fans leaving no appreciable odor while he rolled the cigar between his fingers. "You are correct, except if it were not for Tina's grandmothers, one of whom is my mother and the other my mother-in-law, you would never have been permitted anywhere near Tina now. Look around this room, Mr. Collins."

Nico did and noticed he was the center of attention from every man in the salon, including Ronald Forman, Tina's current squeeze.

"With the exception of a few, these men have known Tina since she was a gleam in her mother's eye. I understand from George someone tuned you up Chicago style for following her last week."

"That's true."

"Expect an apology from those who are responsible."

"It's not necessary."

"It is, yes, and it will be delivered. Now, why do you believe Tina has been unresponsive to your inquiries?"

"I have no idea. When my people have spoken with Mr. Hopper, he insisted my company "sweeten" the deal. Each time the offer was improved and his percentage raised, we were told Tina felt it was not enough."

"Claude Hopper? He's the person you've been negotiating with?"

Nico put down his cigar, reached into his pocket for his phone and paged through several apps. "That's the name I was given." He noticed Tina's brother, Keenen Justice, the police detective pull his phone from his pocket and leave the salon.

"Ah," breathed Redmond. "What position did Mr. Hopper indicate he held with Sweet Justice Productions?"

"We were led to believe he is the key contact for the company. Is this not the case?"

"He is not. He is Tina's publicist, not her business manager. For future reference, you would have to be vetted through attorney William Chandler at Advantage Entertainment. George and Clarence Bryant are legitimate contacts for Sweet Justice Productions as well; usually for contract positions inside the company. They handle her in-house talent contracts and other human resource business."

"I know who William Chandler is. However, you said 'vetted' by him."

"That's correct. No one speaks for Tina, except Tina. If you have something she wants, she'll reach out to you. Apparently, you don't have something she wants. Still, you were mistreated; something that doesn't sit well with us. Therefore, you will be granted an opportunity to speak with her."

A bit miffed, he asked, "When will this meeting take place? I've already been in Chicago far longer than I intended. I hadn't come prepared to stay more than a few hours."

A toothy grin crossed Redmond's face. "Whenever the hell she wants, so settle down, Mr. Collins. I can guarantee this is going to be a bumpy ride."

Nico believed him, but again, he never backed down from a challenge. However, looking around at the men in the smoking lounge, he believed he was in good company... except with Ronald Forman.

Nico relaxed into his comfortable chair and took a long pull of his cigar while eyeing Forman. Yeah, I'm coming after Tina Justice, he thought as he and Forman continued a visual combat. Your time, brother, is over.

"He has no one, this one. He is alone in the world," said Anna Lettie to her granddaughter, as she sipped a rich, robust Amaretto. "He does not know what family is."

"That could be his choice," Tina argued irritably and squirmed under her grandmothers' glare.

"Your father and grandfathers are not happy about how he was treated. You will do this thing to ease their minds," said her grandmother Alicia. "Yes?"

"You might as well do it, Tina," said her BFF Kristen Catherine. "My Lydia Martine went right to him, crawled up into his lap, and went to sleep. She doesn't do that with just anyone. Children have good instincts. They're too young to get it wrong."

"I agree," said Tina's other BFF Cheryl. "My girls were just as taken by him. Besides, I like the way he stepped up and helped us win the game today."

"The man played professionally for years. What would you expect?" Tina whined annoyed.

"He played out of his position, pal, and marched you right up the field," Cheryl argued grinning.

"He also stepped up when it was time to clean up. He isn't afraid of manual labor. He's as rich as Midas, but he blended right in and went with the flow. The babies and your grands like him and he's impressed the rest of us. He's a captain of industry just like you. No one gave him what he has, just like you. He did it the hard way, just like you. He earned it," commented Cheryl.

Tina wouldn't disregard her friends' advice. Besides, the fact they were closer than sisters, like triplets, they had good heads on their shoulders. She would hear this Nicholas Collins out. Of course, she didn't have much choice in the matter. Both grandmothers and her mother weighed in on his behalf.

Though her mother was giving her the Jedi, mind-control treatment, her dad was clear as crystal: Just do it! Even her grandfathers who she could usually wrap around her little finger were impervious to her pleas for intervention. Her brothers, her champions, had forsaken her. Now her BFFs were presenting a united front. No one stood by her side against the interloper.

Well, she'd see what he was offering just so she could say she did it, but he was going to have to work for it.

10

If a man with Ronald's attributes, brains, brawn, and bed expertise, was continuing to bore her senseless, something might be seriously wrong with her. The chemistry between them had died a natural and timely death, thought Tina, as she climbed out of bed before dawn. She showered, dressed, and left the house without waking him from his post-coital sleep. He was unsettled enough about Nicholas Collins' presence in her family and friends' inner circle. What she was about to do would give him heartburn, but she'd deal with that later.

She searched the designer closet for warm men's clothes and then searched the in-home computer for the bedroom where her security team indicated Nicholas Collins was sleeping. It was after two when the party finally broke up. Since there were eight inches of snow on the ground and more falling, everyone stayed at the mansion. She knew her mother and grandmothers would be up shortly preparing for a seven o'clock Monday morning breakfast, so she didn't have much time to get done with what she had to do.

She found Nicholas asleep alone in a third-floor bedroom right where the computer said he would be. He slept on his back with the blankets down below his waist. It was clear to see with the flashlight he had indeed taken a beating. She'd have a word with the Greene Team about his treatment and with BoBo, too. However, there was no way to deny Nicholas Collins was beautifully built. He was tall, most of which were strong legs, a narrow waist, and a solid torso without an ounce of fat. He obviously stayed in shape. He handled the football game well and her families' vetting process which, for the unsuspecting, was pretty intense. Yet, she'd see for herself how he handled ... other things.

"Up and at it, Collins," Tina barked and tossed the bundle of clothes at him.

Nico slowly came awake at the sound of Tina's voice. He looked at the time on his wrist watch and then frowned at her. "Why," he asked but did not move to sit up.

"I need the exercise."

He snorted a laugh. The woman danced her butt off last night after dinner until 2:00 o'clock this morning and she needed exercise at 5:00? He couldn't do any of the intricate Latin dances she, her family and friends executed, so, for the most part, he just watched. "If you wanted exercise, you should have slept with me a few hours ago."

"If I wanted to sleep with you, you wouldn't be sleeping now. You'd still be showing me what you're working with. You've got five minutes, pal," she said and left the room.

Nico was sure she was right. The woman wasn't still in one place for a second. He washed up, dressed in the clothes she brought, surprised they fit him perfectly. Even the boots were his size.

He opened the bedroom door fully dressed to find her leaning against the opposite wall, long legs crossed at the ankles, arms folded across her impressive breasts, and carrying on a conversation through a headset.

She checked her watch and nodded. He dressed with time to spare. "This way," she said and started off at a fast clip leaving him to follow in her wake.

Though he dearly needed hours more sleep, Nico realized he had to have his faculties about him when in Tina's presence. She had surprised him more than a few times on this odyssey weekend, so he kept his mouth closed and followed her into the industrial-sized kitchen. If he was surprised her mother and grandmothers were already there, he didn't show it. She handed a heavy shearling coat, watch cap, and gloves to him while the grandmothers passed each a thermos. Before he could get his coat zipped, buttoned, and a bright red scarf around his neck, Tina was walking out the back door and across the field of fresh snow where the day before, they played a successful football game. He noted there were footprints coming to the castle from what looked like a large igloo beyond a stand of trees.

When he turned back to face forward, it was just in time to not go tumbling down the shallow slope of stairs leading to a boathouse. Once inside, he found three boats docked; the first one a yacht, the second a racing cigar boat, and the third a sailboat.

Tina was climbing down onto the deck of the sailboat named **The Outlaw Justice** and stowing her coffee thermos down below deck. She reached for his coffee while he got the gist of what they were about to do. This was going to be an experience he hadn't had for a very long time and he didn't know how to feel about it...except exhilarated. A garage-sized door crawled high up into the ceiling and opened onto the vast expanse of Lake Michigan just as the sky began to lighten. There was a thin layer of ice on the water. The sun turned the heavens into a picture-perfect kaleidoscope of color that cast beautiful reflections on the water causing it to sheen.

"Are you going to stand there gaping or are you going to cast off?" Tina chided.

He turned his head and grinned at her. "Those aren't my only options, but for now, I'll cast off."

She was afraid he was right. He cast off the ropes and nimbly jumped aboard continuing to push the boat away from the berth as she started the engines and guided it out into the placid, icy water. *The Outlaw Justice* was her baby and the sixty-footer, from stem to stern, handled like a dream when under its three sails. When far enough from shore, she cut the engines and untied the mainsail while Collins handled the remaining two. With a push of a button, the wrenches pulled the sails into position while Nico tied them taut. She yelled, "tacking" in time for Nicholas to duck before he could have been knocked overboard by the boom of the swinging sail as the wind snapped the sheets tight and lifted the boat across the water like a hydrofoil.

Nico held onto the center mast, his heart pounding like Tyco drums in his chest. He looked out to the vast horizon of dark blue water and ice-cold air whipped and slapped him about. He remembered Lana Norton took him out on her twenty-foot sailboat a time or two and what an exhilarating experience that was until she wanted sex at sea on the deck. He put the memory aside and enjoyed this early morning ride. He had gone to college in Wisconsin, but there was nothing as cold as the Chicago Hawk on Lake Michigan. He loved it!

Tina settled back in her seat at the rear controls with her coffee and watched the sheer pleasure in Collins' demeanor. She had to give him points for his ability to roll with the punches without one complaint. She had subjected him to a great deal since he showed up on Sunday afternoon, less than twenty-four hours ago. He was undaunted by the quick changes. It impressed her he was steady under pressure, but then she remembered his performances on the gridiron in both college and the pros. He had been steady there, too.

From what she had time to read of her brother, Tyson's CIA and FBI files on Collins, he had never been implicated in or arrested for anything. She scrutinized his businesses and those he was in business with. Some she knew, but none of the others sent up red flags. His reputation as a corporate raider was well earned she read, however, it didn't move the meter on the point scale she had put him on. She had the resources to pull a hostile takeover of NICO Communications if she chose, but she was more interested in the partnerships he held to launch a new satellite.

She never liked the idea of working for someone else, so if she could buy a transponder on his satellite, Sweet Justice would have multiple media outlet channels. This would mean launching entirely new subsidiaries of her company. She would not be relegated to a single, primetime, two-hour window for her show. She could go twenty-four/seven and three-sixty-five on multiple channels. She could even launch an all-news channel to compete with CNN. As she had once envisioned, she could even launch an ad-free educational channel for children and teens based on the superb program her friends, former Ambassador Jeff Logan in Summer County, South Carolina, and Roselyn Hunter Greenfield in Washington, DC, instituted. That program had students performing academically superior to the national average. She might even partner with them for the service for a new educational children's television network.

There was no time like the present to get the ball rolling as she put in a call to her friend and former college classmate, US Supreme Court Justice Vivian Alexander Montgomery. Vivian's father, South Carolina State Senator Bernard Alexander was the first to institute the unique program. She would need his advice and counsel if her project was to work.

As she talked and guided the sailboat across the water, other ideas began to crowd her mind. When she ended the call with Vivian, she was so deep in thought, she didn't register Collins had retrieved his coffee and taken a seat next to her at the controls.

Nico sat silently beside Tina thoroughly enjoying the bracing morning air and excellent black coffee. At this time of the morning, were he at home in New York City, he might be jogging in Central Park or in any city he found himself in. He also had a membership in his pal's sports and health club facility where he worked out during inclement weather. However, although unbelievably cold, he much preferred this race across the water to the mundane run in the park, his gym or on a warm, sandy beach in the tropics.

"How long have you been doing this?" he asked.

"Since I could crawl. My grandfather's great-grandfather worked on boats on The Lakes, so boating became the Justice family's way of livelihood for several generations and was a tradition in my grandpa's family. Grandpa Justice became a minister, but by then The Lakes were in our family's blood. My father and uncles brought us and all the kids with them when they went sailing. My brother, Diaz, is a Coast Guard Captain here on The Lakes."

"I can certainly believe that. I talked with Diaz yesterday about his experiences in the Coast Guard on the Great Lakes. You handle *The Outlaw Justice* with finesse and skill. I'm glad you brought me along, but I don't think you just needed a shipmate. Your father said when you were ready to talk, you'd reach out to me. Am I correct; this is the time you selected?"

"I have questions. What's your schedule for the next few days?"

He shrugged. "My time is what I decide it will be."

She nodded. "Good. Let's head back to shore. Breakfast should be ready."

They turned about catching the wind again and enjoyed a mutual silence on the return trip. Nico was sorry it had to end. The sails were lowered and he lashed them down, while Tina guided the twin engines into the boathouse berth. They had only been gone ninety minutes, but Nico believed it to be the best and most memorable period of time in his recent memory.

He had been with many women, but not one who intrigued him as did the all-encompassing Constantina Justice.

When Tina pulled him out of the breakfast hall and into an empty salon, Ronald Forman could feel what was coming. He decided he wouldn't go easily. After all, his job as her liaison with his television network and his livelihood were on the line. "What's going on, Tina? When I woke up, you were dressed and gone. On my way to the house, I caught sight of *The Outlaw Justice*. I used the binoculars in the kitchen to see you and Collins coming back."

"You're right, Ronald. I was out for an early morning sail and I took Collins along for the ride. However, it's the beginning of the work week for me and that's business. It has nothing to do with what's between me and you. I'm not enjoying our relationship anymore. We have almost daily disagreements for the past month or two. We've had a good run the past six months. Some of the times have been fun, but like all trips on a merry-go-round, at some point, the music stops and people get off the hobby horse. I'm at that point."

"You don't feel anything for me, do you?"

"Nothing lasting, no. Look," she said sighing. "I'm in my mid-thirties and doing exactly what I want to be doing at this point in my life. I made it clear at the beginning of this relationship I didn't want or need a man as a permanent fixture in my life. At the time you said you understood and agreed. If your feelings have changed in the interim, then that's on you. Mine haven't changed. There is no reason for me to interfere in your need to marry and have a family."

"We can keep going the same way we have. We'll work through our disagreements. Maybe you'll feel differently over time."

She shook her head. "I'm moving on."

"It's Collins, isn't it?" he said between gritted teeth.

She shrugged. "Maybe. Possibly. I like what I see. I'll probably seduce him into my bed sometime soon," she said facetiously. "So, we best call it a wrap before it happens, don't you think?" She didn't mean it, but his presumption that she was only dumping him for another man rubbed her the wrong way.

Ronald was so nonplussed at her nonchalance he stalked from the salon and never noticed Nico in the hallway.

Nico hadn't been intentionally listening. He was returning from the washroom when he heard his name used in anger and stopped. When Ronald stalked away in the opposite direction, he moved into the doorway of the salon and leaned a shoulder against the jam. "You'll be sure to let me know when you're ready to seduce me into your bed, won't you? You move so fast I wouldn't want to miss it."

Tina rolled her expressive eyes at him. "You'll just have to keep up, pal. I don't telegraph my moves, but when I'm ready I expect you to get naked."

He shrugged his right shoulder. "Sure. I can drop trou at a moment's notice."

"I've been so informed. I'll use a stop watch to time you."

His laugh was deep.

***

After an enormous breakfast and the best coffee he ever had, Nico again found himself as part of the clean-up crew. However, he was not the center of attention this time. No battery of questions came his way. There was just lively conversation mostly about the next time the family and friends would come together for Thanksgiving. He, George, Peter Brock, and Tyson Justice formed the floor-mopping crew and there was quite a bit of floor to mop in the breakfast hall and kitchen. An hour or so later when they put their mop heads in an industrial-sized washing machine, they were finished, and Nico felt a measure of accomplishment for a job well done. Not one man complained.

Nico had never mopped a floor in his life, but for some reason, he didn't find the task odious. He was the head of a multibillion-dollar conglomerate. The other participants in the floor-cleaning crew were Peter Brock, a wealthy attorney with his own prestigious law firm; Tyson Justice, a CIA operative; and Thomas Ashton Marshall, a lawyer and a renowned international law expert. A cleaning crew could have easily been hired to do the menial tasks, but Nico learned that just because they had the means to do something, it didn't mean jack shit to this closely-knit cabal. Besides, servants would likely want to covertly snap pictures or listen in on private conversations, meaning that the families and trusted friends couldn't be completely relaxed and uninhibited. Everyone had a hand in making the time they spent together memorable. Even the children participated by helping to make floral arrangements, fold napkins or make name cards.

With many hands at the tasks, it took no time to put the few halls they used in the castle back in order. When he finally found his way back to the room he had slept in the night before, the bed was stripped and the luggage packed with the cleaned clothes he had used since coming to Chicago. The luggage also contained more clothes than he had used. Now he knew what the women had been doing while the men cleaned the kitchen and breakfast hall. Linens and used towels were stacked on the floor outside each bedroom door as if waiting for pick up. He found it somehow extremely intimate to think Tina Justice selected his attire, packed his bags touching and selecting his underwear to suit her taste. If someone suggested the incomparable Constantina Anna Alonza Justice would be taking care of him, he would have had the person committed as certifiably insane.

"We have things to do, Collins," Tina said from the doorway.

He had not heard her come up behind him. She had changed her clothes it seemed, but he had no time to dwell on it.

"Grab the luggage and let's move," she said, but then pulled a head mike to her mouth and began speaking to someone named Bruce. He followed her quick march to one end of the corridor where an elevator stood open and waiting. Without a break in her conversation, she leaned back against one of the elevator walls as the box descended.

She was looking in his direction but seemed to be looking through him.

"Yes, thirty to forty minutes max."

The doors opened, and he followed her out into another corridor carrying his luggage by a strap over his shoulder. This hallway twisted and turned. One needed a map to find his or her way around what he considered a castle. A few paces down, she opened a door and walked in. Through a top, half-glass wall, he saw BoBo Carter in a hospital bed with his right leg elevated in a splint-and-weight contraption. A svelte man stood by holding BoBo's hand.

A scowl grew on BoBo's face when he spotted him and Tina.

"How goes it?" Tina asked BoBo.

"Alla dis ain't necessary, Tina."

"According to Juan and *Mamacita*, it is. You want me to call her in for another little chat?"

BoBo's dark complexion seemed to pale at the thought of calling Tina's mother into the room. He shook his head in reaction, crossed his massive arms across his chest, and pouted.

"Good enough. Big Red also had a talk with you, too, didn't he?"

"Yeah," BoBo said obviously aggrieved.

"Well?" Tina said and waited.

BoBo turned back and looked at Nico. "I apologize for what happened to you, man, but ..."

"Uh-uh," Tina inserted. "No buts. If you believe someone is out to do me harm, what are you and the Greene Team supposed to do?"

"Tina," he whined.

"BoBo," she said, elongating the name until it brokered no argument.

He sighed looking away. "Detain and call the police. Then call Keenen and Commissioner Ned." Still, he pouted.

"Exactly," she said and then hugged as much of him as she could get her arms around. Turning to the man beside the bed, Tina said, "Walk me out, Rayne."

Once outside of BoBo's hospital room, the thin man palmed his face, tears leaking through his fingers. "He's scarred, Tina."

"I know, Rayne, but his job is secure. I'm not going to fire him. Stay with him. Convince him."

"You're not going to need me in the studio?"

"Not for the next few days. Once BoBo is moved to *Mamasita's* house, come back into the studio if BoBo seems stable enough."

Rayne seemed to breathe a sigh of relief. "The roads should be clear enough by tomorrow to move him."

"So I'm told. Will you two be all right for a few days?"

"Yes, I'll take care of my man. Don't worry."

"I won't. *Mamacita* is staying to take care of the meals and Big Red has crews out clearing the roads. Juan and the doctor he's dating will stay until BoBo can be transferred to the house. The regular cleaning crew is scheduled to come in to do the laundry, dust, and vacuum."

"You go on, now, Tina. I know you're on a tight schedule."

"I'll see you both soon," Tina said hugging Rayne.

Rayne shook hands with Nico and returned to BoBo's side.

Silently, Tina and Nicholas went out a side door and across a walkway cleared of snow to a helipad. A helicopter with **JUSTICE** emblazoned on the tail section sat with blades still.

"Stow your luggage behind you," Tina ordered as she climbed in one side.

He did as instructed and then climbed in the opposite side.

Tina fired up the engines and continued her conversation with Bruce as she went through her pre-flight checklist.

When the bird was ready to fly, she switched to a control tower frequency and received permission to lift off. She absently gave more points to Collins. He didn't barrage her with questions about BoBo when clearly he could have. He also didn't question whether she could fly a helicopter. Rather, he strapped in, settled back in his seat comfortably, and watched the landscape fall away as she lifted off and gained altitude.

Nico saw other helicopters in the vicinity, but she stayed well away from them and the other air traffic going in and out of the area airports. Before he knew it, the blades were blowing snow off the helipad at her studio as they set down. Once secure, she shut down the engines.

"Leave your luggage in the copter," she said as she climbed out.

A rooftop door opened. A man stood waiting while the helicopter blades slowed to a stop.

"How are we doing on time?" Tina asked.

"You have time to spare," he answered and turned to Nico extending his hand. "Hello, Mr. Collins, I'm Bruce Joyner, Tina's executive assistant. If there is anything you need while you're here, please don't hesitate to ask me." He then hurried to catch up with Tina.

The hallways were busy with people moving quickly from place to place. Most nodded an acknowledgment to Tina and then to him, but otherwise moved about on what appeared to be important missions. Once in Tina's inner office, Bruce handed a cup of coffee to Tina before asking whether he would also like a cup. Nico nodded in the affirmative, but his attention was riveted on Tina as she conducted a conversation on her headset and reviewed reports on her desk concurrently. She never sat down or seemed to relax, always moving. This activity was conducted on what had to be no more than three hours of sleep. She was a ball of energy but seemed to have a handle on several things simultaneously. After providing the coffee, Bruce stood by watching and apparently privy to every conversation Tina was conducting and at the ready to handle whatever Tina handed to him.

It fascinated Nico she could switch so effortlessly from the pre-dawn sail, to family and friends at breakfast, packing a bag for him, concern for her friends Rayne and BoBo, flying a helicopter with skill and efficiency and hit the ground running with her busy day's activity already underway. This activity was conducted on what had to be no more than three hours of sleep without yawning once. It was also clear to him the time she took away from work to be with her family and friends was equally as well orchestrated as her work schedule and very precious to her. She took time for what mattered to her but never lost sight of her goals or objectives. He appreciated the fact he got to observe her up close and personal. No dossier could have captured everything about this phenomenal woman.

11

The chatter continued in the conference room until Tina entered with her executive assistant (EA) Bruce Joyner and a man some recognized as Nicholas Collins. The group of twenty production crew silenced immediately. Tina stood, her back to her special projects team, a cell phone to her ear. After a period of silence, she said, "Keep me posted," and then hung up pocketing the phone in her pants pocket.

Turning, she eyed the group. "As you are aware, it's been some time since anyone has heard from attorney Jillian Harris. The FBI is pursuing the theory that, because her family is wealthy, she's been kidnapped for ransom; however, no ransom demands have been made. It's my opinion the FBI is clueless."

"This seems to support your theory she was not kidnapped for ransom. Since her body has not been found, she, along with other high-profile people, have been abducted for other reasons," reasoned Octavia Anderson, a top investigative reporter and analyst with Sweet Justice Productions.

Tina nodded in agreement and then turned to her EA. Bruce sat and queued up a group of photos on the wall video screens. "Here you see twelve relatively high-profile women and seven men who have gone missing under suspicious circumstances in the last couple of years. In the case of Jillian Harris, she was last seen on Martha's Vineyard with our own Chicagoan Strickland Briggs," said Bruce.

"Wasn't he interviewed and detained by the FBI?" asked Leo Fontaine, a photojournalist.

"He was, yes," answered another team member, "but his story was corroborated by Judge Clarence Bryant who is the Chief Justice of the Illinois Supreme Court and Attorney Sheila Duckworth Marshall. They verified Jillian walked away in Lola's Restaurant parking lot while Briggs stood talking with them. Several cars left the lot and others pulled in while they stood there. I've eaten there. It's a popular restaurant. Since the car she came in was still there and she could not be found, they called the police," said Tina.

"Octavia, I want you to lock on to this story and pick two others to work with you. Give me several perspectives in an hour. Hollis, you and a team you select focus on the other missing persons. Give me fresh angles. Forrella, let's see what you and Lennox can dig up on the friends and families of the missing. Martinelli and Kertz, team up on the money end of human trafficking. Rimmer, you and Berlin grab data on what countries aren't having problems with human trafficking and why. Are the punishments more severe if caught in those countries? You know the drill. We reconvene here in two hours. I want reports and suggestions for a special edition before two o'clock. Everyone move. Go now. Learn things."

"Are we scrapping today's scheduled show?" Assistant Producer Jodi Morgan asked.

"No, we'll do it. Bill Chandler will sit in for me as originally planned. He confirmed an hour ago. He'll be in the studio on time."

The young producer seemed to sigh in grateful relief.

As the group of staff members scrambled to perform their assigned tasks, Bruce shut down the equipment and followed Tina and Nico to her office. He grabbed his iPad from his desk and began rattling off tidbits of information for Tina. When he finished, he fell silent.

Tina nodded her acknowledgment of the information he gave, then asked, "Is Claude here?"

"He is," said Bruce.

"Let's have him next."

Bruce nodded, tapped his earpiece and said, "Bring him."

Shortly, two security guards brought Claude Hopper to her office.

"Tina, what is the meaning of this?" he demanded belligerently, but his eyes went wide when he spotted Nico.

Again, Bruce queued up a video on one of the monitors on Tina's office wall. When it digitized, Claude could be seen pleading unsuccessfully to convince her to allow the in-home exposé. When she left her office, the cameras caught the unflattering things Claude said, his behavior behind her back, and the conversation he had with Nico.

Though the video lasted less than ten minutes, Claude seemed to have aged considerably in that time.

Bruce produced a contract from the stacks on Tina's desk and a pen for his signature.

Though Claude looked pleadingly in her direction, Tina never said a word. She was standing behind her desk reviewing and signing off on other projects.

Claude, apparently aware his fate was sealed, took the pen and signed his dismissal letter. Bruce made a quick copy and handed it to Claude. Security marched him out while Tina took a call on her private line.

"*Sí, abuelo, el hombre está conmigo. Estoy en mi oficina, abuela. Prometí yo y voy a hacer como pedido. Sí, te amo tanto demasiado. Bendiciones,*" she said and hung up, a smile rimming her lips.

Nico didn't let on he understood bits and pieces of her side of the conversation with her maternal grandparents. They must have asked whether she kept her promise and he was still with her. She assured them he was, and she loved them. Thrilled her maternal grandparents were bringing pressure to bear on her to give him an opportunity to talk with her, he entertained himself on his smartphone for a while. So deep into his own work, he didn't notice Tina was watching him. He ended his call and slipped his phone and hands into his pockets. He stood regarding her as she did him but uttered not a word.

They could say more in silence, Tina acknowledged, than a full-blown conversation. Nicholas Collins was an extremely patient man. He did not have a need to fill every moment with conversation or inane chatter. As he looked at her, she found she couldn't read his thoughts, but she knew instinctively wheels were turning in his head. She found that quality in him intriguing. *More points in his favor,* she thought. He was racking them up. It seemed his stock had grown not only in her family's estimation but also in her BFF's. Both Cheryl and KC, before they left for their homes that morning after breakfast, wanted her to listen to what he had to say. She wasn't quite ready yet, but she was moving in that direction, particularly if he could give her something she wanted in return.

Bruce came back into Tina's office and nodded to her, signaling the completion of some task she had given him. She looked at her watch and headed toward the door. "Let's move, Collins," she said and set a quick pace out the door to a waiting elevator. Bruce followed them in and pressed the button for the second floor. When the doors opened, they stepped out into a wide room with cubicles rows deep and wide with people talking on headphones. Reader boards up along the ceiling indicated three hundred calls were underway, but that number constantly changed.

Nico assumed it was some type of call center, but he wasn't sure what was going on. They went into another conference room that was absent of the noise. Tina pulled the headphone mike to her lip while Bruce stood by. When Tina shook her head at him, Bruce moved toward him.

"This is one of Tina's law centers," he began by way of explanation. "It's called The Justice Center. People call our 1-800 number here when they have questions about the law or are in crisis. Lawyers use us to do legal research for cases, but they have to pay for the service. Others don't. The people you see here and in the other locations are, for the most part, law school students. They work here between classes. Others are first, second or third-year lawyers who are gaining experience working here. They assist the students with a wide variety of cases that have become more complex. When a court appearance may be required, the case is transferred to a lawyer who specializes in that type of issue and has signed up to do *pro bono* work for the Justice Center. Whoever handled the initial call is dispatched to work with the attorney who agreed to handle court appearances."

"This is just in Illinois, right?" asked Nico.

Bruce shook his head. "No, this is nationally. We have an international section, though it's not very large. Thomas Ashton Marshall usually handles international clients through his Washington, DC, or Portland, Oregon, law firm, Marshall and Marshall. The other locations are Washington, DC, Denver, Colorado, and Seattle, Washington. They come online starting in DC at 6:00 AM and stagger startup across the time zones."

Nico turned and looked through the glass-panel wall to the panoramic view of people on calls. Occasionally, a light would go on at someone's station and a person would hurry over.

"What's going on there?" Nico asked.

Bruce followed his line of sight. "Someone may have found more evidence in an illegal scheme. In the databases we use are indications something in a court case is coming to a head. Any number of situations may be taking place, but one of the law school students thinks she has a match. I can follow it up if you're interested."

"I'm curious," said Nico.

"Say no more. I'll let you know what's what after Tina meets with the Justice Center's Director," he said nodding to a middle-aged woman who was heading in their direction. "Mom," Bruce said as the woman entered the conference room.

"Hi, honey," the woman acknowledged hugging Bruce and then turning to Nico. "You're Nicholas Collins," she said extending her hand.

"I am, yes," he said accepting the hand she extended.

"Charlotte Joyner," she said while she shook hands.

"A pleasure to meet you."

"Thank you. I presume it's Tina's wish for you to be here."

"She hasn't kicked me out so far today."

"Mom, Mr. Collins noticed a light go on at Station 82. Do you know what that was about?"

"A car dealership pulled another bait and switch in Jackson, Mississippi. Fourth one we've been alerted to. We're preparing a case file for the Mississippi State's Attorney General."

"You help law enforcement as well as defense counsel?" asked Nico.

"Yes, but it depends. It's about getting justice for the people least able to protect themselves. We can't save every puppy in the pound . . ."

"Still, you do for people what needs to be done," Tina interrupted and hugged Charlotte.

"We're getting there," she replied. "Tina plucked me out of obscurity as the dean of a law school and plopped me down here where I work harder than I ever have and love it more."

"It's not my fault. Blame Bruce and KC. They are the ones who sealed your fate."

"I do," she said and laughed. "Let's get started." So they did. Mrs. Joyner brought Tina up to date on interesting cases that had been discovered while Tina considered how to fit them into potential exposés. Bruce took notes on what Tina wanted to be done in each instance.

"I'm concerned about the number of threats made against your life, Tina. I've given everything I've found to Ned, Keenen, and Tyson. They believe some of these threats are actionable. Now with BoBo incapacitated, I think you should bring on more skilled security."

"I'm aware of it, Charlotte, believe me. So are my family and friends, but I'm not going to live my life in a box."

This news gave Nico a mental jolt. He hadn't imagined the work she did would scare her enemies into threatening her with bodily harm. Something swelled in his gut causing a severe sense of protectiveness toward her. He silently vowed no one and nothing would harm one strand of the hair on her head. He would talk with her Uncle Ned and brothers to determine what measures were being taken to protect her and what he could do to help. He would also talk with Tina.

An hour and thirty minutes later, the meeting had ended. They were on the move again to the production arm of her operation. This time, when she went through the steps and stages, Nico could see how anyone involved in human trafficking might want to silence the maven of Sweet Justice production. She was integrally involved, detailed, and digging deeper into the crime. He had a better understanding of why he had been so severely attacked for tailing her. Fear coated those who care about her; both family and friends. However, the fearless Constantina Justice still wore a face that screamed **I dare you**.

"Hungry?" Tina asked Nicholas as they left her office well after one in the afternoon. She arranged for the Greene Team to offer their apologies for assaulting him.

He accepted the apologies but had the distinct impression that, given the same set of circumstances, the next intruder would fare no better than he had.

"I could eat," he said and shrugged.

"Good. I'm hungry, too. Let's head out."

He thought they would head to the cafeteria in the building on the first floor, but instead, they went to the rooftop again and headed for the helicopter.

She wasn't ignoring Nicholas she assured herself, but her day had been busy. Still, she set things aside to make room in her schedule to hear Nicholas out. She had gathered a great deal of information and set wheels in motion for what she had in mind to do.

As she piloted the chopper north, skirting The Lakes to the upper peninsula of Wisconsin on Lake Superior, she plotted and planned how to approach the tasks ahead of her. She loved this view of the Great Lakes from twenty thousand feet. In no time they were approaching her wild horse ranch west of Houghton. She watched the bright orange, wind-direction cones that circled her landing zone. The wind was far more fierce and the snow much heavier in this area that jutted out into Lake Superior and edged her property on the northwestern side. The roofs of the huge red barns held at least a foot of snow, but ranch hands still guided the wild horses from pastures to corrals and paddocks.

Several of the horses were due to deliver within the next twenty-four hours and Tina planned to be there to witness the events. She set the bird down and scrambled to lash down the skids. The wind was serious on the open land with nothing but a stand of trees as buffers. Several ranch hands rode up on horses to assist. She hailed them all by name and bending into the wind led Nico to a massive, modern-looking log cabin.

Once inside, the heat wrapped around them like a moist, warm blanket.

"*Tao,*" Tina called out once she unraveled from her hat, gloves, scarf, and coat.

"Come to the kitchen, Namida," a male voice returned.

She could smell the beef stew half a house away.

"*Hola!*" a big, rawboned man with a ruddy face, black streaked hair, and a long braid down the middle of his back called out when they entered the kitchen. He was placing large soup bowls on the wood-plank, raw-edged, trestle table next to mugs of water. A bowl of fresh salad stood in the middle of the setup. The aroma of freshly baked bread permeated the air. "It was a good flight?"

"A little turbulent, but we were able to fly above it for most of the trip. I wasn't sure I'd be able to land."

"A Nor'easter is coming through later tonight. It should be calmer in a few days." Then he turned after putting a large, covered soup tureen down on the table before offering a hand to Nico. "Twin Tao Outlaw," the man said shaking Nico's hand. "You're Nico the Brave," Tao said and laughed.

"You have to be when you're around Tina Justice."

"Then you know you're no fool. Sit. Eat. Beer or wine?"

"Red wine if you have it. I need to wash up," said Nico.

"There. That hall, second door on the right."

Nico followed instructions and left to take care of his needs.

Tina watched him go, then washed her hands at the farm sink. "Smells good in here."

"Until this snow, we had a good harvest."

"It's early in the season."

Tao nodded. "The boys are scrambling to bring the herds in before nightfall. Others are stringing rope lines and bringing in fresh bales of hay and feed. It's going to get messy, but we should have enough cat litter to hold us for a week if need be. Then we have to use the horse wash to survive. The dump trucks are ready to handle the mess."

Nico re-entered the kitchen and heard the "horse wash" comment. He was curious but didn't ask as his stomach needed immediate attention. They had breakfast at seven and coffee once they arrived at her office, but nothing since and he was starving. Still operating on three hours of sleep, Tina hadn't slowed down or yawned. Her father was right. It was indeed a bumpy ride.

Tao served the food but didn't stay. He had work to do preparing food for the ranch hands he told them.

Tina and Nico talked while they ate, both filling their bowls twice with the chunky beef, garlic, carrots, peas, potatoes, celery, onions, and thick, savory gravy. The crusty, fresh-baked bread was still warm from the oven and the salad tasted fresh picked. When they finished, they stowed the leftovers and stacked their dishes in the dishwasher.

"Come," said Tina, carrying two mugs of hot, mulled-wine punch, "let's get comfortable."

Nico noticed she didn't have on her headset for a change and led him to a long, wide divan in front of a roaring fire in a great room. She sat at one end and encouraged him to remove his boots and stretch out as she had facing her. "Now tell me about satellites and transponders." She passed a mug to him.

"That's what you want to know about?" he asked surprised, yet again.

"Yes, how does it work?"

"A rocket launches a satellite into a geostationary orbit above the Earth. The satellite is made up of one hundred transponders. Each transponder contains a number of channels on different frequencies. Each transponder is preset to receive and send digital signals directed at it from earth uplink locations. The signals can be audio, video, data or a combination. The signal or signals send downloaded information to the earth to satellite receivers in a wide, broadcast area attached to homes or businesses in a specific area or across the country. It's not particularly complicated."

"Each transponder can handle many channels of information interactively?"

"Yes, it can. It is likely to be able to function that way for many years. Since it's digital, the signals uplink and those downlinked are much leaner, clearer than analog signals with little or no atmospheric distortion or interference."

"What happens to it then when it stops functioning?"

He shrugged. "It becomes so much space junk. However, Dr. Tate Kennedy and Astronaut Benjamin Alexander have started a company which will collect space junk and return it for disposal or reconditioning."

"Benny Alexander?" she asked and brightened considerably.

"Yes, I believe you know his sister, Vivian."

"I do, very well. I know the entire family. Vivian and I were in undergrad together at Spelman University. Benny's going to leave the military?"

"Not yet, no. Eventually, yes. What I read about the operation was preliminary. You and Benjamin were close?"

She laughed. "At one time I had this monstrous crush on him, but no, not in the way you suggest. He married a local Chi-Town girl, Stacy Greene. She's now Admiral Greene. She trained the Greene Team. The ones responsible for your tune-up last week."

He rubbed his still sore ribs. "I'll remember to mention it the next time I run into her."

"They apologized to you, something they've never had to do before. They won't soon forget it. You shouldn't have a problem with them again."

"Good to know."

She laughed at his deadpan delivery and he noticed how that gesture changed the angles and planes of her face into something spectacular. Her eyes danced with merriment, surprising him yet again. He noticed she downplayed her beauty, yet he only caught glimpses of it until now.

"Why are you looking at me like that?"

He shook his head as if to clear it and took another sip of the warm wine. "Sorry. You laughed and it's the first time you smiled at me."

She shrugged. "It's the first time I haven't been annoyed with you. Tell me more about your satellite and its transponder space."

So he did, sharing his knowledge with her. She was an extremely quick study, asking serious questions most people would never have thought to ask. Then again, he remembered she was a trained attorney. The afternoon sank into the evening as they sat at opposite ends of the divan sipping cups of hot wine with a Native American blanket over their legs and the fireplace still ablaze with huge logs crackling and popping in the grate.

Into the comfortable silence came the sound of boots and spurs on hardwood floors.

"*Tina,*" a voice called out.

"Great room," she answered and a man in authentic heavy western gear entered. He wore a grin on his rugged face when he spotted her on the divan.

"You play footsie with this man, but cannot answer your phone?"

"What can I say, Uncle Geo, he gives good foot."

He let out a bawdy laugh, plucking her up from the sofa and giving a noisy kiss on her mouth. "If I didn't love my wife so much and I wasn't your uncle, I'd show you what good foot feels like."

"Where is she?"

"In the stall with her other husband waiting for you."

"Okay, okay. This is Nicholas Collins, Uncle Geo," she said as she stuck her feet in her boots.

"Yes, so I've heard," he said shaking hands with Nico. "The Brave One who comes to your home uninvited. Why is he not dead?"

"Big Red gave him a reprieve."

"Must have been Anna Lettie's doing that saved him."

"*Abuela* Alicia was in town, too."

"Ah, yes, the football weekend. Did you win?"

"Of course."

"Then Bouchard has to wait until next year again to challenge you to be the quarterback."

"Builds character," Tina said and grinned wide and salaciously.

"Maybe I do him a favor and get you pregnant by one of my ranch hands and you'll be out for the season."

"Don't even speak it into the air, Uncle Geo."

"My sister let you run wild too long. You need to settle down and raise a family."

"We have enough family as it is. You, Tao and Ayanna have nine children."

"They have yet to produce as many grandchildren as we want."

Finally bundled, they went out a side door into a world of furious white snow.

"Grab the rope, Collins, and don't let go," hailed Tina as hand-over-hand she grabbed hold of the rope pulling herself through the blizzard.

He sensed she was ahead of him, but he could not see her as he squinted through the snow storm. It seemed like forever when he came to the end of the rope inside a horse barn. He expected it to be cold with a door wide open to the elements, but, surprisingly, it was warm inside what looked like a huge arena. He could feel the heat rising up from the floor. Giant ceiling fans turned forcing the heat down to the floor, dissipating the cold. There were horses in paddocks moving restlessly from place to place.

"They haven't settled down yet," said Tina, who stood beside him in a fenced corridor between the paddocks. "They're wild horses not accustomed to being corralled so don't get too close to a gate."

He had no intention of getting anywhere near the huge animals. He followed Tina and her Uncle Geo to another connected building just as large as the previous one where a woman stood holding the tail of a horse with one hand and her arm up to her shoulder in what seemed to be the horse's ass. She wore what looked like a black, diving wetsuit from the neck down and black rubber boots. Her grey-streaked hair was plated and twined in a ball on top of her head. A clear shield covered her head and face.

"Namida," Star Dancer in Chippewa, the woman called out.

"Nekoma Kiwidinock," grandmother, Woman of the Wind, Tina responded.

"One moment. This colt is hard to turn in the womb, but I almost have it. Otherwise, it would be a breech birth. Feel it now, Geo," she ordered.

Geo stepped forward and, as Tao held the horse's head with a cover over its eyes, Geo felt the horse's belly. "Twins, I think," he said, grinning.

Nico noticed Tao and Geo were nearly identical. Tall, rawboned, but obviously strong. When he looked back at the woman, she had both arms in the horse pulling with all of her strength. The horse whinnied and tried to twist away, but the woman soon pulled the colt out of the womb. Others stepped in and covered the newborn with straw cleaning away the sack and fluid covering the colt as it lay on the fresh hay palate. The woman again had her arms inside the horse pulling a second colt free of the mother's womb. This time after the second colt was born, everyone cleared out of the stall while the cover was removed from the mare's head and eyes.

Immediately the mare sought her offspring nudging them until they began to gain their spindly, unsteady legs. Instinctively the twins found the mare's teats and began to suckle.

"I'd hug you, but I'm a mess and I have eight more to deliver tonight."

In the meantime, someone was hosing the woman down with some type of soapy solution and water.

"Diablo's been busy," grinned Tina and leaned in for a kiss on both cheeks. "My Abuela Alicia gave him to me for my twenty-first birthday," she told Nico. "He's sired many of the wild horses you see here. Dr. Kiwidinock Outlaw, this is Nicholas Collins. Kiwidinock is my grand aunt and the best veterinarian, bar none, in the state."

"I've been hearing about Nicholas Collins, The Brave, but no one told me he was such a big, handsome man. You do like your men well built, Namida."

"Thank you . . . I think," said Nico.

She laughed at his chagrin. "Don't worry, son, I'm not a cougar in training. Those two men are my husbands and we have nine children, but only eleven grandchildren. I have my hands full with them. However, if I can't marry my Namida off to you, I have several single granddaughters."

He wasn't sure he heard her right, but he wasn't about to ask for clarification with the threat of marriage hanging in the balance.

"Kiwidinock means Woman of the Wind in Sokaogon Chippewa. She is my gram Anna Lettie's sister-in-law. Uncles Geo and Tao are my grandmother, Anna Lettie's twin younger brothers."

"They have nine children?" asked Nico.

"My granduncles were a bit busy, too."

Tao swatted Tina on her bottom and she laughed dancing nimbly out of the way.

"We are Oneida," said Geo. "What would you expect?"

"You're Outlaws, too," she said and then turned to Nicholas. "My grandmother's great-grandfather helped runaway slaves escape the South up through here into Canada. No one ever knew his given name though we know he could read and write. Everyone just called him Outlaw and the name stuck. Legend had it he was a Buffalo soldier who hated what slaves were subjected to. Some said he was Black; others claimed he was Oneida. DNA shows both traits in the family tree."

"Come, we have time for genealogy and history lessons later. We have work to do," said Kiwidinock as she marched off to check on other horses who were due to deliver. She was helping them along by breaking their water sacks to induce labor.

More introductions were made as the evening progressed with more births. By three in the morning, Nico's eyes were ready to cross from fatigue. Tina led him back to the house using the rope line through the blizzard, but no one else followed them in. Rather, the Outlaws stayed in the horse barns to see to the mares and tag their colts.

"Want something to eat or drink?" Tina asked as they stripped out of their heavy weather gear in a mudroom.

"After wading through seminal fluids, uh, no. I don't think so."

Tina laughed, then said. "Get some sleep. It looks like we're not going to be able to fly out later this morning."

"Aren't you going to bed?"

"I will shortly. Rest well. You've had a long day."

He shook his head and walked away. He was dog tired and not ashamed to admit it. After his shower, he headed to the kitchen for a bottle of water. All of the lights were out. Tina was showered and asleep on the divan. She had apparently put more logs on the fire. Her laptop was on her lap. He picked it up and powered it off, placing it on the table behind the tall divan. Rather than go off to his bedroom, he climbed in at the opposite end of the divan as they had been before, covered them both, and promptly went to sleep.

When she heard his even breathing, Tina sat up and looked her fill of Nicholas by firelight. She wasn't sure, but she was beginning to like this Nicholas Collins. He thought she was asleep and could have snooped in her computer, but instead, he put it away, made sure she was covered, and crawled onto the divan opposite her. Yes, she was beginning to like him . . . a lot, she thought before she let sleep finally have her.

12

Initially, it was the scent of robust coffee and frying sausages that awakened him from a deep sleep. A glance at his watch surprised him that it was half past eleven. He never slept late as a rule. The tall trapezoid windows assured him it was daytime, but the white snow that blocked any view of the landscape proved to him they were not going anywhere soon.

Then he heard it. The sound of a female voice somewhere in the house singing the Whitney Houston classic, "I Want to Dance with Somebody" and surprisingly on key. He climbed out from under the heavy blanket and off the divan following the sound of Tina's voice as she went into the chorus about wanting to dance with someone who loved her. Wanting to feel the heat from someone. Yeah, he felt the heat, all right, and not from the heated floors or warm kitchen cooking. He leaned a hip against a kitchen counter as she jammed to the music swinging her very impressive hips provocatively into an energetic and complicated Latin dance, probably a Salsa, her feet moving as if choreographed and drum beating the handles of a pair of long wooden spoons on the countertop, upper cabinets, and then pots hanging from racks attached to the ceiling as if she took lessons from Sheila E.

When she swung around still singing, playing her sticks, and spotted him, she mischievously grinned but kept singing and dancing what now looked like a Samba. Earbud wires hung down into the breast pocket of a too-large red plaid shirt that skimmed just above her bare knees. The sleeves were rolled up to her elbows and her feet were covered in thick, gray socks that were stacked around her well-toned legs like dancer's warmers well above her ankles. Her hair was loose, a profusion of dark auburn curls that flew around her gamine face, shoulders, and down her back as she continued to sing and dance to the conclusion of the energetic song.

Nico pushed himself away from the counter toward her, took one of the earbuds from her ear placing it in his own. The beginning strains of "I Have Nothing Without You" played while he nudged her into a slow dance around the kitchen island. The sticks forgotten, she moved into him, going up on her toes, her arms going to circle his neck causing the shirt to rise, too, as they matched step for step to the sultry music and Ms. Houston's incredible voice.

Tina closed her eyes inhaling the natural scent of him just under his jawline. His strong arms cocooning her against his bare chest fitting down to his firm thighs. He turned her in his arms, her back to his bare chest without missing a beat as they danced. One arm came across her above her breasts while the other fit across her abdomen guiding her movement to match his. He leaned down, his lips brushing her ear for the final breathless words of the song.

They stood still for ponderous moments as their hearts beat strongly in their chests.

"Breakfast smells great. What can I help you do?" Nico asked into the humming silence. If he didn't move to neutral territory, he'd have her spread eagle on the island's quartz countertop with his thickening member buried deep inside her.

Tina opened her eyes and slowly moved out of the warmth of Nicholas' embrace. "Brunch, and you can turn the potatoes, onions, and peppers in the skillet. Then check the biscuits in the wall oven while I scramble the eggs."

"With cheese, I hope," he said as he lifted the lid on the beautiful, nearly done hash brown potatoes. He felt uncomfortably bereft without her in his arms or close to his needful body. "Do you mind if we eat in here?" he asked. He reached for a covered bowl for the potatoes that would keep them warm.

"Not at all. Plates in the glass-fronted cabinet. Fresh apple juice in the fridge."

"Silverware?"

"Behind you in the second drawer to your left."

Together they managed to arrange the meal on the long, tall, quartz countertop where moments earlier he imaged having unbridled sex with Constantina Justice. They blessed the food and then dug in.

"This is good, Tina. Thank you."

"You're welcome, but don't mention it to anyone that I cooked."

"Your secret is safe with me."

"I want something else from you besides your promise to keep my secret," she said and had him looking up at her from his plate.

He eyed her suspiciously. If this was a pick-up line, he hadn't seen it coming. He wasn't sure how he felt about it if it was. "Okay, I'm listening. What do you want from me?"

"Space on your satellite; a broadcast transponder."

Folding his arms over his chest, he sat back in the tall seat and stared at her in thought and contemplation. He for sure hadn't anticipated that. Her beauty kept edging into his conscious thoughts, preventing him from thinking strategically. "You know every one of the transponders has been sold."

"Sold, yes, but not all of them have been paid for. You have several customers who have not yet come up with the cash or financing to seal the deal."

"You know this because how?"

"Research. I've made an offer yesterday to the startup internet company, Star HyperNet, to buy them out. I expect a signed contract today."

Star HyperNet was, indeed, one of the companies his top man, Jerrod Duncan, negotiated with. They weren't well organized or run efficiently and he had considered buying them out himself. "I gather you made the offer before you had me explain the operation to you." At her nod of agreement, he said, "You've been busy."

"When I know what I want, I don't waste time going after it."

He nodded in contemplation. "I want your show on my network for five years or you don't get the transponder."

Her brows winged up in surprise. "Three years."

"Four years. Simulcast on both networks; yours and mine with an option for ten."

"Five-year option."

"Eight years."

"Seven, and that's my bottom line."

He shrugged. "Okay, done. Seven-year option and I get the first right of refusal beyond year seven."

She considered his proposal. Actually, he was holding all the cards. She wasn't negotiating from a position of strength and he knew it. It was his satellite to do with as he pleased. He was spending billions on its launch. Her only other alternative was to wait for the next broadcast satellite to be launched several years from now. The problem was, she didn't want to wait. A bird in the hand was worth more to her now than the promise of two in the bush later. "Contracts signed today?"

"That's doable. Where's your printer?"

"In the office. I'll show you after brunch."

"Good. Would you like more coffee?"

"I would, yes, thank you," she said and handed her mug to him. She liked he didn't expect her to wait on him. *Funny,* she considered, *Ronald wouldn't even have thought to offer to get coffee for her.*

They chatted amicably while they finished eating.

"So, your grand aunt and uncles weren't just pulling my leg. She actually lives with both men?"

"It's true. I forget which one she's actually married to. Geo is the older twin, but, yes, both men are her husbands."

"Interesting. I guess it works since they've been married so long."

"Forty years, I think, so it does. They've known her since she was a girl. They both fell in love with her and when she came back to set up her practice here after graduating from veterinary school, they popped the question. There still aren't a lot of single women living up here. There is only a population of six or seven thousand people living in the closest town to here and that's still hours away. Sharing a wife or husband is commonplace in this area. It's very rural and isolated. There are no laws that prohibit it. The weather is not often hospitable."

"Which leads me to believe you were aware the weather conditions were going to become severe. You packed a bag for me with heavy weather gear. You wanted to get me alone."

"I did, yes. However, I did actually want to be here to see the horses born. We leave them in the wild and keep track of them and their health most of the year. Then we bring them in to check up on them before heavy weather sets in. In a few years, I'm going to have to think about thinning the herd. They need more space than I have here on this ranch. I want a bigger place. Probably someplace warmer with plenty of land for the horses to roam. Since I was going to be here anyway, I promised my family I would hear you out. Bringing you along kills two birds with one stone so to speak."

"I see. The storm?"

"Yes, I knew it was coming and I had to push some things around to arrive before it hit."

"You already knew what you wanted before your parents put pressure on you to talk with me."

"No, actually, it didn't occur to me until I read the dossier on you."

It was his turn to be surprised. "I should have known you'd do your due diligence before considering buying a company like Star HyperNet just to get access to a transponder."

"It made sense to me. I can lease back transponder space for channels I won't immediately need for broadcasting or cablecasting programs."

"You'll recoup your investment immediately if you decide to do that."

She grinned. "Yes, I know. Shall we begin the re-negotiations on the price of the transponder?"

***

It was mid-afternoon, and they were still in heavy negotiations. This time it was about the fees for the insurance coverage should something happen to the satellite during the launch or after it was deployed in a geostationary orbit. Generally, Nico would have had Jerrod negotiate the fine points, but he found he was thoroughly enjoying the debate with Tina...Tina Rabbit, he corrected; Namida, Star Dancer.

The nickname her brothers gave her was on point. The woman wasn't still for two minutes at a time. She thought on her feet and looked damn good doing it, too. Occasionally, he'd put a roadblock in the mix just to see her fists punch her hips and her expressive eyes narrow to slits on him as she figured out a way over, under or around him. He had her skidding to a stop from time to time, but she always found her way around him to get what she wanted in the end. If there was a term she wasn't familiar with, she called a timeout until she could research it. That usually meant they made a foray into the kitchen for something to nibble on or a bathroom break while she consulted with someone at her call center. When they resumed ten to fifteen minutes later, she was raring to go.

What was distracting him was the red plaid shirt she wore. He was fairly certain she was naked underneath, but her legs and thighs were clearly a distraction.

Tina loved this negotiation and she was not afraid to admit to herself she was enjoying Nicholas Collins. Neither of them had taken time to dress for the day. There was no point since they were snowbound. They couldn't even wade through the field to the barn because it was too deep. He still wore the red plaid pajama bottoms to the shirt she wore. She had packed his bag but saved the shirt for her own use. She admitted to herself she liked looking at his muscular bare chest and arms and made no apology for her voyeurism. He looked his fill of her thighs and legs, so she considered it a fair deal. However, watching his muscles move, when he locked his fingers together behind his head, was to her way of thinking, pure poetry in motion. The bruises on his upper body were beginning to fade, but she still wanted her lips on what was left. His six pack abs were pronounced and his pecks well-cut and defined.

The four-thousand-foot cabin was comfortably warm and quiet except for their voices. They worked through the standard contract he downloaded. If she haggled over a minute point, it was just to see him roll his eyes up to the ceiling praying for divine intervention. She enjoyed tweaking his nose on certain points and grinned when he acquiesced and changed the terms or conditions.

When he held her in a slow dance earlier, she didn't want the music to stop. That was a first for her she realized. Never before had a moment existed for her like the one they shared while dancing in the kitchen. She could feel him pressed firmly against her back, his member thick between her cheeks. Yet, the moment wasn't about sex, but intimacy. At that moment she had only to turn her head slightly to capture his mouth, but she didn't do that. It took all the restraint she could muster to deny herself the pleasure. However, she did it as much for herself as she did for him.

He had been subjected to women taking advantage of him since he was fifteen, she learned. Clearly, he was over twice that age now; a child no more. However, if she could, Tina felt she would have had Lana Norton incarcerated for the sexual abuse she had subjected him to when he wasn't much more than a child. As a result, according to his dossier, he was never able to form a normal relationship with a woman...not even close. He had the typical male response to women he wanted or who wanted him in high school, college, and the pros, but it was purely physical and superficial. No emotion included. It was more of a mechanical process. She wasn't about to tap him for emotionless sex the way others had. There was no doubt she wanted him, but he would have to make her feel the heat for more than a physical release.

"Okay, so that appears to be the last detail," said Peter Brock over the satphone connection they established.

"Agreed, Colton? Rommel? Zack? Jerrod?" asked Nico of his team.

"Agreed," they all answered.

"Good working with you again, Zackery. Final contracts coming through now," said Peter. Immediately the fax machine began to spit out the multi-paged documents.

"Where is Cheryl?" asked Tina of Peter about his wife, her BFF.

"She and our girls are in the kitchen mixing up something for tonight's dessert."

"The girls are only two and three years old. They don't need to know about kitchen duties already. What's wrong with Cheryl?"

"Hormones. I think we're pregnant again."

"Oh. Well then," said Tina, delighted.

"Nothing's confirmed, but I know my wife. She's definitely feeling very maternal. She jumps my bones often and continuously."

"Yeah, I'll just bet you fight her off with all your strength."

"Well," he said with a long sigh. "She just overwhelms me each time."

Tina laughed as she pulled the copies from the fax machine.

"Are we done for the time being? I want to go play house with my wife."

"Yes, Peter, hug Cheryl and the girls for me."

"Will do," he said and disconnected.

"Yes, that works for me," said Nico to his advertising agency head and public relations officer. "We'll release the announcement to the press before the evening news cycle on the West Coast. Sweet Justice Production revealed, in a joint statement with NICO Communications, yadda yadda."

"This is unbelievable news, Nico! Man, this will rock the telecommunications industry to its foundation! You've pulled off a miracle getting Sweet Justice Productions to come on board!" said Jerrod, ecstatic.

"You really did it, boss. I know Tina. She's tough," said Zack.

"Yeah, yeah, let me see the announcement for final approval before it's released."

"Yes, sir! Right away!" Zack gushed and then disconnected.

Nico dropped the phone in his lap and dug the heels of his hands in his eye sockets. He and Tina had been negotiating for a solid four hours before they finished ironing out the details of their contracts for the transponder. She was a tough and savvy negotiator, but in the end, there were compromises on both sides and they each got what they wanted out of each deal.

He was good, Tina thought as she poured a mug of mulled wine punch for each of them. She was more than satisfied with the deals they struck. She was even excited about the broadcasting freedom she was about to undertake. It certainly meant she would be working harder and expanding her operation. She needed to get on JaiHonnah Baylor's schedule to design a larger facility to house her much larger operation and on Roderick Baylor's schedule to begin construction. Roderick or JRock, as he had been known as the sports icon, now built homes and businesses using container units which meant he could fabricate the spaces off-site and truck them in fitting them together like a Lego set in no time. It saved time and a great deal of money. If she could get on the husband-and-wife team's schedule, she could be operational in less than four months.

She handed a mug to Nicholas as he continued to talk with his people in his New York City office. She curled into the opposite end of the divan from him and dialed her college friend.

"Hey, Tina," said JaiHonnah Hawkins Baylor.

"How's life treating you, Jai?"

"Better and better. How was the football game?"

"We won, of course. Sorry you couldn't make the trip."

"We are, too, but I'm actually so pregnant, I'm waddling like a duck. Roderick is hovering like a mother hen."

"When are you due?"

"Around Thanksgiving, so about a month from now. At least this time we don't think it's twins," she said laughing."

"There is that. Did you ever think, when we were back in undergrad at Spelman, you'd become the mother of so many?"

JaiHonnah hooted a laugh. "I never envisioned anything other than becoming an architect, structural and civil engineer. Now, between us, Roderick and I have five children and another on the way. We're spending more time parenting than at our careers."

"You're happy, though. I can hear it in your voice."

She sighed. "Deliriously happy. What about you, Tina? When are you going to slow down and let someone catch you?"

For some inexplicable reason, Tina looked up a Nicholas and found him looking at her while he continued to talk business with his office staff.

"I'm the seventh child of Redmond and Marguerite Justice. I'll consider settling down after all of my brothers are wedded and bedded. Until then, a man just has to be able to keep up with me."

"Yeah, right. You know your brothers are confirmed bachelors," Jai said and laughed. "So, other than the Mission: Impossible, what's up with you?"

"I've just agreed to sign Sweet Justice Productions on with NICO Communications and purchased a transponder on their satellite that is about to launch."

"*Whoa!* Talk about burying the lead, Tina. That's fantastic! Congrats! You need what, more office space?"

"Exactly. Can you fit me in?"

"I can, yes, but I'm going to put you in touch with my cousin Lizelle Fiona Lowry. She's a brilliant architect in her own right. We've collaborated on several projects. She's single and not pregnant," Jai said laughing. "Roderick and I are going to take a little time off once the baby is born. Lizelle will step in to handle my projects with my staff. Wesley Greenfield will step in for Roderick on current contracts. Will that work for you?"

"If she's as good as you say she is, then yes. She need only duplicate what you did with Sweet Justice Production's studios. Wesley is familiar with my operation. I envision a triangle-shaped building forming an inner courtyard and maybe two to three additional levels added to what already exists. I want the inner courtyard covered at the rooftop level so that the ground and balconies can be used year-round."

"That's a great design idea, Tina, and it will cause the least amount of disruption for your existing facility. The buildings can be connected by breezeways on each level. I'll have to figure out how to form a triangular bubbletop to withstand the heavy Chicago snowfall. I can personally work with that fairly quickly and then I'll work with Lizelle on the prototype. Give me a few days to pull her in and put it together."

"Thanks, Jai. What about JRock's schedule?"

"I'll put it on his calendar and Wesley Greenfield's. We'll get back to you by the end of the week with their projected construction timeframes."

"Works for me. Thanks, Jai."

"Hey, what are besties for?" she said.

"By the way, I'm going to race. You want in?"

Jai's scream was loud and long. "Oh, yes, definitely! It's just what Roderick and I were thinking of doing for a family retreat. When and where?"

They talked for another thirty minutes making plans for the sailing holiday.

Nico watched her while she talked with someone who was obviously a close friend. She was warm and affectionate with people she cared about, he noticed. When it was purely a business relationship, he could sense that about her, too. She had a clear and direct approach to the discussion…very methodical. Details didn't escape her notice. Nothing much of importance was left uninvestigated. He very much liked and appreciated what he saw. He had to get up and walk away. She was becoming embedded in his psyche and that couldn't be good for either of them. These feelings and emotions were new to him and he wasn't at all sure how to handle his reactions to them. What he did know was the longer he sat looking at her, the harder it would be to walk away once the deal was inked.

13

Nicholas stretched for the third time that Tina noticed. Either he was fatigued or succumbing to cabin fever. They really hadn't been in more than a few of the many rooms in the cabin, but he had been working steadily reading reports on his iPad for the last few hours. So had she and she was mentally tired. Her stomach told her she needed to fuel up soon, too.

"Come on, Collins. Let's get some exercise."

His brows winged up as he looked at the whiteout through the windows. No way were they going outside in that. He looked at her as she stood and reached a hand to help him up from the divan. "The last time you said that to me, you took me sailing. I know we're on the shore of Lake Superior, but I don't think we should sail in this whiteout."

"Oh, I think we can do better than that. How do you feel about swimming in this weather?" she asked leading him by his hand down a corridor to double doors. She dropped his hand and opened the doors with a flourish. *"Voila,"* she said grinning.

He walked through the doors into a heated, cedar-paneled room with a high ceiling that contained a swimming pool. It was long, but only four lanes wide and, according to the scale along the perimeter, about eight feet deep. The opposite wall was glass providing a full view of the snow piled about twenty-inches deep and more falling. Lounge chairs and small tables occupied areas of the pool deck with live, green trees and plants strategically placed. There was a dressing room and restroom with shower stalls. The back wall also appeared to contain a kitchenette with a long bar and stools providing additional seating.

Tina watched the surprise on Nicholas' face dissolve into a pleasant smile.

He turned and looked at her. "I, uh, don't have swimwear."

She raised one eyebrow and began unbuttoning her shirt. She let it fall to the decking and stepped out of it and her socks. "You don't need it, but if you're shy, I promise I won't look," she said and executed a perfect dive into the water.

"O-kay," he said and dropped his pajama bottoms, removed his socks, and followed suit.

They swam laps *au naturel* in the comfortably warm waters doing both breast and back strokes and finally lazily floating on their backs looking up at the ceiling.

A while later they climbed out of the water, minds relaxed, muscles sufficiently limbered, and dried off. Tina retrieved a couple of terrycloth robes and slippers from a closet and wrapped her hair in a towel. Then they headed off to the kitchen.

"Steak, baked potato, and fresh steamed cauliflower and broccoli sound good to you?" she asked.

"It does, yes. It's the one thing I can prepare without screwing it up. You prepared brunch. Let me do the dinner."

Pleasantly surprised, she nodded in agreement and took a seat at the long, quartz-topped, center-post workstation to towel dry then blow dry her hair.

Nico hunted up the ingredients and seasonings needed for the meal, then downloaded Down to The Bone's *Staten Island Groove* on her iPod audio system. He handed two wooden spoons to her and had her hooting in laughter. She picked up the beat and played drumming along while bouncing in her seat to the music. She was really a very good drummer.

She watched him as he seasoned and then seared the Porterhouse steaks on both sides before placing them in the wall oven to broil. By the time the Idaho potatoes baked through in a microwave oven, the broccoli and cauliflower had steamed to perfection in a double boiler on the range top. He sautéed onions and peppers in butter and Worcestershire sauce for a nice topping for the steaks.

Within thirty minutes they were adding sour cream and chives to their piping hot potatoes and red wine to their goblets.

Nico waited while Tina took a testing bite of her steak. She looked up at him, her eyes smiling conveying her pleasure. Then she dug in with gusto.

"Can you keep another secret?"

"Sure, as long as I don't have to keep it from your grandmothers or mother. They intimidate me. One look from any of them and I'd spill my guts. I'd tell them anything and everything they want to know."

Tina had to cover her mouth as she laughed. "Then you know how the rest of us feel, but no you don't have to keep the secret from them."

"Then, okay, I can handle that. What is it?" he asked lifting the goblet to his mouth.

"I'm having a boat built to enter the America's Cup next year."

The goblet never made it to his lips. Instead he sat staring at her, searching her eyes as he placed the delicate piece of stemware down on the quartz countertop. "Well, hell," he said just above a whisper, before picking up the wine bottle and pouring generous portions into each glass. Then he lifted his in toast. "Anchors away and give 'em hell!" he said touching his glass to hers. Then taking a sip.

"How about *we* give 'em hell?"

Slowly the goblet left his lips. "I've been on a sailboat before, but I've never raced. Monday was really my first experience on a sailboat that large," he said though remembering Lana Norton's sailboat when he was a teen."

"You have good reflexes, an agile mind, and superior upper body strength. You obviously work out regularly. A few lessons to get your sea legs and routines added to your regimen and you'd be good to go. What do you say?"

"Yes, I say yes."

She nodded and again touched her goblet to his; the touching of fine crystal making a pleasant sound. This time they both drank deep, eyeing each other.

"Besides your brothers, who else have you selected to crew?"

She laughed. "You're beginning to know us very well. Let's see, the list includes Cheryl and Peter Brock, Kristen Catherine and Thomas Marshall, and George and Clarence, Junior. Then there's: JRock Baylor, his wife, JaiHonnah, and their children; Jai's sister, LaiLoni and her husband, Jefferson Logan, and their family; and Vivian Montgomery, her husband, Chuck and their twenty-five children. Maybe even

Benny Alexander, his wife Stacy and their seven children if they can manage it. All of the usual suspects. It's going to be big fun with about seventy of us. JRock and Vivian both own sailing yachts and have homes along the route we'll take to get to Argentina for the competition."

He understood the significance of the lineup. All were family to her and she was including him. He was the only outsider being permitted into the inner circle. It humbled him. He had never been included in any group except on the gridiron and that was work. He had no friends to speak of, but Constantina Justice was changing that dynamic in his life. He filled with sensations he never felt before and didn't know what to do with. It was necessary to talk, or his emotional inexperience would show on his face. "Tell me more."

"Peter Calloway is an engineer who spent several years designing sails used to win, place or show in the America's Cup. I've commissioned him to build *The Outlaw Justice II*, a hundred-fifty-foot, J-Class sailboat for the next racing season that begins in Buenos Aires, Argentina, next year. In the meantime, our crew has been taking *The Outlaw Justice* out on Lake Michigan for preliminary preparation for the race. She's only a sixty-foot sailboat, not J-Class, but the winds have been good on the lake. We've raced her before from Chicago to Mackinac Island. We put in three solid days of work before Sunday's annual football game. Peter has never designed a boat before, but he's confident he can do it. We're taking a chance and seeing what he comes up with."

"How did you find him?"

"Through Gregory Alexander."

"The basketball player?"

"He and Peter Calloway were roommates in college. Greg is Vivian Alexander Montgomery's brother."

"Ah," he breathed. "You and Vivian are friends."

She nodded. "Best buds."

"Undergrad at Spelman."

"Yes. You apparently did your due diligence."

"A complete dossier on you, your family, and friends."

"I would expect no less."

"It had facts and figures, but it didn't tell me nearly enough. Spending this time with you, your family, and friends still is only the tip of what I believe is a very big iceberg."

"You're not intimidated by what you've learned. That's points in your favor."

"Except for your mother and grandmothers, I'm comfortable on this roller coaster that is your life and is similar to a ride through the pitch black of Space Mountain at Disney World. I imagine there are more twists and turns ahead that I won't see coming."

"You have absolutely no idea," she said smiling and touching her glass to his again.

He believed her but was not wary of what lay ahead for them. She wasn't either, he felt. They had reached a level of intimacy he had never experienced before ... and he liked it.

After dinner, they cleaned up the kitchen together, and then returned to the great room for a lively game of chess. Halfway through, they stopped playing and stared at one another.

"I, uh, want to be with you, Tina, but not at the risk of damaging what we've begun as business associates, and more importantly, as potential friends."

"I know what you feel. I feel the same way. I want to be intimate with you, but I don't want it to get in the way."

"Can we do this, Tina? Can we have sex and . . ."

"It's been a busy day and it's late. Let's sleep on it."

He nodded his agreement and they went to bed in separate rooms.

Nico was looking at a west coast basketball game when he noticed Tina leaning against the door jamb of his bedroom. He was reclining on the bed, but without a word between them, he clicked off the game and sat up on the edge of the bed. With his elbows on his knees, he interlaced his fingers and waited.

Tina had thought and thought some more about Nicholas Collins. She instinctively knew he wouldn't come to her bed uninvited, but would welcome her if she chose to come to him. It was risky to make this move and she knew all of the reasons why she shouldn't add sex to the equation. Still, when lust chased heat in her blood, she didn't deny herself what she wanted...and, without question, she wanted Nicholas Collins.

Wordlessly, she moved toward him until he unlaced his fingers and ran his warm palms up the inside of her legs and thighs to the inverted Y axis of her heat. He opened her shirt and buried his face against her sensitized skin, pulling her in so that his mouth could taste and tease. She stood, but her head fell back, and her eyes closed on a breathless moan. His clever tongue was doing amazing things, causing stars to ignite behind her eyelids.

Standing, Nico shed his pajama bottoms while finally getting his hands and mouth on Tina's warm, pillow-soft breasts and firm nipples. They were unbelievably sweet, tasty morsels on his tongue, and he luxuriated in pleasuring them and her. Placing hands on the back of her thighs, he hiked her up until she firmly locked her legs around his waist. His shaft strained with the need to mate, but he held off the need clawing inside him. Instead, he lay her across the bed and feasted between her open thighs.

His intimate kiss turned molten and lit her up like a tinder-box fire. He clamped his mouth on her with incredible accuracy and intensity. With no barriers between them, he continuously buried his face, needing like breath to take her scent into him. The thrill so intense she thought she would levitate up off the bed.

They didn't bother with the light but took time to prepare to cover Nico's pulsating member for when the time came. "I didn't expect our meeting to be a prelude to this, Tina, but I'd be lying if I said I didn't want you from the very first day I saw you. You should also know that I want you so much that this could get a little rough. Stop me . . ."

Tina leaned up taking his mouth and ending his ability to have coherent thoughts. They lost track of time in the time-honored 69 position, tasting themselves and each other on their lips and tongues.

"Since we're doing true confessions," she interrupted, "I should tell you that I've had these fantasies about bedding you since you invaded my home. However, if you don't get into my body soon, you're going to see a grown woman cry."

He took her hand, clamped it around his shaft, to cover him, and then guide him home. While he began the agonizingly slow feeling of burying himself balls deep, Tina simultaneously latched onto the slightly-raised chest tits on his beautiful body. Pecks like his deserved to be worshipped and adored, and she did her best to meet the challenge. He moaned deeply, loudly and long as her hands and mouth went to work enjoying the pleasure of having him rock her world. "Tina," he moaned like a mantra or a fervent prayer in his ear as his body expertly brought her to and through another peak. He was so thick, hot, and huge inside her, and didn't seem to need any direction. Instead, he read her body like it was yesterday's news.

He rolled her over onto his hips without losing their connection. When she was atop him, she rode him as if she was an experienced belly dancer, his strokes so firm and exciting inside her. She had incredible control of her PC muscles to the point that his penis felt as if it were in a velvet vice. Palming her breast, he molded her flesh until her nipples were as hard as pebbles. Her hands went up into her hair and loosened her locks to glide her fingers through the strands while his long, blunt fingers and thumb went to her tangle of nerves, massaging aggressively. Still, her internal muscles held him shuddering through successive releases.

He could not seem to slow; it felt too amazingly good being inside her tight, wet portal with this new experience. Even though she had cum several times in succession, she was still virginally tight. Her body still gripped him as tightly as if fisted in her hand. Each second, he knew it couldn't get any better, but then it did when she tightened those kegel muscles even more and he found himself near asphyxiation from his heavy breathing. He had never experienced what he heard called the Singapore Kiss before, and now that he had, he didn't know whether he would ever be satisfied with ordinary sex again.

Then she palmed his face, ravished his mouth, and pumped him harder and faster than before, this time sliding back and forth while on her knees to give her center the friction she

138 | Ann Jeffries

wanted. Grabbing her hips, he helped her glide, his member slick with her creamy moisture. His nuts contracted into him before he lost control and came again harder on a strangled cry than he ever had before. The spasms went on for what seemed like an eternity, his heart thundering and his muscles bunching taut against the exquisite pain of a hard, pleasurable release.

In his haze, he felt Tina follow within seconds of his earth-shattering release. Lightheaded from the rush, he thought he might pass out. With eyes closed, he tried to focus on taking slow, deep breaths, but her tightly flexing and spasming inner muscles were lethal on his still too-sensitive penis, making it tremble involuntarily.

She loved the way Nico made love with her. Her kegels clamped so tightly around him he couldn't pull out of her without hurting himself or her. For a while, the pleasure was so great, so intense her muscles froze, causing a series of orgasms to flash over her in rapid succession. Once he was released from her body, she took off the condom and again mouthed him into life, again tasting what was left of his release and desiring more. His recuperative ability and stamina were amazing. He wasn't a passive lover, instead he gave her wave after wave of unbridled and unbelievable pleasure. His warm hands, chased by his mouth and tongue, glided over her body as if he couldn't get enough of her. It was a good thing that, after tonight, she wouldn't see him again anytime soon. Otherwise, his touch could easily become addictive.

The next morning, Nico woke to the sounds of loud, heavy equipment outside the cabin. He looked around, but Tina was not in the bed where they had spent the night together. Checking his watch, he noted it was barely six, but the snow had stopped, and the sun was out. He crawled out of bed and went into the attached bath to shower and dress. When he made it into the kitchen, one of the twins was there rolling steak and eggs into what looked like soft tacos.

"Hola!" he hailed, a smile bright on his weathered, but still handsome face.

"Hola," Nico responded, not sure which of the twins he addressed. "I see the storm has passed."

"It has. Sit. Eat. Namida is checking the bird."

"Namida?"

"Ah, you call her Constantina. Namida is her Chippewa name. It means--- "

"Star Dancer," Nico interjected.

"Yes. The Ancestors sent her here and she has never been still since she arrived. She dances fast through life. Can you keep up with her?"

"There's a question," he said and thought after last night in her arms the rest of his life depended on whether he had the stamina to keep up with her.

Just then the focus of his thoughts opened the kitchen door and marched into the mudroom from outside unraveling the heavy weather gear she wore and placing it in the mudroom. He just looked at her seeing her in a whole new light. Her hair was braided from the crown of her head down her back. A piece of rawhide secured the thick end.

"Just in time," said the twin. "Eat and I'll fill your thermos for the trip."

"Thanks, Uncle Tao, I'm starving."

"Is your bird okay?"

"She is. She's warming up," Tina said, hugged her grand uncle from behind, and then washed her hands before sitting next to Nico at the bar. "How are you this morning?" she asked him.

"Good. How long have you been up?"

"A few hours. I needed to get my day going early." She dug into the steak and eggs breakfast burrito with the gusto of the ravenous. "This is delicious, Uncle Tao," Tina said around a healthy bite.

It was good, Nico agreed. The steak, eggs, onions, and hot peppers were held together in the soft taco with a healthy amount of horseradish cheese. He finished three with two glasses of orange juice and a big mug of black coffee.

"Ready to fly?" Tina asked.

"As ready as you are," he said but wasn't sure how he felt about her seeming omission of what transpired the night before. Of course, they weren't alone in the kitchen and certainly didn't have time to discuss it as they packed up to leave.

Before they left, her grand-aunt and her other grand-uncle joined them in time to say goodbye. A wide enough swath had been cleared up to the helicopter and around it by a big red farm tractor with an enormous scoop. With the blades whirling, snow was flying away in all directions. Once secured inside, Tina contacted air traffic control and lifted off waving to her family as she did so. She swung out over the dark blue of Lake Superior with the sun bright on the horizon. She wore a pair of shaded aviator glasses and passed a pair to him before she bulleted south.

Nico didn't want to distract her as she continually communicated with the control towers of each air traffic control sector they crossed. The closer they got to Chicago, the busier the air traffic became. Eventually, they were landing at Midway Airport where his odyssey started on Thursday nearly a week earlier.

It was harder than she thought it would be to bring Nicholas Collins to this point where they would part ways. They had come face-to-face on Sunday afternoon for the first time. In the interim period between then and now, they shared so much of themselves with the other. In many ways, more than she ever expected to share with any man.

She needed time and space to think about that…and him. They would come together again she knew. She would try to make time to join him for the launch of the satellite from the Kennedy Space Center in Cape Canaveral, Florida, and then, once he was ready, they would meet periodically to practice for the regatta. She was looking forward to those times.

Tina had cut the engines and the blades had slowed to a stop before the ground crew airport personnel approached to remove his luggage and begin to service the bird. He sat a moment longer looking at her as she studied him. He reached his left hand behind her head and brought her mouth to his for what was intended to be a short kiss. Once their mouths touched, he wanted more slanting his lips over hers and opening to the warmth he found waiting.

It seemed like a lifetime before Nicholas pulled away, but Tina still felt bereft at the uncoupling. She searched his eyes and found the same confusion he must have seen in her eyes.

"To be continued," he said before kissing her again. He climbed out of the helicopter and climbed aboard a golf cart that took him to his waiting flight back to New York City.

Tina climbed out to allow the ground crew to provide the service checks necessary before she could leave.

Approximately twenty minutes later, she watched Nicholas Collins' Adventurer Executive Air flight take off and gain altitude. Shortly, the servicing complete and gassed up, she received permission to lift off and head for her office back in work mode. If she was right about how the abductions were executed, she would be working on another exposé very soon. She had work to do.

14

Several weeks passed before Nico was able to take time to view the special exposé on The Sweet Justice show about the number of high-profile men and women abducted and never found. He remembered sitting in on Tina's production meetings. She and her teams did a masterful job on the exposé. There were already calls from the public for more on that story.

Now he made it a priority to record her show every evening and watch it when he had time for dinner, usually alone in his penthouse. He didn't find a lot of time during the day to think about her or what he experienced those days while in her company. His schedule was too jam-packed with preparations for the satellite launch. However, alone at night she consumed much of his quiet time.

There was also a great deal of work related to his new Financial Empowerment Network (FEN) which would proffer deals that could be made by starting new businesses or partnering with individuals or groups to finance companies and investments.

He was making more contacts in the states and abroad and taking more meetings which grew out of the joint announcement that Sweet Justice Production was to be a key feature on his satellite. He had a number of meetings out of the country to attend. However, he was keeping his schedule fluid so he could fit practice time for the regatta in when possible.

He hired a coach to teach him about sailing and actually progressed to the point he had learned port from starboard and would soon be out on the waters around Manhattan with Peter Galloway learning the ropes that controlled the sails. They were planning a series of lessons at daybreak come rain or shine in the unpredictable November weather. Peter and his wife, Joyce, owned a forty-foot sailboat, *The Lucky Duck*, they kept moored in a Manhattan boat dock. They also owned a boatyard where *The Outlaw Justice II* would be built and lived above the boathouse in a five-thousand-foot loft.

Nico was meeting other people who were avid sailors and participated in regattas worldwide. Peter and Joyce talked him into attending a ten-thousand-dollar-a-plate gala at a local yacht club. Little did he know or expect Joyce would arrange for her unmarried friend, Margo Chandler, to be in attendance, too. However, also in attendance were Gregory Alexander and Jackson Chase, two members of the prestigious and relatively new Wall Street brokerage house, banking institution, and securities firm, Compliant Trading and Investment (CTI) partnership. He had read good things about the brokerage house. Joyce and Margo were also founding members of CTI. Gregory and multi-billionaire Supreme Court Justice Vivian Alexander Montgomery were siblings. He also learned Margo was the sister of actor, top fashion model, entertainment lawyer, and Tina's confidant William Chandler. That fact still didn't raise Margo's stock in his estimation. As avid investors and single men, he, Gregory, and Jackson hit it off and conversed during most of the gala. Jackson shared that his brother, Isaac, was a Merchant Marine and an excellent sailor. That fact intrigued Nico.

Margo did join in during their conversation but seemed more interested in getting him alone. She was a very attractive woman who was very bright, aggressive, and not shy about expressing her interest in seeing him again after the yacht club event. Under ordinary circumstances, he would have taken her up on her offer, but for some inexplicable reason, he passed on the opportunity. He didn't want to question why considering he hadn't been sexually active since the days before he met Tina.

Margo's wasn't the only interest shown to him since he last saw Tina, but none of the women sparked his interest as Tina had. He wondered where she was and what she was doing at that moment.

***

"*Mamacita*, Tina's reading at the table," Bouchard chided, rustling his sister's hair as he sat down between her and Miguel with a full plate of food.

"What are you, two years old?" she parried frowning and swatted his big hands off her hair.

"No working at the dinner table, Tina," her mother reinforced from the kitchen counter. "You know that."

"Yes, *Mamasita*," she sighed, and then to Bouchard, she said under her breath, "Blabbermouth."

"She called me a blabbermouth, *Mamacita*."

"Oh, for Pete's sake," fussed Tina.

"Stop teasing your sister," said Redmond as he sat down at the table with his plate of food. "You've been at it for a while. What are you reading so intently anyway?"

"Nothing, Dad."

Juan plucked the report up from under Tina's nose. "CIA Investigation of Abductions," he read aloud while Tina leaped up trying to retrieve the report from her much taller brother. "What are you doing with a CIA file?" he asked holding it out of Tina's reach.

"Tyson, did you give your sister that file?" asked Redmond of his son, the CIA operative.

"She used some of my notes for her exposé," he admitted while filling his plate from the buffet.

"Why do you still need to review Tyson's notes? The exposé already aired," commented Keenen, the Chicago PD detective.

"It's not important," Tina said tickling Juan's ribs, so he had to lower his arm while she snatched the report out of his hand.

Redmond stopped eating and stared at Tina. "'Not important?' What are you up to, Constantina?"

She shrugged warily under her father's penetrating scrutiny. "Just some details I want to follow up on," she said placing the report in her briefcase and collecting a plate to fill with her dinner from the buffet.

"JC told me he is concerned about threats made against your life, Constantina. You never mentioned it to me before. Why?"

"It was just rumor, Dad, nothing concrete."

Dead silence reigned around the table as everyone stopped eating and stared at her. Marguerite came to the kitchen table and stood behind Redmond with a hand on his broad shoulder regarding Tina.

"He does not tell me this, why?" asked Marguerite.

"Spill, Tina," demanded Tyson.

Just then Diaz made his appearance and stopped short when he noticed the tension-filled room. "What has Tina done now?" he asked, his arms going akimbo.

"Apparently, she failed to mention threats have recently been made against her life," said Redmond pushing his plate away and folding his big arms on the table while staring at his daughter. "JC mentioned it to me today. He thought she had told me about it already."

"It was about the mob piece I did a while back. It's nothing to be concerned about."

"You do not tell me what I am to be concerned about, Constantina!" said her mother furiously. "You are *my* child. No one dares harm any of my children or they have hell to pay!" Her dark Argentinean eyes flashed ominously.

"You've been out and about without BoBo by your side since his injury. That stops now!" thundered Redmond. "You do not make a move unless or until you have security around you. Is that understood?"

"Yes, sir," Tina said, sighing. She was a grown woman in her mid-thirties, but she didn't want her parents to worry and the way her brothers were looking at her, she knew they were concerned, too. Age was nothing but a number to her family so, for their sakes, she would do as ordered.

Everyone seemed to relax and began eating again, but there was a definite pall over the usually lively dinner conversation when all of the children were at her parent's table for a meal.

"So, you have talked with Nicholas Collins, have you?" asked her mother as she sat down next to her husband with her plate of food.

Tina shrugged. "No, there was no need. We completed our business and signed the agreements. Once the satellite is launched, I'll have several channels of programming ready to go national. I'm expanding the studio space and gearing up for a twenty-four-seven operation."

"Aren't you going to the launch of Nicholas Collins' satellite?" asked Miguel.

"Probably. If I can fit it into my schedule. I've been very busy."

"Then you will invite him for Thanksgiving dinner and weekend, yes?" asked her mother.

"Why?" Tina asked, aggrieved.

Her mother frowned at her. "He has no one to share the holiday with. He will come to be with us for the weekend. See to it."

Tina rolled her eyes to the ceiling. "Yes, *Mamasita*."

***

"There is no use pissing and moaning about having Nicholas Collins join us for Thanksgiving dinner and the weekend, Tina," said Cheryl on a three-way call with Tina and Kristen Catherine. "Personally, I like him."

"I do, too," commented Kristen. "I especially like him with you more than I did what's-his-name, the walking pretty boy. My Lydia Martine is still talking about Nicholas."

"She's a toddler, KC. Who knows what she's saying," Tina deadpanned.

"Her father and I have it on good authority from her brothers."

"Geeze, KC, they're not far out of diapers themselves."

"The question of whether he's to be included has been settled, hasn't it?"

"Maybe he has other plans," Tina offered.

"Text him and see," suggested Cheryl.

"*Mamasita* didn't say I had to do it immediately. I can do it if I have a chance to go to the launch."

"Why don't I give her a call and ask when she wants the invitation to be extended?"

"You're not my friend anymore, KC."

"You're already in hot water, Tina, so I suggest you send the text."

"Or I can call him on his cellphone, loop him into this call, and we can all ask him to join us."

"Stop! Don't do that, Cheryl! I'll send the blasted text," she huffed and did so immediately.

"Good girl," teased KC.

A reply came in moments later accepting the invitation to join her, her family, and friends for the Thanksgiving weekend. KC and Cheryl laughed like loons at Tina's dismay.

***

Nico was pleasantly surprised to receive a text message from Tina inviting him to spend Thanksgiving Day and the weekend with her, her family, and friends.

He had a feeling the invitation had not been entirely her idea, but regardless of its origins, he was pleased to receive it.

He had never been invited to spend a holiday with anyone's family. He usually had something to do, mostly work-related, but if the mood struck, he might spend a few hours in mindless sex with a woman of the moment.

He wasn't sure what, if anything, he should bring for the occasion. He didn't want to show up empty-handed. Certainly, flowers for the women served to make them happy. Perhaps a box of cigars or a case of wine for the men would do. He would have to think about it and have a florist prepare something special for each woman. For Tina, he would personally pick something exotic. She wasn't an ordinary woman. Selecting something for her would take more time and thought.

He was looking forward to sharing with her what he had learned about sailing and would be prepared if she decided to take him out on the lake again early one morning. He still felt exhilarated when he thought about meeting the challenge sailing provided. Being part of the team was also a new occurrence that gave him a new level of joy. Again, a new experience, because of Constantina Justice.

He flicked on the flat screen to view her show and stretched out on his bed, his fingers laced behind his head. He was so intent on her face he missed much of what her editorial comments entailed. He sat forward in his bed, she was still raising awareness about abductions, and the criminal element involved in the human traffic trade. Issues that could draw dangerous attention to her and her efforts. An uncomfortable sensation skittered up his spine. He picked up his phone and speed dialed someone who could give him answers.

"Slade," came the response once the phone was answered.

15

"Tina?"

"Yes, Bruce?" she answered when he stuck his head in the open door of her office.

"A Strickland Briggs is here in Reception to see you. He doesn't have an appointment."

"Briggs?" she asked, surprised. She hadn't heard anything about him for several years. He was the jerk who used to date her friend KC, Kristen Catherine Bryant, when she was a law school professor and then a state court judge; before she married Thomas Ashton Marshall. Briggs had visions of grandeur to rise to the presidency of the United States using KC's *bona fides* and celebrity as a springboard while he carried on an open affair with Shannon, the supermodel. Now Shannon was dating Clarence Bryant, much to everyone's dismay.

Briggs went up against Thomas Ashton Marshall in federal court and lost so badly he dropped out of the social scene in Illinois and Washington, DC. Tina wondered why he was there to see her. They were never friends or even friendly toward one another. She really didn't have time, but curiosity got the better of her.

"Tina? What do you want to do?" asked Bruce.

"How much time do I have?"

"None," he deadpanned.

She rolled her eyes at him. "Have him brought up."

"Okay, I'll postpone your staff meeting."

"Do that."

Bruce tapped his earpiece, conveyed the message, and added Briggs should be escorted by a security team. Then he tried to find time in Tina's schedule for her staff meeting.

Shortly Strickland Briggs arrived at her office escorted by a security man and woman. She was surprised by his appearance. Generally, he was a clean-shaven and dapper dresser. The man who appeared looked nothing like the one she remembered. Her curiosity about his drastic change was peaked even more.

"Tina," he said by way of acknowledgment but didn't extend his hand. He simply nodded. "Thanks for seeing me."

"Strickland, what can I do for you?"

"I've been following your exposés on the missing women and wondered whether there was more information you hadn't released."

"Why, Strickland? Is there something you know that hasn't come to light yet?"

"I, uh, I know one of the missing women."

Light began to dawn, but she kept it to herself. "Which woman?"

"Jillian Harris."

"Oh yes, you were questioned by the Martha's Vineyard PD and the FBI about her disappearance. You two were vacationing together as I recall. That was during the time you were bound and determined to marry Kristen, right?" she said, her tone sarcastic.

He dug his hands in his pockets. The anguish she read on his face almost made her feel sorry for him. Obviously, Jillian's disappearance was wreaking havoc on him.

Tina took a mental step back and tried another approach. She called Bruce into her office to take notes. "Tell me what you remember about that time, Strickland."

"It was during the *McElroy v. Wayne* case. Do you remember it?"

"Sure, it was all anyone talked about. It was KC's first case as a federal appellate court judge. Cheryl and I were clerking for her. Peter was her chief of staff. It was one of the biggest cases in legal history. The press and news media were like rabid dogs for every scrap of information for weeks."

He nodded. "Thomas Ashton Marshall was lead counsel for Wayne Agra Industries. Jillian stepped in as his second chair to handle the case. I was representing McElroy. We had argued the case before the federal appellate court's three-judge panel and were waiting for a verdict."

"You and Jillian were on opposite sides, but you decided to bury the hatchet, so to speak, and go on a holiday together? All the time professing how much you were in love with KC and having an open affair with Shannon?" Tina asked, skepticism coating her voice.

"Okay, Tina, I get it. You and I were never going to be friends. I didn't respect KC the way I should have. It didn't start out that way with me and Jillian. Although we were adversaries in the courtroom, we were both curious about why KC had been pulled from the judges' panel and what Thomas Ashton Marshall had to do with it."

"Why would any of that matter to you or Jillian?"

"We thought there was something going on between them, but we didn't know what. We each learned that, shortly before the trial commenced, KC and Marshall had been on a vacation to some undisclosed location. We were trying to figure out where they went and whether they were together. You should remember that time. As it turned out, KC and Thomas married and now have three children."

"They married in the chief judge's chambers *after* the verdict was released."

"Don't try to blow smoke up my ass, Tina. They had to have known each other intimately before the trial started to have married a matter of hours after the decision was issued. I also note their first son was born eight months after the date of their wedding. I may not be much in your eyes, but I took the same bar exam you did and passed. Jillian and I were right. Thomas Marshall and KC knew each other intimately *before* the trial started. That's why he backed out of the case to let Jillian handle it and she got the chief judge to replace her on the bench."

"Even if you are correct, and I'm not saying that you are, what are you planning to do?"

"Nothing. I wish them no harm."

It was true, Tina thought, Strickland Briggs may have been an arrogant tool at one point, but he wasn't stupid. Vaguely, Tina remembered KC went on nearly a month-long vacation while she, Cheryl, and Peter packed up KC's Chicago office in preparation for her move to the Federal Appellate Court in Washington, DC; a judgeship KC still held today. Tina made a mental note to check with KC about that time.

"What was Jillian's reason for hunting information about Thomas or Kristen?"

"She wanted to marry Thomas Marshall. His mother, Sheila, had laid the groundwork for Thomas to run for the Oregon governorship as a springboard for the presidency. Sheila also picked Jillian as the perfect wife for him. Jillian wanted to be the First Lady of Oregon as well as the country. However, Marshall had no interest in running for political office or in Jillian."

"You had the same aspiration as I recall," Tina remarked.

"I did, yes, and I pursued the relationship with Kristen for that reason. At the time I thought she would have made the perfect ornament on my arm. I was slated by my parents to step into former Illinois Senator Tolleson's place when he stepped down. I would marry Kristen, get her installed as a Supreme Court Justice, and, based on her celebrity, I would run for the presidency. Her father and my parents believed we would have been the perfect power couple. None of that for me or Jillian was going to happen when Kristen's father and Thomas' mother found me and Jillian together *in flagrante delicto* in a restaurant parking lot on Martha's Vineyard. It was stupid for us to be so public about our relationship, but Jillian is adventurous like that. What were the odds do you think we'd be discovered? Jillian and I thought we were sufficiently *persona non grata* on frekkin' Martha's Vineyard that we could . . ."

"Never mind, Briggs. TMI. Regrettably, I get the picture."

"That's the night Jillian disappeared."

"What was the plan?"

"Jillian was going to find out where Thomas vacationed, and I was going to do the same with KC. If we could prove Thomas and KC were together *before* the Wayne trial, Jillian and I planned to use the information to coerce Thomas and KC into going along with our plans. He would marry Jillian and I would marry KC. Still Julian and I planned to continue our sexual relationship with each other even after we were married; KC and me and her to Thomas. All of that disintegrated when we were discovered together."

"Essentially you were going to blackmail them."

"That's true. Back then I would have done anything to appease my parents. Jillian and I thought her plan to find the information would be enough to keep Thomas and Kristen apart and in line."

"Who was Jillian going to tap for that information?"

"She didn't say a name and I didn't ask. She only said she knew someone who could tell her about all of the private resorts someone like Thomas Marshall, with his wealth and need for privacy, might vacation. I had the impression the man was someone wealthy who would frequent exclusive resorts. If her source could suggest some places, then she would try to find out whether KC had been to any of those places on her secret vacation. I suspected if you or Cheryl or even Peter knew where she was, none of you would tell me. The same would be true of her brothers. They never liked me, so I was going to get her father to find out where she had been."

He was right about that, thought Tina. If they had known where KC was, they would never have told anyone where she was. The thing was they respected KC's need for privacy and didn't pry into that information. She and Cheryl never gave it a second thought. Now Tina was even more curious. Shortly after that, the fact KC and Thomas married secretly in a Polynesian wedding after only knowing each other a few weeks sparked even more interest.

"You asked whether I have more information than I have released. The short answer is yes and no, however, I'm not sharing what I know yet or dropping my inquiry into these disappearances. More exposés will widen the focus in the weeks to come."

He seemed to brighten some at the announcement. "Thank you, Tina. If or when you have more information you can share, I hope you'll let me know."

"She means something to you, doesn't she?"

Slowly he nodded. "She means everything to me. I appreciate that you're continuing to follow this up."

"You're welcome. I should have more soon," she said opening her office door. The two guards stood waiting as a rather dejected Strickland Briggs walked out.

"How sad," commented Bruce. "I'll have his comments for you within the hour."

"Would you clear my schedule for the rest of the day?"

Bruce seemed to considerably pale but then uttered, "On it. Consider it done."

She knew what she was asking him to do was monumental, but it had to be done. "Good. Call KC, Thomas, Peter, and Cheryl. Tell them I want to meet with them for dinner tonight if they are available at one of their homes. Since they live in the same community, it doesn't matter which one."

"Done. I'll have a jet ready for your departure at around four. I'll also alert security."

"Do all of that," she said and proceeded to prepare notes on what she needed to discuss with her friends.

***

"So, to what do we owe the honor of your presence, Tina?" asked Cheryl as the group finished an excellent dinner in Cheryl and Peter Brock's home and settled with coffee and cognac in one of the salons in their home. Also in attendance were Kristen Catherine and her husband Thomas Ashton Marshall, III.

"Yeah, Tina, even for you this is a surprise," commented Peter.

"It's about the exposés Sweet Justice has been producing."

"Excellent work, Tina, but how can we help?" asked Thomas.

"I had a visit from Strickland Briggs earlier today."

There was dead silence around the room and stunned expressions before Peter said, *"Whoa!* Talk about a blast from the past."

"I'll say," said KC. "How is he involved with your story?"

"It has something to do with the disappearance of Jillian Harris, doesn't it?" asked Thomas.

"She used to work for you before she disappeared, didn't she?" asked Tina.

Thomas nodded. "She did, yes. My mother brought her on board at our law firm literally behind my back and without my knowledge or consent. She was at one time lead in-house counsel for Wayne Agra Industries. When we went to court against McElvoy, Wallace Wayne, president of the company, wanted her on my team as his eyes and ears. I figured it couldn't hurt to have someone already familiar with the case as my second chair. She, however, wanted to make it into something more. I wasn't receptive."

"Okay, I didn't know that. She had only been with your firm for a short time. Before that she worked for your client?" asked Tina.

"That's correct. She was an excellent trial lawyer, but I didn't want her in my firm because of her relentless pursuit.

I didn't need or want the sexual harassment her employment with my firm would encourage. I told my mother, who was the managing partner of our firm, either Jillian had to go, or I would."

"Before the case ended up in federal court, you went away on a month-long vacation," stated Tina.

Surprised, Thomas nodded. "I needed a break. I'd been going non-stop for several years, mostly on cases out of the country."

"You and KC met during that vacation?"

"We did, yes."

"Where is this going, Tina?" asked KC.

"Stay with me, KC. I'll connect the dots in a moment. Did you know each other before that?"

"No, we didn't," said KC. "We accidentally met on an island, Plaza de Masquerada, in the Archipelagos."

"Our reservations were connected. We ended up sharing the common areas of a two-bedroom, two-bath suite," said Thomas smiling at his wife. "Luckiest screw up of my life."

"Did anything unusual happen while you were there?"

KC looked at her husband, her brows drawing together. "No, not that I recall, but that was years ago, Tina."

"How about you, Thomas? Do you recall anything happening while you and KC were on the island?"

"No, but KC left abruptly without saying goodbye and I didn't know how to find her. For a time, I feared she had been kidnapped. Imagine my surprise after searching everywhere for over a month when I find out she is one of the judges assigned to adjudicate one of my biggest court cases. Then I learn she had dated opposing counsel, Strickland Briggs."

"I remember this part," said Cheryl. "KC had to withdraw because she and Strickland used to date and he was threatening to blackmail her into ruling in his favor on the case. However, until the day of the trial, she didn't know who you were, Thomas. We teased her about that fact. Everyone had heard of you, but not KC."

"I remember that, too," said Peter. "We couldn't figure out why KC looked so shocked when you stood up in the courtroom before the case was started, Thomas."

"That's right. It's the credo of the Plaza de Masquerada, the Place of Masks, that you don't disclose who you are or what you do. KC and I had no idea we were both lawyers or even what each other's real names were. I was as shocked to see her in court on the bench as a federal court judge as she was to see me."

"Getting back to when you first met. That's all you remember from that time?"

"Well, yes."

"Yet, you mentioned your concern about KC's unannounced departure from the island. Why did you think she may have been kidnapped?"

"I learned after I returned to Portland, two women did go missing from the island. That's what initially had me worried something like that may have happened to Kristen."

Tina leaped on that information. "I don't have information about that in my reports about missing women."

Thomas shrugged. "I don't know why not, except it didn't get picked up by the mainstream media. The Plaza de Masquerada management is manic about protecting their clients' privacy. However, the disappearances were investigated by the local island police, I understand."

"Then how did you learn about it?" asked Tina.

"I asked a friend to help me track down who KC was and where she went after leaving the island. However, my mother put him on another assignment to Japan. He only had time to begin a preliminary investigation starting with the island."

"This person, your friend, worked for your firm?"

"Did and still does. Slade Richardson."

"Richardson Investigations and Security," said Tina. "I've met him. He was the best man at your marriage to KC. Where is he now? I'd like to talk with him."

"I haven't a clue. He's like you, Tina, he could be anywhere. However, if you want to talk with him, that's something I can make happen."

"Good. Now getting back to your time on the island, did you know anyone else?"

Both Thomas and KC shook their heads. "Thomas drew a lot of female attention," teased KC. "He was beating them off with both hands tied behind his back."

Thomas snorted a laugh. "Oh, yeah, talk about beating them off; no pun intended. What about you and that Tolliver Bunkley character or the one with the grab hands?"

"Minor incidents, but Thomas went caveman on them. He tried to castrate that Webster jerk."

"Someone got physical with you, KC?" asked Tina.

"He was drunk and stupid," said KC.

"Who was he?"

"I really don't know. I only danced with him a few times."

"Most of the men and women at the resort were wealthy," added Thomas. "You had to be to stay there. I got the distinct impression he felt entitled to treat women as if they were his personal possessions."

"He certainly was an arrogant man," commented KC.

"His name was Webster?" Tina asked making a note.

"Maybe. As we said, no one used their given name at the resort. We didn't. Most people went to the extreme and paid with cash to avoid leaving a paper trail and to protect their anonymity."

"He wasn't staying at the resort," said KC, her brows drawn together in thought and memory. "I remember he wanted to take me to his yacht anchored somewhere offshore. The man had a serious creep factor. I wouldn't have gone to church with him."

"I'm still not making the connection," said Peter.

"Me either," commented his wife, Cheryl. "What does how Thomas and Kristen met and where have anything to do with missing women?"

"Just before Jillian Harris disappeared, she was trying to find out whether Thomas and KC met secretly before the trial. According to Strickland, if he and Jillian could have proven Thomas and Kristen were together, they would have used the information to blackmail you both into going along with their nefarious plans."

"That sounds like something Jillian would have done. She took every opportunity to insinuate herself into my life."

"Strickland, too," said KC, "but instead Jillian went missing."

"Yes, and although innocent, you two did meet and have a relationship, even married before the federal trial."

"As far as I was concerned, it was just a lark. Thomas and I only knew each other for a matter of weeks before we participated in an impromptu island wedding for grins and giggles," said KC. "I didn't believe Polynesian weddings were considered legal in the US. However, I never practiced international mediation law like Thomas. I was shocked when he proved we were legally married. So, yes, technically, I had an intimate relationship with Thomas before the trial, and although I didn't know it at the time, he was legally my husband.

"Before the trial date when I learned Strickland would represent McElvoy, I confessed to Chief Judge Hathaway that Strickland and I had a prior intimate relationship," continued KC. "He ruled there was no judicial indiscretion since my relationship with Strickland was over months before I was appointed a judge on the federal circuit court bench. I felt I had done my due diligence, but my continued participation was tenuous at best. However, when Thomas stood up and I realized who he was, I was shocked. Because I had an intimate relationship with him that I had not reported, I knew I had to withdraw from hearing the case."

"That's why I had to stop the trial before it started when I saw KC on the bench with the other judges. I believe that's when Jillian became suspicious of what was going on and my relationship to KC."

"You did stop the trial before it started, but if they had learned you were married and tried to blackmail you, what would you have done to protect KC's position as a federal appellate court judge, Thomas?"

"If they threatened KC, I would have destroyed them."

"It's a good thing you never had to go that far," commented Peter.

"You didn't have anything to do with Jillian's disappearance, Thomas," stated Cheryl.

"I didn't, no, but what Tina seems to be hinting at is perhaps whoever Jillian was going to talk with to get a list of places I might have stayed did have something to do with her disappearance."

"Exactly," said Tina. "Especially now that I know other women went missing on the Plaza de Masquerada which translated means The Place of Masks. That's where Jillian's research may have led her."

Thomas looked at Tina critically. "What else are you thinking, Tina?"

"These abductions seem to take place around water or exclusive resort areas."

"I'll put you and Slade together. Maybe he can contribute more."

"Thanks, Thomas. That will help."

16

It was late when her Adventurer Executive Air flight landed at Midway Airport, but Tina was still feeling energized by what she learned from her friends at dinner. They were also concerned about her safety for pursuing this line of inquiry.

Tina was also concerned about them, too. After all, it hadn't been that long ago that Cheryl and her group of twelve at-risk young girls she mentored had been accosted by African terrorists and renegades. The terrorists were looking for twenty young African female students who were royalty in their own countries and rescued from an English-speaking school in Africa by secret American military forces. Cheryl and her Lawrence Twelve Crew of young American female students defended themselves admirably against three terrorists until the authorities arrived. Yet Tina didn't want to put her friends or her family, for that matter, in danger. However, she felt compelled to continue her search for a way to stop the abductions of prominent individuals and the wider crime of human trafficking.

It was possible, had it not been for Thomas' intervention, she feared Kristen Catherine could have been one of the women to go missing. Tina felt she was on to something with the idea people who were abducted disappeared from places wealthy yacht owners were known to frequent. She would contact Tyson in the morning to determine what he could dig up in the CIA files about the two missing women from the Plaza de Masquerada. She would also start researching more about the yacht owners who frequented private resorts.

When she arrived at her home in the Gold Coast on Lake Shore Drive she was told by her security team to stay in the elevator while her penthouse apartment was searched, but she ignored their instructions and stepped off the elevator into her condo only to be brought up short by the sight of a tall, handsome, impressively dressed man who stood in her living area talking on a cell phone. He didn't end his conversation when guns were trained on him, but merely took his hands out of his pockets and held them up in a non-threatening gesture.

Just then Keenen came from her kitchen eating an enormous hoagie followed by Tyson.

"Whoa!" said Keenen, "Put the hardware away. He's friend, not foe."

"Thanks," said the man who Tina now recognized as Slade Richardson. He ended his call but stayed still until the guns had been holstered and the threat of imminent danger passed.

Tina walked up to him, her hand extended. "Mr. Richardson, thank you for getting in touch so quickly."

"Call me Slade, Ms. Justice."

"In that case, it's Tina. I presume Thomas reached you."

"He did. I was on my way from San Diego to Philadelphia and decided to make a stop here in Chicago. I contacted your brothers to clear the way to speak with you. How can I help you?"

She liked he was a man who could get straight to the point. He stood casually with his hands in his pockets, feet apart, head up, and back straight. From what she was able to learn about him, his parents were killed in India, their homeland, when Slade was still a toddler. He was raised in the United States by his father's half-sister and her husband, Millicent "Millie" and Walter Turner. They lived in Portland, Oregon. Millie worked for several generations for the Marshall family as the house majordomo while her husband, after retirement from the Special Forces military, became the Marshalls' groundskeeper. They had no children of their own but raised Slade as if he was their child.

Slade and Thomas were the same age and were raised together in the Marshall household attending the same schools through college before going their separate ways. Thomas went to law school while Slade became a Navy SEAL officer following in the footsteps of the uncle who raised him. That training must have carried over into his current career as the head of Richardson Investigation and Security, Tina thought. She had the distinct impression that Shade's clandestine career never truly ended. His piercing eyes, thick, curly black hair, and beautiful olive-brown complexion made him stand out in a crowd. Yet though he stood casually, his muscular body seemed lethal even under a well-made Italian suit. He closely resembled the actor Sendhil Ramamurthy in stature and beauty.

"My production company has been following up on the disappearance of certain high-profile men and women."

"Yes, I've seen the exposés. Excellent work, by the way."

"Thank you, but I'm not finished with the series. I've come across certain additional information about one of the women, Jillian Harris."

"Ah," he said, "Information you no doubt learned from Strickland Briggs."

"Geez, Tina, where'd you dig him up from?" asked Keenen before taking a healthy bite of his sandwich.

"He came to see me at the studio today. He wanted to know whether there was additional information I hadn't released."

"You told him what?" asked Tyson, "That you have me searching CIA files?"

"I told him I was still following the story and planning to expand the focus."

"You talked with Thomas about his knowledge of Jillian before and after she came to work for Thomas' law firm, Marshall and Marshall," Slade commented.

"Yes, but Thomas said her association with the firm was conditional and short lived. His mother was grooming Jillian to be Thomas' wife, but fired her when she caught Strickland and Jillian in the act on Martha's Vineyard."

Slade nodded. "That's true. Thomas' mother, Sheila, was fit to be tied until she learned Jillian had gone missing. Sheila and Kristen's father, along with Strickland had been the last to see Jillian before she disappeared."

"My theory is that Jillian's and other disappearances occurred in resort areas where the wealthy are known to congregate near great bodies of water. Places like Martha's Vineyard and the Plaza de Masquerada."

Though the south sea island name registered with Slade, Tina believed she would have missed his reaction if she weren't so intently monitoring his expressions and body language. "You know something about this, don't you?"

She was not only bright and beautiful but also very perceptive, Slade thought, as he analyzed what he could tell her without jeopardizing several years of covert work he and other active members of the super-secret organization, known only as The Nursery, had undertaken. "I'm aware there is a correlation between these abductions and certain exclusive resorts, yes."

"You probably know much more, but I sense you're not going to tell me everything you know, are you?"

"I understand you have some of the best researchers and analysts on your staff at Sweet Justice productions. That's why you earned a Nobel Peace Prize for your in-depth investigations and reporting."

"That's perhaps one of the most cleverly ambiguous statements I've heard from someone who is not a lawyer."

Slade grinned. "My association with Thomas was time well spent."

"I don't want to put my family and friends in the crosshairs of some global human trafficking organization."

That knocked the grin from his face. "Then step back, Tina, and let the authorities do what has to be done."

She was shaking her head before he finished speaking. "Not a chance. I don't give up, especially when this could endanger people I care about. My family has daughters no older than the ones forced into the sex trade. Every time I hear someone else's child has been taken whether in Africa or on any other continent, I feel I'm not doing enough to stop it. So, I'll keep doing what I'm doing until not another female goes missing." She offered her hand. "Thanks for stopping by."

Slade took her hand for a farewell shake, nodded to her brothers, and then exited her condo. When he was secured in his car, he took his cell phone from his pocket and asked, "Did you hear all of that?"

"I did, yes. I'll pass the message to Delta Dawn when he checks in. Tina Justice needs to be protected. I'll see who we have to shadow her. She's already rubbed certain elements the wrong way."

"I've already had a call about her safety and I'm on it. Still, Tina Justice is up to something. Do what you do, Satin."

"Will do, Cobra Khan. Move on to complete your next covert op in Philadelphia. There's a yacht club meeting scheduled for tomorrow. I've reviewed the very solid investigative work you completed about the San Diego Yacht Club. The sooner we gather all of the evidence needed for the World Court in The Hague, the sooner we can ensure Tina Justice's safety."

"I'm reading you five-by-five. On my way. Over and out."

***

"Come on, Tyson. How difficult could it be to get satellite surveillance images of certain areas around the globe during the times the abductions took place," Tina wheedled.

"I work for the CIA, not Sweet Justice productions. I have cases of my own to work on. Besides, if you want that type of Intel, you need to contact NSA."

"You know all the right people to contact. Weren't you dating an NSA attorney a few months ago?"

"How would you know who I was dating?"

"Uh, brother, remember who you're talking to," interjected Keenen. "Our sister has more spies than China."

Tina pursed her lips at her brothers. She knew they would help her; they always did. They were lounging comfortably in her media room eating popcorn and drinking beer. After Slade Richardson left, they sat feet up on ottomans watching the recorded version of the Sweet Justice show that aired earlier that night with William Chandler in the anchor's chair. Since Keenen and Tyson had all but taken up residence in her penthouse every night for her protection, at their mother's insistence, she took advantage of their presence to bounce theories off them.

"Actually, I think you're on to something, Tina," said Tyson. "I'd like to get a look at that footage as well, but it's not my case and I don't believe the CIA has what you're looking for. Interpol or NSA is the more likely intelligence-gathering organs for satellite images. Particularly since you're looking at multiple locations where the abductions took place and over several years. That's a lot of footage to overlay for comparison."

"You should ask Diaz what data the Coast Guard keeps. Since you suspect the abductions are made via seaports, he may have some suggestions."

"Good idea," she said leaping toward her cellphone.

"Hold up," declared Tyson. "It's nearly two in the morning. Diaz had a hot date tonight with the school teacher. He hoped to get lucky."

"Women go for that man-in-uniform look, believe me," said Tina.

"Ha! You didn't," teased Keenen. "You dated that lieutenant friend of Diaz's for all of two weeks."

"Ewe, he had ink all over his body," she protested. "When he got naked, it looked like he was still wearing clothes. When

I say he had ink everywhere, I mean *everywhere*. His penis and balls were inked too. I was reading his body art so intently, I lost interest in having sex with him."

"TMI, Tina," Tyson said laughing.

"Really, Tyson, someone had to hold his balls to ink 'the butt stops here'."

Keenen and Tyson were cracking up laughing when Bouchard aka Butch Justice walked into the media room. "What's so funny?"

"Now we know why Tina drop kicked Diaz's friend."

"Ink Man?" Butch asked. At their collective nods, Butch grinned. "Yeah, she told me about him."

"Did you close the restaurant early?" asked Tina.

"I did, yes. It's snowing again. I let everyone go a few hours early so they could get home before it got worse."

"Why didn't you go home?" Tina asked.

Butch gave her a meaningful look. "Your mother wanted me to make sure you ate a good dinner. She sent me to cook for you."

Tina grinned. "She's your mother, too."

"Yeah, but she never sent anyone to cook for me."

"That's because she wouldn't let anyone but her cook for you, her baby boy," deadpanned Keenen.

"Hey, I was the baby of the family until Tina came along. I was entitled to the perks."

"We were all 'the baby of the family' until the next one came along," said Tyson.

"Did you have your dinner, little girl?" asked Butch.

"Actually, I had dinner with Thomas, Kristen, Cheryl, Peter, and the little people last night in Maryland. We had fantastic crab cakes."

"*Mamasita* will be pleased. By the way, Uncle Ned wants to have Thanksgiving dinner in town at my restaurant. He has to ride in the parade and his police officers are all on duty."

"Is something up?" asked Tyson. "I didn't get any alerts about suspicious activities."

"You'll have to ask Uncle Ned about that. He checked with Granddad, who agreed to the change of venue. We're all expected to serve Thanksgiving dinner to the poor and indigent at Granddad's church as usual. All the uncles, aunts, and cousins are going to be there. Granddad is going to preach the eleven o'clock service."

"With the parade, church, and serving breakfast and dinner, the issue is settled. We have to have our dinner with family and friends in town instead of at Point of View."

"We can go there after dinner and spend the night and the rest of the weekend as usual," said Butch. "We will still have the basketball game on Friday afternoon. Maybe we'll get some practice time in on the yacht on Friday morning and then on Saturday and Sunday as we originally planned."

Tina nodded. "That'll work."

"Is Nicholas Collins coming?" asked Tyson.

"He says yes. I'll let him know about the schedule change."

"Good. *Mamacita* wanted to make sure. Nana Anna Lettie wanted him to come to church, so make sure he knows about that, too."

"Why?" Tina sighed, aggrieved.

"Isn't it obvious? The grands like him. They don't spend this amount of time and effort on someone they don't care about."

"Hey, kid, it doesn't have to be about you, ya' know?" said Butch.

"Fat chance," teased Tyson.

17

Nico had to admit, even to himself, he was looking forward to seeing Tina Justice face-to-face again. He had been working harder than ever before dealing with details related to the launch of his satellite and making up for the unexpected time he had spent with Tina. He had wrapped up one business meeting after another, putting together like-minded people who would partner to share transponder space for their various endeavors. He even met with some of the established broadcast networks looking to secure space on his all-digital, interactive equipment rather than the aged analog and more expensive facility. Indeed, this would be a banner year for NICO Communications. He was hedging his bets by contracting for the development of the next generation satellite. If anything went wrong with the launch of the bird, he would be ready with the launch of a replacement in little or no time.

Now he was finishing up the last of his busy schedule for his other company, NICO Enterprises, as the Adventurer Executive Air (AEA) jet set down at Midway Airport in

Chicago and rolled to a stop at the private AEA's jetport. It was Wednesday evening, but for the next four days, he cleared his schedule intending to focus all of his time and attention on one thing…getting better acquainted with Ms. Constantina Anna Alonza Justice.

He had watched her television shows religiously and was more aware of the effort that went into putting on a two-hour production of the caliber of her show. He had been taking meetings with his newly created production house chief, Gail Simons, in preparation for the launch of his Financial Empowerment Network (FEN). She had gladly given up her position as his Talent Agent to take on this expanded role. She just wanted to take a week off between positions for a little vacation. He suspected Slade Richardson had something to do with her request.

His new network created a couple hundred fulltime staff positions. It included both on-camera talent and those who worked behind the scenes in every capacity from copy editors to the office managers who bought the paperclips.

Surprisingly, William Chandler was helpful in introducing him to people with name recognition who were interested in taking a leap from their existing positions in the television or journalism or movie industry to joining his new communications operation. He was particularly keen to get Gregory Alexander to take on a financial expert role with FEN. William Chandler represented Alexander in his sports career as his agent. He was hopeful Chandler could persuade the young icon, known as Alexander the Great, to do with business what he accomplished with sports.

Then he learned from Chandler it had been Tina's idea to help jump-start his new operation. At her request, Gregory agreed to a one-year contract with an option. The publicity was sending the potential ratings through the roof. That was one of the reasons why he was looking forward to seeing her again. Another reason had nothing to do with business.

It was with surprise and no little amount of pleasure that, when he exited the private jetport, there stood the woman of the hour leaning against a town car, ankles crossed and hands dug deep in her pockets. Although it was as cold as a witch's tit, a grin started on his mouth the moment their eyes connected and held until they were a breath away from one another.

She looked up at him with that "I dare you" expression he had come to enjoy.

"Hungry?" she asked.

He shrugged. "I could eat."

She nodded toward the car at her back. "Climb in."

The porter placed his luggage and briefcase in the trunk of the town car while the driver opened the rear door. Nico tipped the porter and then climbed into the warm interior behind Tina while the driver closed the car door and then the trunk.

He sat turned toward her while she leaned forward and strapped him in. Yet her eyes never left his. Once they were underway, the shield was raised between the front and back seat. He leaned forward and sampled her lips. He felt her smile before they separated.

"How long have you been planning to do that?"

"Since you walked into an LA nightclub nearly twenty months ago."

"That's a long time to wait."

"It is, but it was worth it. I plan to make up for lost time."

"You're awful sure of yourself."

"Are we spending the night together?"

"That's up to you. I know you have reservations at the McCoy Grand."

"Of course, you do. Is that where you've decided I'm staying?"

She grinned at him. "There are other options."

"I'll take option number two."

"Without knowing what it is?"

"Option number one was the car service I hired to serve my transportation needs. Option number two was finding you waiting for me. I'm sticking with option two."

"I hope you're hungry."

He laughed. "Yeah, that, too."

The car pulled into an alley and was surrounded by security. Moments passed before the rear doors were opened and he and Tina were ushered into the rear of a restaurant. They immediately peeled out of the heavy coats, scarves, and gloves they wore. He only had to sniff the air to determine no matter what he ordered for dinner, the meal would be superb.

They were led into an intimate private dining room where the only table was already set beautifully for two. Candles were lit around the room and soft music filled the air. Logs in a fireplace burned cheerfully further adding romance to the ambiance. He finally had time to just look at her; to really see her. He noted her hair was longer and she seemed to have lost a little weight. She was a perfect size he thought, but with her schedule weight loss was probably normal to her. However, it was her eyes that always captivated him. She had her Grandmother Alicia's eyes, dark and dramatic, hypnotic in fact. He could look at her for a lifetime, he thought.

"Let me guess, the menu has already been decided."

"Probably. It's my brother, Butch's restaurant. It's called Bouchard's Place. He doesn't let me dictate what he serves."

"Ah, that's why everything has been arranged. However, what's with all the security? There was a car ahead and one behind from the time we left the airport."

Tina ducked her head and looked away. That gave Nico pause. A finger to her chin, he turned her face to meet his. Concern immediately filled him.

"What's going on, Tina?"

"It's nothing really."

"It's something. Do I have to call Tyson or Keenen to find out what it is?"

She shook her head. "I've been getting an increased amount of hate mail. That's after a family friend mentioned to my father rumors he heard about threats to my safety."

"I know someone I'd trust with my life," Nico said pulling his cell phone from his pocket. "His name is Slade Richardson. He heads ..."

"Richardson Investigations and Security," Tina finished for him.

He put down his cell phone. "You know him? Is he investigating these threats and handling your security?"

"We've met a few times, yes, but I haven't hired his company. The cars you saw were driven by off-duty cops I've hired at my family's insistence."

"Yet you stood in the open to meet me when I came through the doors at the airport. Anything could have happened."

"Believe me, I was only standing out there for a matter of moments before you came out."

"I liked that you were there to welcome me. No one has

ever done that for me before, but don't do it again. I want...
no, I *need* you to be safe, Tina. I don't have friends or anyone
I care about except you. I don't want to lose you or destroy
people because they threaten you."

She smiled at his serious expression.

"I'm not joking, Tina."

"I know you're not. I'm smiling because Thomas Marshall
said essentially the same thing with the same dangerous
inflection in his voice about anyone who would threaten
Kristen."

"She's not only his wife, Tina, she's his best friend."

Tina nodded. "I know what they mean to each other.
You're exactly right."

Just then the door opened. Butch entered carrying a tray
with soup, salad, and a bread basket. His sommelier followed
carrying bottles of wine.

The conversation shifted to the meal, but Tina's thoughts
stayed on Nicholas' staunch declaration. She believed him. If
someone threatened her, he would destroy whoever just as
Thomas would do to protect his wife. That declaration had a
warm sensation engulfing her heart.

Several hours later, Nico was pleasantly sated. The main
course, chateaubriand for two and a couple of bottles of an
excellent red wine had him enjoying Tina's conversation and
company immensely.

"Ready to go?" asked Tina.

"Where?"

"I have a few stops to make."

Indeed, she did. The first being her attendance at a rally

for a candidate for the city council and giving a speech of support that had the large crowd raising the roof in support.

Next, they visited a nightclub owned by the husband of one of the members of her production crew. She had helped the gay couple arrange the financing through Gregory Alexander's bank in New York City. Her appearance would guarantee the club would be in the top ten in the city for the gay and lesbian community. While there she danced like a kid still in her teens. He could hardly keep up with her or the men who wanted to dance with him.

Finally, they stopped by the hospital room to visit a woman who was losing her battle with pancreatic cancer. Her name was Patty. She was a single mother of five who worked her way out of poverty and had just graduated from college along with her youngest daughter. She had helped all five of her children attend and graduate from college while she worked as a waitress in Butch's restaurant. She wouldn't let Tina, Butch, or anyone help pay her way. Rather, she was bound and determined to do it herself as an example to her children to rely on themselves and never give up. For that visit, her children left the room while Tina sat holding Patty's hand and talking quietly.

When they were again in the car, Nico pulled Tina into his arms and sat without talking. He sensed the visit to the hospital had shaken her.

"Where to now?" he finally asked.

"That's up to you. I don't have anywhere else I need to be tonight."

"Then if the offer is still good, I'll take option two."

The penthouse was a surprise. It wasn't lavish, but homey

and comfortable. It was large consisting of four bedrooms and four and a half baths, but not ostentatious. The open-concept kitchen, dining, and living areas were modern, but it was obvious she assigned her creature comforts to her media room. There were eight large flat screens on the walls, a kitchenette, free-standing popcorn machine, and a tall beer and wine cooler easily accessible. All of the furnishings were plush and roomy allowing space to sprawl and lounge.

Keenen and Tyson were there watching the end of a west coast basketball game. They greeted them as he and Tina came in.

"Good game?" asked Tina.

"No bad. Cal State looks impressive this year."

"Any incidents?" asked Keenen.

Tina shook her head. "No, nothing. I'm done. I'll see you in the morning," she said and left.

Nico sat waiting for her to close the door before he looked to both men. "How bad is it?"

Tyson and Keenen didn't pretend not to know what he was talking about. Nico learned it was worse than Tina had indicated, but so far there was no clear indication whether there was one or several threats to her safety.

Someone had hacked her system at Sweet Justice Productions and accessed her schedule wreaking havoc with what was real and what wasn't. Her team resorted to paper rather than electronic copies that went into burn bags her father's company collected and incinerated periodically during each day. Now, only Bruce, her EA, was privy to where Tina might be at any given moment of the day, and even he was not always aware if she decided to change her schedule on the spur of the moment.

Tina kept her time as fluid as possible, Nico learned from

her brothers. They had homes of their own at the family compound on the south side Jackson Park area of Chicago but had been spending as much time as they could protecting Tina. If one or both couldn't be with her, they arranged for trusted, off-duty, police officers to take their places.

After spending nearly forty minutes with Keenen and Tyson, Nico went to Tina's slightly-ajar bedroom door. She was sitting up in bed reading a number of reports spread out around her. He walked in and closed the door behind him.

Tina looked up into Nicholas' worried expression. She figured her brothers filled him in on what had transpired since he left nearly six weeks earlier. Without a word passing between them, she stacked the reports she had been reading and placed them on the nightstand beside her bed. She then scooted over and folded back the covers in invitation.

Nico undressed without taking his eyes from hers. When finished, he climbed into bed, turned out the light and folded Tina into his embrace. Her warm, scented skin comforted him and somewhat allayed his concerns. She knew the danger she faced but was taking no unnecessary risks. Her concern was for those who might be injured or killed in her defense he knew. Still, that didn't stop him from wanting to wrap her up and tuck her away somewhere safe. Instinctively, he knew it was not the best outcome for Tina. She would never live her life behind shatter-proof glass. She had a zest for life and living unmatched in anyone else he ever met. There was a barely contained effervescence in her. It was shown in her arresting eyes and her "I dare you" countenance.

No, Tina Justice was to him a beacon of light and loveliness both inside and out. No one was permitted to threaten harm to her; not as long as there was breath in his body. Those were his last thoughts as he permitted sleep to take him.

***

The smell of bacon and baked goods woke Nico. As before and as expected, his watch still set for east coast time indicated it was well before dawn and Tina was already out of bed. He showered and dressed in a suit and tie in preparation for the church service Tina indicated they would attend that day at her grandfather's church. However, when he arrived at the breakfast bar in the penthouse's common area, he found Tina, Butch, Keenen, and Tyson all casually dressed.

"Happy Thanksgiving," the Justices' chorused as they went about setting the bar with breakfast foods, coffee, juice, and fruits.

"Happy Thanksgiving," he responded. "It seems I'm overdressed."

"You have time to change after we eat."

"O-kay, but according to the schedule I received via text, we're slated to attend church this morning."

"True that," commented Tyson. "However, we're going to be providing services of our own at church, but before church services start. No one dresses up for church on a service day. You'll see why shortly. For now, let's eat and get going. Nana Anna Lettie opens the church doors at precisely six and we dare not be late."

They talked while they ate, filling Nico in on how they expected the day to go.

"Isn't that an invasion of their privacy?" Nico asked.

"It is, yes, but it's the decision the people make when they walk through the church doors. No one forces them to make that decision. However, they know they are required to adhere to the rules in order to enjoy the benefit of the services they receive free of charge."

With a sturdy meal under their belts, they wrapped up warmly and began the journey across town to the huge, stately-looking, non-denominational church and school that took up an entire, south side city block. It was just shy of six in the morning central time when they pulled into the church's secured multilevel parking structure and quickly entered the building on a subterranean level. Many of the Justice family members were already assembled, checking on supplies for the awesome tasks ahead of them.

People were lining up outside down the long block in the frigid weather patiently waiting to get in. Nico was shocked to see not only the Justice family members, but also their close friends, the Brocks, Bryants, and Lawrences, he met at the football weekend and prepared to accomplish a great deal of work. They were all scheduled to go to Tina's castle, Point of View, after they had Thanksgiving dinner at Bouchard's restaurant for the traditional basketball game and annual weekend get-together. He was also looking forward to the practice time on Tina's yacht.

At a dizzying speed, he was introduced to members of the church who were gathered to do work on a holiday. At exactly one minute to six o'clock, six bells began to chime in the church steeple. All commotion ceased while a prayer was recited by a child over the loudspeaker. The doors were opened, and the poor and indigent began to stream in.

In assembly-line fashion, a church member stepped up to each person and ushered him, her or a family to an area where they disrobed and went through a restroom complete with private showers. Towels and robes were provided while the people proceeded to the next station to have mani-pedi services and barber and hair salon services provided by expert members of the church community. Then the person was interviewed about general health issues before undergoing physical and dental exams. Afterward, clean clothes and shoes were provided.

Tina's call center law students were there in full force to determine what services these people needed to improve their lives. Families were interested in safe and secure housing and schools while others were in need of jobs. The students were attempting to provide whatever service was required.

Nico was assigned to kitchen duty along with Butch who was supervising the food preparation for both breakfast and the Thanksgiving dinner. By hour three, Nico's arms were beginning to ache after lifting heavy pots and trays of food between the kitchen and the huge dining hall where people lined up at different stations and were served by people who wore white aprons, gloves, and hairnets.

A time or two, Nico glimpsed Tina being consulted by one of her law students or introduced to someone or a family. On one occasion, he was standing and staring at the overwhelming number of people in need of help when someone at his back said, "Pardon me. You're Nicholas Collins, aren't you?"

He turned to the attractive woman with unusually light, crystal brown eyes and the man who stood beside her. "I am, yes," and accepted the hand she extended.

"I'm Stacy Greene Alexander and this is my husband, Benjamin. I understand you were assaulted in one of our buildings recently by members of the Greene Team. I apologize for what happened to you."

His brows beetled in confusion. "It isn't necessary, Mrs.

Alexander. I've received apologies from the people involved." There was something about Stacy Alexander other than her extraordinary eyes that triggered a sense he was in the presence of a warrior. She had a type of city quickness about her that put him on alert. That was particularly true when a tall, beautiful, female teenager approached, and Stacy turned before the young person reached them.

"Pardon me, Mom, Dad," she said. "Shannon is talking with a little girl she believes may have been molested."

"Nicholas Collins, this is our daughter, Whitney Ivy."

"Hello, Mr. Collins," the young woman said shaking his hand and smiling brilliantly. "Please pardon my interruption."

"Hello," Nico said stunned by her beauty, poise, and was sure she would break many hearts in her lifetime. "It's not a problem."

"We hoped to talk with you a bit more, but we need to see about this," said Stacy.

"Certainly. I'll make sure we speak again," he said shaking her hand as her husband and daughter shook his hand before walking away. It was then he realized who they were. Benjamin Alexander was five-star Air Force General and Astronaut Benny Alexander. Stacy was Navy Admiral Alexander. Benjamin was the younger brother of industrialist Kenneth Alexander and Kenneth's wife California US Senator JeNelle Towson Alexander. Kenneth and Benjamin were the older brothers of Gold Medalist and Supreme Court Justice Vivian Alexander Montgomery and professional basketball icon Gregory Alexander. The same man Tina enticed into joining FEN. He had met Gregory at the Yacht Club dinner and hadn't made the connection with his illustrious family until now.

"Are you okay?" asked Tina, suddenly standing before him.

"I just met Admiral and General Alexander. In a church basement, I just shook hands with an astronaut."

Tina smiled at his surprise. "Uh, yeah, and ..."

"Well, hell, Tina, you may know them, but I've never met an astronaut before."

She shrugged. "Okay, if you're over your bromance and infatuation, the pot you're holding needs to be washed and used to make the turkey giblet gravy," she said grinning.

He shook his head and laughed. "Yes, ma'am. By the way, the Alexanders went to see about a little girl..."

"Who may have been molested. Yes, I know. Don't look now, but the man in question is being arrested as we speak by Keenen as quietly as possible. The woman he was living with showed signs of abuse during her physical exam as did her ten-year-old son and seven-year-old daughter."

He could only stand and stare at her. She, her family, and friends were truly amazing people. They had provided critical services to a couple hundred needy people and were continuing to ensure their needs were met beyond this event. Each church member stayed with the person he or she met when the doors opened and chaperoned him, her or them each step of the way. For the indigent, clothes and shoes from Tina's closet and elsewhere were being provided while their old clothes were being washed or dry cleaned in another part of the church basement by Peter Brock's father who owned laundry and dry-cleaning establishments throughout the state. Medicine was being dispensed for those who couldn't afford it by Juan and his team of volunteer doctors and nurses. Temporary housing was being located for the homeless. Much of it in the remodeled tenements now cooperatively owned by the residents and secured by the Greene Team. Fingerprints were taken along with DNA samples and run against AFIS, the Automated Fingerprint Identification System, to weed out the criminal element. Badges with pictures were issued so that the successful new tenants could access the building through the improved security system using a palm print. Cash and other donations would help to furnish the apartments and provide other amenities like dishes, pots, pans, silverware, sheets, blankets and towels. Each person received a gift bag with the basics like toothbrushes, toothpaste, soap, combs and brushes, deodorant, lotion, and shaving kits for the men and coupons for the women for the purchase of other personal hygiene products. Nico realized this event was not only a church social, but all about service to the community.

When the church service began, the Justice family was seated front and center. There was not a seat in the massive auditorium or the double-decker balconies to be found. Extra chairs were brought in so people could sit along the walls and down both sides of the aisles. There had to be nearly eighty members of the choir who brought tears to everyone's eyes with their joyous sounds. Reverend Ellis Justice's sermon was more a discourse on the true meaning of service. Surprisingly, it was succinctly delivered and lasted only twenty minutes. By the time Thanksgiving dinner was served and the last people were out the door with food sacks of sandwiches, fruit, and cake, it was approaching three in the afternoon.

Although the Alexanders left before the church service started so that they could fly to their home in a place called Goodwill, Summer County, South Carolina, Nico did have a chance to talk with them and meet, in addition to their daughter, Whitney Ivy, their two sets of triplets; one a set of girls and the other a set of boys.

With so many hands willing to help, the barbers and

beauticians packed up their equipment, the medical and dental doctors and students lead by Dr. Juan Justice stacked their charts, Tina's law students gathered to ensure all details were recorded, and Butch made sure the kitchen was set to right. As each task was completed and Nico helped carry huge bags of trash out to Big Red's waiting trash trucks, everyone began to relax.

"A good day's work," commented Anna Lettie Justice.

Her husband, Reverend Ellis Justice, kissed her. "You always do good work, babe," he commented and hugged her to his side. As the wife of the senior pastor, she was responsible for everything they accomplished that day and was gearing up to do the same thing for Christmas Eve with gifts for everyone and for Easter, too. They had been doing these events for more than thirty years and had many success stories to show for their efforts. Regrettably, the number of those needing help never decreased, but few needed more than one intervention to set them on the road to living a life above the poverty level.

"Where was JC today?" asked Big Red of his wife, Marguerite.

"We sent meals over to the housing development for him to distribute to the shut-ins. He opted to stay and do that rather than come here. He was also checking the housing to make sure everything was ready to receive the new tenants when they were bused over."

"Who is JC?" asked Nicholas of Tina.

"He's the man who manages the buildings where you were assaulted," advised Tina. "He's a loner who mostly stays to himself. He's good with the people who live in the building. My mother and grandmother have been trying for years to get him to join us for our get-togethers, but he always wheedles his way out of coming."

Nicholas, physically weary after more than nine hours of heavy physical labor, only nodded his understanding.

The family and friends did a final inspection of the church, stacking chairs on table tops and mopping floors before locking up and heading to Butch's restaurant to enjoy their Thanksgiving dinner. His staff had cooked the meal and once everything was set up, a skeleton crew of workers had volunteered to stay behind to serve and clean up for the Justice family and friends. Many of Butch's restaurant workers were found at his grandfather's church in years before in need of a future. Butch helped them through culinary school or the beginning of junior college to learn the business and then helped find positions to enhance their careers.

Nico was amazed at the testimonials he heard from different people who had been helped in one way or another by some Justice family member or close family friend. Teachers, police officers, truck drivers, cooks, nurses, even doctors, dentists, lawyers or corporate types and small business people like the barbers and beauticians, the list went on and on. However, there were also stories about some whom, despite the best efforts of the church, family or friends, perished by their own hand in drug dens or other means. The fingerprints and DNA samples helped the police notify the next of kin when bodies were discovered with no identification. Church members continued to keep up with their charges as best they could, but still, some slipped through the cracks. The success stories were great, but those who refused to be helped weighed heavily on the minds of church members.

18

Nico remembered the bright, white-hot pain that bloomed in his chest, but not the sound of a gunshot. Rather, he saw a middle-aged man rushing forward who strangely resembled the man he remembered as his father. He was distracted, however, by Tina's and Juan's teasing each other before the blood splattered on his face and in his eyes. Then there was the screaming he heard but couldn't figure out who was making the noise. The last thing he remembered clearly before everything faded to black was looking up at Tina from the ground.

"We've got to get you out of here, Tina!" demanded Keenen.

"No!" she said vehemently as she paced the waiting room outside the hospital operating theater. "Whoever shot us could have been aiming for anyone. Uncle Ned was the first one out the restaurant door followed by Dad and then Juan. Then JC ran up trying to say something. He was shot in the back. The bullet grazed my arm before it hit Nicholas who was directly behind me."

"If the sniper hadn't hit JC first, you would have been shot dead center of your head!" Tyson thundered.

"Don't you think I know that?" she blared rubbing her bandaged right arm that was in a sling. For a flesh wound about the size of a nickel, it hurt like hell. "Instead JC is in surgery fighting for his life and we don't know what Nicholas' condition is. Why the hell hasn't Juan come out to tell us anything?" she demanded.

"Tina, sit!" her father said succinctly. "You're wearing a hole in the carpet. Your mother needs you."

Tina had been marching from one end of the waiting room to the other; fear and nervous energy guiding her steps. She still had JC's and Nicholas' blood on her clothes as well as her own.

Ned Justice entered the waiting room that was surrounded by Chicago's finest. The local FBI station chief was with him. Others were processing the crime scene and interviewing witnesses.

Redmond stood and faced his oldest brother. "What do you know?"

"The sniper was in a building under construction over a block away from the restaurant. By the time the Crime Scene Investigators figured out the location of the sniper's roost, the perp was gone. The techs are checking street cams, both public and private, to see whether they can spot anyone carrying a rifle with a scope and using hollow-point bullets."

"That's a needle in a haystack," said Redmond frustrated as he looked at his wife and daughter sitting holding hands and talking quietly.

"I want to get Tina out of here to a safe house," said Ned.

Redmond snorted. "She refuses to go anywhere until she knows JC's and Nicholas' conditions. Even her mother can't convince her to leave."

"I want to know how the press and news media was on hand," said Tyson. "The restaurant was closed for the day. Bouchard only had a skeleton crew working."

"My officers tell me the news media showed up about ten minutes before we were ready to leave after dinner."

"Someone had to tip them off. I don't believe this was some type of coincidence. We were heading to the mansion for the rest of the weekend. That's where the press usually camps out. This is the first time we had Thanksgiving dinner at the restaurant instead of the grands' place or the mansion."

"You're right, Keenen. This was no coincidence. I and the FBI have people conducting background checks on the workers who were still in the restaurant and those who left. Someone had to be tracking our whereabouts today. We don't usually use the restaurant's front entrance. We usually enter and exit by the kitchen door in the alley because it's more secure.

Juan's appearance in surgical scrubs garnered everyone's attention. "They are both going to be all right," he announced immediately to allay everyone's fears. He pulled off his surgical cap and sighed wearily. "JC is going to take a while to recuperate. He has a pretty big hole in his back and chest. However, Nicholas' wound is also a through and through. The bullet was pretty well spent when it passed through him, but it left a hole nonetheless. Usually, a hollow point bullet expands upon entering a target in order to decrease penetration and disrupt more tissue as it travels through the target. That didn't happen this time. The bullet broke a rib and collapsed JC's left lung, but that deflected the bullet enough that when it left JC's body, it grazed Tina's arm and shot straight through Nicholas without hitting anything but muscle."

"Lucky for everyone," commented the FBI agent.

"When can we see them?" Tina asked.

"They are both going into critical care. This is the thing though. We did a blood type and match on each of them. It's routine when we have to give a blood transfusion. It turned out that they are both AB negative. That's more rare than Type O. A preliminary DNA test indicates they are a match. JC is Nicholas' father."

Silence reigned.

"How could that be? Are you sure?" asked Tyson.

"I'm sure," said Juan.

"It's possible," said Tina into the void. "Nicholas told me he hadn't seen his father since he was fifteen years old. Some twenty-two years ago."

"Well, hell," said Redmond. "I never made the connection. JC's legal name is Jock Collins. I had forgotten that. We've called him JC for so long no one calls him anything else."

"He must have been in his mid-teens when Nicholas was born," said Ned. "Still, I need to have him questioned by my detectives about why he came rushing up to us."

"It will have to wait at least twenty-four to forty-eight hours, Uncle Ned. He's heavily sedated and I don't want him moving around in his condition with a broken rib, damaged lung, and a hole in his chest and back the size of a golf ball. The only way I can ensure he stays quiet is if I keep him sedated."

"Can I see him?" Tina asked.

Juan nodded. "He won't know you're there, but considering he saved your life, you can go into Intensive Care, but only for a few moments." He embraced her, kissing her forehead and then placing his head against hers, his eyes tightly closed as if in prayer. He knew the outcome could have been quite different as they all did.

***

Nico felt the blood pressure cup inflating on his right bicep and heard the beeps of medical equipment. He was fighting to rise from the deep, foggy sleep and was finally able to open his eyes to the dim light. The first person he saw was Tina asleep in a chair turned with its back to the door, but her left hand was interwoven with the fingers of his left hand. Her right arm was in a sling. He shifted his head to his right to the male nurse recording his vital signs on an iPad.

"Welcome back, Mr. Collins," said the nurse. "You're in the Intensive Care Ward of the hospital. You were shot in your upper chest, but you're going to be all right. Your doctor is Juan Justice. He's really good and he'll be in to see you at six this morning. So, you don't have long to wait to talk with him about your prognosis." He nodded to Tina. "She hasn't left your side since you came in from the surgical theater late last night. She was given a mild sedative and pain pill, but the wound to her right arm is going to be fine, too. She just needs a little rest. Are you comfortable?"

Nico nodded; his voice too rusty to speak. The nurse completed his tasks and then left the cubicle.

Nico turned his head and studied Tina in repose. His mind was still foggy, but he remembered her face, her hands holding his head demanding he talk to her and keep his eyes open and on hers. He remembered trying to talk, but pandemonium seemed to be all around drowning out his words. Then he remembered seeing Juan's face as he ripped the shirt and sweater away permitting ice-cold air to chill his skin and blood. He was fading when he felt as if he was being lifted onto a gurney and then into the ambulance, Tina still talking to him as the vehicle screamed through the streets. He was in and out of consciousness until now.

Tina felt the slight movement of Nicholas' fingers in hers. The sticky grip of sleep was slow in leaving. Her mother forced pain medication and a sedative on her that had her down for the count within moments. Still, when she felt Nicholas' fingers flex and grip hers more securely, she opened her eyes and found him awake and looking at her. Slowly, she levered herself up out of the chair without breaking eye or hand contact. She leaned toward him and rubbed her lips against his, their eyes still open on each other. He opened to her kiss and joined her tongue in a warm greeting.

It shouldn't have happened in his condition, but his member went thick. "I want you in bed...now."

She smiled. "I know, but we can't do that here."

"I should say you can't," said Juan as he entered the cubicle accompanied by med students. "Your vitals just shot through the roof, Nico. You may feel a little randy at the moment, but you're not in any shape to do anything strenuous. Tina, step out so I can examine my patient. You're causing him to have carnal thoughts."

Before she could move away, Nicholas tugged her hand until she leaned to his lips for another kiss.

Her mother waited outside Nicholas' cubicle with a change of clothes for her and directed her to a lavatory where she showered and dressed. Her mother changed her bandages and began drying Tina's hair as they sat talking.

It was motherly concern Tina read in Marguerite's eyes when she said, "We will shortly leave this place."

When Tina would have protested, her mother raised her hand silencing her. "Only for a little while. You will do this for me because I ask it of you."

"I don't want to leave Nicholas and JC ..."

"They will come with us. We will go now," she said and led the way out the door. Her brothers were there. Her father wrapped her in her coat mindful of her injury, but still gave her a bear hug and kissed the top of her head. They went to a waiting elevator that took them up to the rooftop where a medical helicopter waited. Tina, her mother, father, and her brothers, Juan and Keenen climbed aboard. JC was already there strapped down on one gurney while Nicholas sat upright in another apparently asleep. Once the doors were closed, the helicopter lifted off and headed to Midway Airport. An Adventurer Executive Airline medically-equipped jet sat waiting in a hanger. They were taken aboard and before long they were airborne again.

She should have known her mother would take charge and orchestrate their escape from the possibility of more danger. It took a strong woman like Marguerite to plan and execute the details including every family member. Tina could only admire her mother's calm but swift deliberation of the tasks ahead of them. She was one of the women Tina most respected, admired, and loved her fiercely.

Eleven hours later, they were shucking their heavy winter attire when they landed in Buenos Aires, Argentina, where another helicopter met them. An hour later, they landed on the grounds of a large sun-bleached, peach-colored hacienda on the coast surrounded by trees overlooking a wide, white sandy beach and the Atlantic Ocean. Raphael and Alicia came out into the balmy spring air to meet the arriving party. Marguerite hugged her parents, followed by Redmond, Juan, and Keenen. JC and Nicholas were wheeled into the house to a special room outfitted with hospital equipment. A privacy screen was stretched between the two beds under a mosquito tent.

While Juan and his mother set up the monitoring equipment for their patients, Redmond, Tina, and Keenen explained what had happened.

"You will be safe here," said Raphael. "No one knows I have any connection to this place. Very few people live here in the area. It is very primitive with no paved roads."

"Where is this place?" asked Tina.

"This land for miles in every direction belonged to my grandfather. It was a part of my grandmother's dowry. It will pass to your mother and then to all seven of you when the time comes."

"It is beautiful here. Why have we not come before?"

"It is a farm for many agricultural crops and too far from Buenos Aires to come often. We have Alicia's parents' villa much closer and where you used to come for visits when you were babies. This place," he shrugged dismissively. "I've had it cleaned and staffed for your visit with people I trust who will not talk about who is here. They and their families work the farm year-round. You'll be free to wander around. You won't be cooped up. Alicia and I have obligations in the city. We do not want to raise suspicion by not keeping to our publicized schedule. When time and circumstances permit, we will come to be here with you. For now, we must return to the city for a state dinner and ball for the English King and Queen at the Palace."

So saying, with a round of hugs and kisses, they left and boarded the helicopter for the ride back to the city.

Tina stared at the beautiful blue Atlantic Ocean stretched as far as the eye could see.

"Quite a place, huh?" commented Keenen. "I don't even remember Granddad mentioning this place before."

"It is because this was not a happy place for him. His grandfather was a direct descendant of the royal family and was not a favored son. He was sent here from Spain to live with a wife he was forced to marry but didn't love or want. She was also royalty but young. Still, he brought other women to live under this roof. If those women became pregnant, they were caused to abort the fetus and then sent away to be replaced by others," said Marguerite. "My father did not want this place where his grandfather did unspeakable things to be a part of the legacy passed down to his next generations. He told me about this place but did not bring me here to meet his grandfather."

"How are JC and Nicholas?" asked Tina to change her mother's sad expression.

"Sleeping, though Nicholas asks for you. He is likely sleeping, too, but you can go in to be with him. I will go to see what the cook has made for us to eat."

Tina entered the room where Nicholas slept in a bed a few feet away from his father. Although JC slept the entire time they traveled, Nicholas was in and out of wakefulness. Juan had sedated him so that he wouldn't feel the take-off and landing of the aircraft. Though it was a medically-equipped, luxury jet, they did hit wind turbulence along the way causing Nicholas to moan in pain.

As she sat beside him under the mosquito tent, she worried had he not come to share Thanksgiving with her, he would not have been shot. Though she was beginning to care for him, she felt perhaps she shouldn't see him again after this for his own protection.

"It's not your fault," Nicholas said as if reading her mind. He was awake and looking at the distress on Tina's face.

She stood and moved closer to his side. "How do you feel? Are you in pain?"

"Stop worrying, Tina. Your brother says I'll be fine. I trust his word. This injury will not have any lasting effects on me. How is your arm?"

"It will heal and barely leave a scar." She hesitated but decided now was as good a time as any to explain who the man on the other side of the curtain was.

"My father?" he asked shocked. He moved to attempt to rise from the bed.

"No, don't do that. You'll open your stitches. Wait. I'll take a picture of him with my cell phone."

She did so one-handed, using her left hand. Then she climbed onto the bed and shared the photos with Nicholas. He studied each one carefully.

"When this man approached us as we were leaving the restaurant, I thought I recognized him, but it was only for a split second. Then I saw the blood on him and you before I felt the pain in my chest."

"He saved us both, Nicholas," she said and explained how the bullet traveled.

"I don't know what to feel. The man abandoned me twenty-two years ago in Chesapeake Beach, Maryland, but saves your life and mine in Chicago, Illinois."

"Then who raised you?"

"Lana Norton, one of my father's many lovers. She kicked him out when she caught him with a so-called friend of hers, but she kept me and put me in a local, top private school. I was fifteen and slept in her bed serving her sexual needs until I earned an athletic scholarship to attend the university. Because her female friends threatened to tell the authorities if she didn't share me, she passed me around like a party favor."

A single tear leaked out from Tina's eyes, but Nicholas used his left hand to thumb the others away while caressing her face. "It's okay, Tina. Once I left Lana's house, I never went back. I stayed on campus during all of the breaks studying and getting ahead in my classes. I worked jobs arranged for me by various alumni organizations. Everyone had to be mindful of the NCAA rules. I had the athletic scholarship that took care of the basics, but the pocket change from the jobs allowed me to take care of the rest myself."

"It's not okay. Is she in jail? They all should be in jail."

"I'm a big boy and I survived. I don't even think about those times anymore," he said, soberly, and then smiled. "I see you and your family and friends, and I know not everyone is out to use you."

"Except Claude Hopper," she deadpanned and made him smile wider.

"Yeah, except him."

"You need to get some rest."

"I need to piss in the worse possible way."

Tina chuckled. "It's the IV. I'll get my mother to reinsert the catheter."

"Uh, no," Nicholas said firmly with a pained expression. "How about calling your brother? He can help me to the lavatory."

"You want a man to hold your equipment for you instead of a woman?" she teased.

"If that woman is you, not a problem, but if it's your mother, serious problem."

"Okay, she's a Registered Nurse and can give you a nice sponge bath, too, but if you insist," she said and reached for the plastic container used to collect urine. She grinned at him. "Since I can only use one hand, you can either hold the plastic or your penis."

"Ha ha," he said lifting the cover for her. She didn't end up holding the plastic and gave him a one-handed sponge bath.

***

"Here, let me cut that up for you, little girl," Juan teased as he cut up the roast beef on Tina's plate into small pieces. "Do you need me to feed you, too?"

"*Mamacita*, can I hit him?"

"Don't tease your sister, Juan," said Redmond. "I'll have Keenen feed her."

"Hey! Why me? Just because she can only use one hand doesn't mean I have to stop eating to feed her. I did enough of that when she was a baby."

Tina pulled a face at her brothers.

"Tina, stop provoking your brothers," said her mother mildly.

It did her heart good to see some of the stress leave her family's faces. Appetites were good for the delicious food that had been prepared. They lingered over the meal and coffee. The hacienda was not outfitted with many modern conveniences. There was no electricity, thus no television or radio. However, the house did have solar panels and a windmill. A cistern collected rainwater they used with propane-fired, hot water heaters for bathing and for cooking. The doors were opened to the ocean breezes, but no air conditioning unit was needed to cool the house. The smell of tropical flowers perfumed the air.

"We'd better not run the batteries long. We'll need them to power the refrigeration and hospital equipment," suggested Juan. "I'm going to check on my patients and then I'm going to turn in."

"We'll see you in the morning," said Redmond as he and Marguerite headed to bed.

"I'm going to check the perimeter security before I turn in," said Keenen.

"Wait for me, Juan," called Tina. She hurried to catch up. After he had checked his patients, Juan said goodnight and left Tina with a sleeping Nicholas. She pushed another bed with wheels close to Nicholas' under the tent, turned out the light before lying down, and linked her fingers with his.

Nicholas smiled in the dark without opening his eyes.

19

It was the middle of the second week when Raphael and Alisha Dela Vega returned bringing their grandsons, Miguel, Tyson, Diaz, and Bouchard Justice, along. There were warm hugs all around with the family together. Marguerite was so happy she had tears in her eyes. No one relished the idea of the Christmas and New Year holidays approaching with the family separated.

Nicholas was up and on his feet, getting his muscle tone back. He, Tina, Juan, and Keenen would take walks around the grounds slowly or sit under the trees of the hacienda a couple times a day. The scenery was so breathtakingly beautiful even with the rows of straight soybean crops that stretched out as far as the eye could see to the west and the setting sun over the mountain terrain. The nighttime rains gave way to bright sunshine days. The peacocks weren't pleased with the human invasion and made their unhappiness known loudly and with the spread of their beautiful feathers.

It was going to be hard to leave this little slice of paradise, thought Tina.

"Well, hell, if I had known it looked like this, I would have come when *Mamasita* first suggested it in the hospital," said Miguel standing on the veranda and looking to the east out to the Atlantic Ocean.

"Man, this is the life," sighed Diaz.

"It is if you can survive the mosquitoes," commented Juan.

"Is that why I see so much mosquito grass, citronella, and eucalyptus planted everywhere?" asked Bouchard.

"Probably, but with everything open air, we have to bathe ourselves in mosquito repellent and sleep under nets."

"How are your patients?" asked Diaz.

"Coming along. Nico is up and moving around as you can see, but JC is still in a lot of pain. Little by little I reduce his pain meds. He's gaining more clarity each day. In a few more days he should be awake long enough for Tyson and Keenen to question him."

"That's good because we can only stay a short time," said Miguel.

"How were you able to get out of the city?" asked Juan.

Diaz laughed. "I took on a new crew at two in the morning."

"I went incognito as the helper to my grocery delivery man," said Bouchard. "The driver and I went about his regular route until closing and then I got delivered to a Coast Guard van in the grocer's parking lot."

"I pretty much did the same thing. I went out on one of the dump trucks riding shotgun," said Miguel. "Tyson did a ride-along with a patrol car as the criminal passenger handcuffed and wearing an orange jumpsuit. We all ended up in the same place, changed into Coast Guard uniforms and reported for duty at two in the morning."

"I took a Coast Guard cutter that was slated for repair out on the lake to make sure we weren't followed and pulled into port at a naval station for repairs in Wisconsin. From there, we changed clothes and caught a private jet out of Milwaukee."

"Slick," commented Juan.

"When we go back, we'll fly from here on a CIA transport. That's an air transportation front for the uninitiated, then into South Bend, Indiana, to drive to Chicago from there.

"I'm sorry for it," said Tina coming into view of her brothers.

They turned at the sound of her voice.

"If you think any of us regret what we have to do to keep you safe, you're crazy," said Miguel.

She went into his open arms as her brothers passed her from one to the other for a warm hug.

Nico stood back and observed. They meant what they said. She was so precious to them they would risk everything for her.

"If you think I'm going to hug you, think again," deadpanned Miguel.

"Yeah, you're not my idea of huggable either," quipped Nico, but he got handshakes, pats on his back, playful jabs, and an invitation to join in.

Juan pulled out a chair for Nico. "Sit. You've been on your feet enough for one day."

Nico sat pleased to be off his feet and included with Tina's brothers. They all sat on the breezy veranda with tall glasses of iced fresh fruit drinks and sun tea.

"Have you talked with your father?" asked Diaz of Nico.

"Not yet. He's still on pain meds that seem to make him loopy."

"They do, but it's for his own good right now," said Juan.

"What's going on in Chicago?" asked Tina.

"Pandemonium," said Tyson. "The news media got video of the shooting, but Uncle Ned put a clamp on any comments from the Chicago Police. He said he and the department don't comment on ongoing investigations. Still, the press is riding on all kinds of conspiracy theories. Some believe Uncle Ned was the target. Others say it was Dad. There was also ink on someone trying to take out Nico because of some past hostile takeover."

"Hell, that could be true," said Nico.

"Sorry, Nico, the smart money is riding on Tina as the target. By the way, Tina, your former publicist, Claude Hopper has inserted himself into the fray as if you didn't fire him. He's taking all the media attention he can get. He's also making the rounds of the talk shows, too."

Tina shook her head. "He would. That's his nature, his stock and trade. His career depends on getting the public's attention."

"Of course, he's pulled in Ronald Forman, who by the way, lost his job with your former network when you signed on with NICO Communications. He was their link directly to you. Without you, there was no need for him to stay on. Together, Hopper and Forman are keeping the stories focused on you and themselves. I think Hopper believes you'll bring him back on board as your publicist or more. They keep alluding to the big deal you struck with NICO as if they were in on the negotiations. Hopper says he was the one who brought you two together. Forman is playing the distraught fiancé."

"What the hell?" said Tina. "I was not even remotely interested in a long-term relationship with Ronald."

"Of course, anyone close to you would know that, but he's playing to the masses and hyping his name recognition by riding on your coattails."

"What a bunch of bottom feeders," commented Juan.

"What can be done to put a stop to this misrepresentation?" asked Nico.

"Nothing," said Tina with a flip of her hand. "If I respond, it will just hype up the media attention. That's what Hopper and Forman would relish. If I ignore them, after a while they have nothing more to say and eventually, they will have to go away. They've had their fifteen minutes of fame at my expense."

"I agree," said Tyson. "That's the best approach."

"Well, Hopper is partly right. If he hadn't been lying to both of us, we may never have met," said Nico.

"There is that," said Tina, grinning. "By the way, how is BoBo?"

"Distraught he was not there to protect you. However, Rayne is keeping him busy. He's up and soon will not need crutches to move around. He's working at the housing project learning the security measures that have been put in place since the building went co-op and helping manage the project in JC's absence," said Miguel. "I've stopped in at least once a week. Things are moving along, but the tenants are worried about JC. They miss having him around to address their concerns."

"Knowing JC the way we do, I'm sure he feels the same way," commented Tina and looked to Nicholas who was staring out to the ocean vista.

"Charlotte Joyner has stepped into your place at the co-op center with a few of her law center students. Bill Chandler,

Peter, Cheryl, and Thomas are rotating doing your nightly show. They say to tell you they'll do it until you get back so not to worry."

Tina was pleased that some of her critical bases were being covered, but she ached to get back to work and find out who did this to her and her friends.

***

"Why did you come running up to us at the restaurant?" Tyson asked JC a few days later.

"I heard dese men were lookin' for a shooter to take out Tina and they found some homeless, former military sharpshooter guy and paid him a lot of money. I don't have no phone. I thought y'all would be at the place on Sheridan Road, but when I went there the security said the plan had changed so I went to the church, but it was locked up. No one was at Big Red and your mama's house either. I figured if y'all were going 'ta have dinner ta'gether like always, it would be at Butch's restaurant. That's when I saw y'all coming out, but I didn't s'pect to see Nicholas with y'all so I hesitated. I didn't think he'd recognize me after all dis time."

"I did recognize you."

"I could see that on your face before ..."

"Before you were shot."

"I guess. I don't remember anything after."

"Do you know who the men were that wanted to hire a shooter?"

"Didn't nobody know 'em, but they was real eager to set up the hit."

"Will you put me in contact with ..."

JC was shaking his head. "I know y'alls good peoples, but they don't. They won't talk ta ya. Not ta' the cops. They might talk ta Miz. Tina. They know her. That's why they told me what they heard."

***

When the questioning was over, Tina and Nicholas sat next to JC's hospital bed alone. The silence would have been deafening were it not for the sound of the ocean meeting the shore.

"Why did you abandon me?"

JC shook his head and sighed. "There was nothing else I could do for ya'. Your mama, she and me was both left at fire stations when we were less than a week old. We had that in common and we grew up in the same orphanage in Chesapeake Beach, Maryland. She was fourteen and I was fifteen when I got her pregnant. She died of somethin' I can't even pronounce when you were born. I wouldn't let the authorities take you away and stick you in some orphanage. You were my son, but I had nothing. Not a high school diploma or a decent job, but this volunteer, a woman in her forties offered to help. I took her up on her offer and we went to live with her in this big, old house. I was her foster child, but all she wanted was some young buck to warm her bed. She was the first in a long line of women who wanted me for my body. I was a big, strapping fellow for my age, just like you. So, I was able to keep you fed and clothed with a roof over your head for long periods of time before some woman got bored with me.

"When I met Lana Norton, I was an established male prostitute living in some woman's home and managing to keep you in school and the social workers away. By then I didn't care anymore about my own self-respect. Lana was very wealthy and so were her high-society friends. She put you in private school and treated you decent.

"One day I was at the house where we were living with Lana when one of her friends stopped by. You were in school that day. I let her in and left her in the library ta' wait for Lana while I went in the bedroom to take a nap. I woke up with the woman naked on me in bed when Lana walked in. She wouldn't listen ta' anything I said 'bout being innocent and kicked me out but kept you. You were maybe fifteen at the time. The woman, Lana's friend, admitted she did it on purpose and tried to get me to move in with her, but I had enough. I said no and tried ta' find work, but Chesapeake Beach is small, maybe six thousand people. They had marinas where rich people kept their yachts. Lana owned charter fishing boats and did big business at the time leasing boats to fishermen. Her husband owned the business, but he was an older guy who had money but dropped dead leaving her at a young age very wealthy. She was very smart though and made the business grow. I couldn't compete with what Lana could do for ya'. She told me she would continue ta' take care of you, but I had to stay away. I stayed around the area and watched you excel academically and athletically. I got offered this job makin' blue movies, but I wouldn't take it even when I didn't have two dimes to rub together.

"When you got the scholarship to attend that Big Ten University, I was so proud. I left Chesapeake Beach hitch-hiking, but I only had enough money from workin' odd jobs to get me to Chicago. I was livin' on the street in an alley when I met up with Big Red where one'a his dumpsters was next to a restaurant I used to go to beggin' food. He brought me to his father's church on Christmas Eve nineteen years ago. One'a the church ladies stuck wid' me. She wasn't tryin' to get me in her bed, but before I knew it that same day, I had a place to live, clean clothes on my back, a job workin' for Big Red, and food on my plate on a regular. So, I stayed in Chicago. I figured I was close enough I could see you play on television and made enough money to buy a ticket a few times to see you play in the stadium. Then you got drafted in the first round of the NFL for a lot of money and I knew you'd be all right."

"Why didn't you contact me?"

He snorted. "What for? There was nothing I could do for you. You were on your way. You didn't need me in your life after all that time. When you left football, I kept up with you on that Internet and through the newspapers in the library where I got my GED and started taking college classes. You had a life and so did I; one where I didn't have to earn my living on my knees or on my back servicing women."

"Well, like father, like son," commented Nico.

JC's brows beetled. "What do you mean?"

"Lana took care of me for sure. I was forced to take your place in her bed for three years until I left for college. Some woman blackmailed her into sharing me during that time."

JC groaned, covering his face with his hands and then winced in pain.

"Don't move around, JC," Tina cautioned. "You're still not in good condition yet."

"I'm sorry," JC said, quietly. "I never wanted that for you, but I didn't want you living from hand to mouth or on the streets with me."

"When this is over, you'll come to New York. I'll put you up…"

JC was shaking his head. "No, boy, I'm staying put. I have work I like and people who depend on me. I want to get my college degree eventually, so I can manage the co-op proper. For the first time in my life, I have my self-respect. When I'm back on my feet, I'm going back to Chicago. I'm no fool though. I know you be rich as Midas. If you want to do something to help me, donate to the building fund for the housing project. That will help me and everyone in the buildings. Miz. Tina, she and others donate time and money 'ta help out, but there are always more things need doin'. If you could see your way clear to donate that would be enough."

"I can do that, but I still want to stay in touch."

JC smiled nodding. "I'd like that, too. Miz. Tina, she always knows how 'ta find me. Ya can come 'ta visit when she comes. I mean if you ain't too busy."

"I'll make the time. In the meantime, I'm giving you a gift of a cellphone. I'll put my number on speed dial for you."

∗∗∗

Five months later, Tina followed the FBI and Chicago PD into Claude Hopper's office where he had his secretary bent over his desk in the midst of an energetic sex act.

"Claude Hopper, you're under arrest . . . man, pull out of her and put that thing away!" demanded the lead agent. "You're under arrest for the attempted murder of Police Commissioner . . ." he continued with a litany of charges.

Claude stood stunned in a tableau Tina thought she would never forget. There were some things she could never un-see.

When she secretly returned to Chicago, JC took her to meet with the people who warned him about the hit someone had put out on her life. That meeting led to others where eventually the names Claude Hopper and Ronald Furman were revealed. They were able to track the money trail to the shooter. Furman had already been arrested the night before half drunk in his home. He had turned states' evidence against Claude Hopper and the shooter they hired in exchange for leniency in sentencing. Claude had promised Ronald a healthy cut of the millions he expected to siphon from NICO Communications as a finder's fee.

Her family connections got her film crew in to record all three arrests. Publicly dispelling the misrepresentations Hopper and Furman had perpetrated was sweet justice indeed.

20

"Careful, Nico, you're pushing it," cautioned Peter Calloway as he watched Nico manually pull the ropes lifting the second sail of three up the single mast and into the air.

The wind caught the sail snapping it into place before Nico could tie it off. The jerk on the ropes pulling his arms sent pain screaming through Nico's chest. The wind was so strong his hands would have been rope burned if he had not been wearing gloves. During the spring, he could go through three pairs of gloves per sail. He also had to be mindful of not letting the ropes get tangled up around his feet and legs again. The first time it happened he found himself swinging upside down over the cold waters of the Hudson River in New York City. His chest muscles hadn't quite healed yet, but he was determined to be fit for the team's first race off the coast of Buenos Aires, Argentina, in six weeks.

The **Outlaw Justice II** was undergoing its final fittings, riggings, and marine-grade polyurethane in preparation for its launch next week. The Justice family and friends were scheduled to converge on New York City by the coming weekend. They would launch her under the cover of darkness and sail her to Argentina to get in a lot of practice for what the big hundred-fifty-foot J-Class sailing yacht was capable of doing. Since it was the season, they were taking a big risk they wouldn't run into any hurricanes along the way. By the time they reached Argentina, they should be well acquainted with her. They would arrive a week early and put into port at the hacienda.

Peter, his wife, Joyce, and Nico took *Nico's Pride*, a sixty-foot sailboat Nico won in a poker game at a yacht club in The Hamptons near his summer retreat, out several times a week. He put up a spare channel on one of his satellite transponders to back the wager. The old billionaire who lost one of his smaller yachts to Nico still paid full price for the use of the channel.

They took *Nico's Pride* out early in the morning to give them practice they needed on a bigger sailboat than *The Lucky Duck*, the forty-footer Peter and Joyce owned. Though Peter was younger than Nico, a friendship developed between them. They both played football in college, but Peter continued his studies in engineering. After graduation, Peter headed to port cities around the world taking on contracts to design sails generally for boats that raced in famous regattas. The commission to build *The Outlaw Justice II* was his first experience with boat building, but he took on the task with energy, enthusiasm, and skill.

Nico would make time to go to the boatyard a few times a week to watch the craftsmen work on the hundred-fifty-foot sailing yacht. She was a big sucker from stem to stern and beautiful. She would be painted navy blue and white with a geometric pattern of the American flag and Native American symbols on the sails.

"Coming about," called out Peter.

Nico nimbly ducked under the swinging jibboom to tackle the straps holding the foresail. Soon he was pulling the ropes of the sail into the air. Thankfully Gregory Alexander had joined them for this practice. It took more than two people to handle *Nico's Pride*. It was a wonder Tina could handle *The Outlaw Justice I* on her own. Joyce, Peter's wife, was there, too, but heavy with her and Peter's second child, a girl this time. Their son, two-year-old Alex, sat fascinated in his father's lap outfitted with water wings and a life jacket, while Peter guided the sixty-footer on the Hudson River.

They would circle Manhattan several times as they had for the past four months always starting before dawn. Sometimes, like today, they could entice Gregory to join them. They weren't the only early morning traffic on the waterways and had to be mindful of other watercraft. However, nothing to Nico's way of thinking was more magnificent than *Nico's Pride* under full sail.

"You're getting the hang of the ropes," called out Peter to Nico.

"Ropes," said his mini-me, Alex.

"Don't get him started," said Joyce, a mother's pride shining in her thin blue eyes. "He'll want to be sailing the rest of the day and won't go down for his nap."

Gregory lifted his namesake from Peter's lap eliciting the boy's excited giggles, placing him on a hip while balancing with feet apart as they pointed and looked up at the sails.

Nico made his way to the stern to join Peter, Gregory, and Joyce who handed a thermos of black coffee to him. He sat and took over the rudder, wheel, and controls from Peter. He considered himself an educated man, but he couldn't put the words together to express how exhilarating sailing had come to make him feel. Nothing, not even watching the successful launch of his satellite matched these sailing experiences. Now he knew and understood why Tina, her family, and friends wanted to take it to another level and race in World Cup competitions.

Still, he had the unsettling feeling there was something underlying Tina's enthusiasm. There were times when they were together over the last six months she would go into seclusion with Tyson and others, who appeared to be CIA agents, leaving him to socialize with her family and friends.

He didn't expect to be included in every discussion she had, but he was always concerned about her safety. He kept Slade's security company on retainer and apprised him of their plans to ensure her safety. Slade's agents were so invisible Nico couldn't spot them, but Slade had picture proof he and Tina were under surveillance and guard. True, now that the shooter who had shot them had been caught, the immediate threat caused by Hopper and Furman ended. The grumbling by remnants of the old Chicago mob had been quelled, so he didn't worry quite as much about Tina's safety. Still, she was one of the most popular faces in the world. Since the launch of her programs on dedicated channels of her transponder, her popularity was constantly trending up.

Tina didn't do anything to increase her media appeal. Rather, she was still staunchly protective of her private life. They kept their private life out of the public's view. When they had time to spend together, they would go incognito to some remote location for a few precious days. More often, they would sneak off to Argentina and spend a week at her grandfather's hacienda. He had granted permission for her to install a few amenities. A heated, screened affinity-edge swimming pool was recently completed, but they hadn't found time to get away to enjoy it. Screens were also installed throughout the hacienda to keep out the mosquitoes. Though they rarely used it, there was a satellite receiver and sat phone installed with one flat screen television in one of the lounges. They mostly lay on the beach or swam in the ocean, ate popcorn, and watched old movies on the television not wanting the real world to intrude on their private time. They became adept at cooking meals when they were hungry but otherwise were lazy about how they spent their time together. However, no work was permitted to be conducted.

He was looking forward to seeing Tina soon. Though they talked often, they hadn't made time to be together in nearly a month. The need he experienced when he thought of Tina convinced him it was more than lust he felt for her. He sensed the feeling was mutual with her.

It was getting on to seven in the morning when Nico, Peter, and Gregory decided to call it a day. They had spent two hours practicing on the waters around Manhattan, but the city was coming alive on a workday. Transportation vessels and sightseeing ferries were starting to compete with the ships and barges. Breakfast, lunch, and dinner boats did a brisk business. There were also the daredevils on jet skis or motor boats who enjoyed zipping around and between the larger, slower vessels causing horns to blow on the water with the regularity they did in city traffic.

One by one, Peter and Gregory, using the thick ropes, lowered each sail lashing them down while Nico slowed to maneuver toward his slip in the boathouse next door to Peter and Joyce's. He had just engaged the engines to further slow their speed when he spotted a woman standing on the dock inside the boathouse. His grin started the moment he recognized her. He had a ton of work to do that day, but it all went out of his head. Gregory and Peter jumped off the boat on either side on to the slip to tie down the yacht to the pylons as it jerked to a full stop and he cut the engines completely.

Tina reached out to take Alex from Joyce while Peter helped his wife step off the yacht. When secured, Nico jumped off and approached the group sharing hugs with Tina. Alex clung to her neck speaking in an undefined language she pretended to understand. She made such a beautiful sight holding the chattering boy Nico felt his heart simply swelled at the vision. He wondered whether she ever saw herself as a mother.

"Okay, big boy, time for you to go to play time," said Peter lifting his son from Tina's arms.

"Play. Bye-bye," said Alex waving both hands.

Tina kissed him farewell and made him giggle, deep dimples appearing in the boy's rosy cheeks.

"Good seeing you, Tina," said Gregory as he, Peter, and Joyce left with Alex to get on with their day.

Nico and Tina were left regarding each other until Tina nodded toward **Nico's Pride**.

"Nice maneuver, Captain. You've learned a lot in a short time. Permission to come aboard."

"Permission granted," he said pleased at her assessment of his newly learned boating skills. Indeed, he had studied and passed the Coast Guard's test to receive his safety certificate.

They climbed aboard. While Tina inspected the vessel, Nico closed the tall garage door with a remote and locked it. A few hours later, Nicholas ran his fingers through Tina's hair as they snuggled nude under the covers in the master cabin.

"She's a beautiful vessel," said Tina. "The previous owner put in a lot of custom features."

"Actually, I had most of the interior redone. It looked like a bordello and a tacky one at that."

"You didn't tell me that," said Tina sitting up in bed leaning on one elbow, and looking at Nicholas critically, her eyebrows bunched.

He shrugged. "For the most part, it needed a serious cleaning. The man didn't take good care of her to begin with, but he has several yachts in different places around the world. This one he kept in The Hamptons."

"How well do you know him?"

"Not well at all. I've seen him at parties or clubs in The Hamptons. We weren't formally introduced until I joined the Yacht Club. I was pulled into a poker game one night at the club. Someone mentioned I just launched a satellite and the man got interested. It was down to the two of us in a big pot when he went all in and put the keys to the yacht into the pot against a channel on my satellite." He shrugged. "I won the pot with a full house. He signed over the yacht on the spot and had it witnessed by the others at the poker table. There were enough lawyers in attendance to hold a shark fest. I took possession the next day. He came to my office the following week with a cashier's check for the full amount of the lease of a spare channel on my transponder."

"Who is this man?"

He told her and watched as she picked up her iPhone to page through several apps. When she finished and input data, he asked. "What's going on, Tina?"

She sat all the way up Indian style and told him about her theory concerning the abducted people and human trafficking. She cautioned that he should say nothing, but she wanted to know more about the billionaire and the people in the yacht club he belonged to.

"I can do that, Tina. The high rollers hang out at the Yacht Club to play poker and baccarat all the time. In fact, because of the upcoming regatta for Sunfish-size sailboats, there's a cocktail party and dinner scheduled for later tonight. I hadn't planned to go because I'm not interested in that size boat, but if you want to get a look at the players, they'll be in attendance."

"I do, yes. Is it too late to accept an invitation to go?"

"Members don't need invitations. We can go, but it's formal attire only. Did you bring anything dressy?"

She grinned at him. "This is New York City, son, and my favorite designer, Carlos Ortega, has his flagship designer store here. Pun intended. Get dressed. We're going shopping."

Nicholas paled at the thought of shopping with Tina Rabbit.

When he and Tina were admitted to the exclusive fashion house, it was as if the red carpet had been rolled out just for her. They were taken into a salon with plush seating and elegant ambiance. Champagne was served with little sandwiches not much bigger than his thumbnail with the crusts removed. When the show began, Carlos Ortega joined them as the models strutted on stage showing off one-of-a-kind, exotic evening wear.

"Stop!" Tina said when a model came on stage wearing what Carlos described as his blue diamond gown. "That's the one I want," she said and followed the model backstage.

When Tina emerged wearing the gown on stage, Nico could have swallowed his tongue if his mouth hadn't gone dry.

It was a sheath that fit her like sealskin with diamond-shaped cutouts that barely held the frock together. The diamond shape rendered it completely backless. Pared with man-killer stilettos, any man looking on risked cardiac arrest, thought Nicholas as he rubbed the ache just below his heart at the sight of her glammed up.

***

Tina expected the usual barrage of paparazzi when she stepped out of the limo following Nicholas and was pleasantly surprised when not one camera flash went off in her face. That was clout, she thought when the press was expertly warned away when famous billionaires were in attendance. That is not to say, however, they weren't noticed when entering the posh and exclusive Yacht Club of The Hamptons. She had seen or met people who approached them at other events in her career. These were not individuals she sought out or wanted to maintain contact with; they weren't her type of down-to-earth folks. These were society connoisseurs more interested in the label in her gown than whether people in Third World countries had clothes on their backs, food to eat or safe environments to live in.

She had to give Nicholas more points for knowing when it was time to move from one group to another in the opulent facility. He steered her to a gallery where pictures of winning sailing yachts dating back to the 1700s were posted. There were few people about in the vicinity providing a modicum of privacy. He pulled her more securely to his side, so he could whisper in her ear without being overheard.

"I know you wanted to get a look at the movers and shakers, Tina, but you and this dress are getting most of the attention."

She grinned up at him. "It's doing just what I want it to do…get noticed."

His brows beetled. "This is not the Constantina Justice who would rather wear old jeans and a ratty sweatshirt, so what gives…" and then it hit him. "You're trying to make yourself a target for abduction," he vehemently said between clenched teeth.

"Don't worry, Nicholas, it won't happen here. However, as handsome as you look, someone might be targeting you."

"Stop trying to placate me, Tina. I will take you out of here if you are going after criminals who are dangerous enough to participate in kidnapping."

"You can't wrap me up in cellophane to protect me, Nicholas. I wouldn't do that to you, though I want to protect you as fiercely as you want to protect me. I almost got you killed for something you had absolutely nothing to do with. Your life is precious to me."

He saw the naked honesty in her eyes. She cared deeply for him and regretted he was harmed. Caring for people was in her DNA no matter what it took. He didn't want her to change who she was, but he wanted to be with her every step of the journey that constituted her life.

"Okay," he acquiesced. "I'll go along with your *research*," he said with emphasis, "but you do not move out of my sight."

She gave him one of her patented impish smiles that melted the sternness in his demeanor. "I'll be your shadow for the evening to prevent anyone from snatching you up, handsome."

He could only shake his head at her, bemused, yet still concerned.

They mixed and mingled, receiving invitations to join various sailing parties for the impending regatta. However, they begged off claiming previous engagements. Most of the people in attendance didn't have to go into an office to make a living. Although neither she nor Nicholas was footloose or fancy-free, others were.

One man Tina sensed kept his eyes on her. Many men had looked at her. A few flirted, even fewer attempted to proposition her, but none studied her as intently. He made her decidedly uncomfortable, but she avoided eye contact pretending ignorance of his attention to her.

"Take me to the bar for a drink," suggested Tina.

"Okay, but you don't drink that much. What's up?"

"Order a white wine for me then lean on the bar facing me." When he did as she asked, "Do you see the tall man with dark hair wearing an Italian tuxedo and white bow tie?" She was pretending to talk with Nicholas while actually watching the man in question using the mirror behind the bar.

Nicholas looked at her but simultaneously moved so he could look over her shoulder. "Yes, I see him. He's been scoping you out, why?"

"He could have been scoping you out. Do you know him?"

"No, he isn't familiar to me, but I've only been coming to the Yacht Club periodically. As I understand it, there are hundreds of members in this club and the club is linked to other clubs worldwide. Many in attendance tonight can be from any number of clubs and will be here particularly this weekend because of the regatta. I don't know all of the ones in The Hamptons Club."

"He doesn't seem to have a date tonight."

"So?"

"If he did it would have been convenient to instigate a little meeting in the ladies room to figure out who he is."

"Why don't I just ask him why he's eyeing my date?'

"Uh, no, that would be too obvious, especially if he has the hots for you instead of me. He might think it's a come on," she said giving Nicholas a winning smile while still watching the man in the mirror.

"All right, let's go to Plan B."

"Which is?"

"I'll go to the men's room and see whether he follows me or approaches you."

"Why don't we both go. I wouldn't want anything to happen to you," she teased. "I want to be the one to peel you out of this tuxedo."

"You did that already, remember? I was fully dressed when you undressed me and had your way with me."

"Was that before or after you got me naked the third time?"

"Hey, I was just trying to keep up," he teased as they headed to the restrooms.

Tina freshened her lip gloss and exited the ladies room to find the man in question standing a few paces from the door. She half expected this maneuver and ignored him attempting to step past him in the crowded hallway when he stepped directly into her path.

"Ms. Justice, isn't it?"

She looked up into eyes that were cold and devoid of softness. "It is, and you are?"

"Most of the people know me as Webster."

The name rang a bell for some reason she couldn't put her finger on at the moment, but just then Nicholas joined them in the hallway.

"Nicholas, this is Webster."

"Mr. Collins, congratulations on the launch of your satellite. Ms. Justice, an honor to have met you," he said and sauntered away.

"Interesting," said Nico.

"Yes, very interesting," agreed Tina.

The dinner bell rang so they went in and were seated. They noted that Webster wasn't among those having dinner.

21

By the weekend, Nico and Tina had returned from his estate in The Hamptons to his penthouse in the Upper West Side of New York City. Although they made time for each other, they both had work that consumed most of their days and were constantly taking meetings via their phones and/or Skype.

Tina was stretched out on one of the plush sofas in Nicholas' open-concept living area speaking with her Chicago office about the construction underway at Sweet Justice studios and other business matters. JaiHonnah Baylor had been right. Her cousin, Lizette Fiona Lowry was, indeed, a very talented architect and easy to work with. JRock, JaiHonnah, and their family, including their new baby boy, were planning to join Tina on the voyage on their yacht *The Navajo Princess.* JaiHonnah's brother, Adam, a vice president of their father's conglomerate, BlackHawk Global, who also raced Formula One cars in his spare time, would sail from Baytown, Texas, outside of Houston, through Galveston Bay, on their family yacht, *The SkaiHawk.* The vessel was named for their mother, Skai, a full-blooded Navajo and registered nurse who died of breast cancer when JaiHonnah was still a teen.

Nico was in the kitchen area doing essentially the same thing, conversing with his office executives while he tried to simultaneously follow instructions for making coq au vin. He dipped a spoon in the broth and carried it to Tina for a taste test. From behind the sofa over her head, he brought the spoon to her lips.

She said, "Hold one," and covered her face mike while she tasted the offering. Her eyes widened in surprise at the delicious flavor as she looked up at him over her shoulder. "Mmm, that's good," she enthused and then without taking her eyes off him, said into the mike, "That's it for today, Bruce," and disconnected. Reaching behind her, when he leaned forward to kiss her mouth, she pulled Nicholas from over the back of the sofa until he landed with his back to her breast. She immediately wrapped her long, bare legs and feet around him. "Mmm," she hummed nibbling on his left earlobe, "this is good, too."

Nico placed the spoon on an end table and continued his conversation with others in his office. He took Tina's hands in his and kissed her palms without missing a beat in his conversation, but his breathing became labored moments later when she began playing with the flat nipples on his bare chest.

"Uh, we'll have to continue this conversation at a later time. Something has come up that needs my immediate attention," Nico said and disconnected the call pulling the earphone from around his right ear and tossing it away. In one fluid motion, Nico turned over, pulled Tina more securely horizontal, and dove into her as she laughed like a loon. Her laughter dissolved into a long, strong moan.

A few hours later, they sat sexually sated for the moment savoring the heady taste of the coq au vin, a loaf of crusty bread, and white wine.

"So, you think this Webster is the same one Kristen danced with several years ago while she was on vacation in the Polynesian Islands?" asked Nicholas.

"Based on the description I gave her and Thomas, it certainly could be. I hacked into the Yacht Club's database, but I found nothing for anyone with the first or last name of Webster."

Nico looked askance at her. "You hacked the Yacht Club's records? You, who has an uncle as the Chicago Police Commissioner, a brother who is a Chicago Police Department detective, one a captain in the US Coast Guard, and another one who is with the freakin' CIA?"

"Who do you think taught me how to hack a computer system?"

"Don't give me that innocent look, Tina," he chastised. "I may have to keep ready cash on hand to bail you out of jail."

"Maybe you should, but until that happens, you can have your way with me," she said and kissed him into oblivion.

***

The Justice family and friends arranged themselves on both sides and the front along the nearly two-hundred-foot dock to view the **Outlaw Justice II**. Hands reverently touched the underside of her hull from stem to stern as all stood in awe of her beauty. Peter stood holding Alex in one arm with his other around Joyce. Unadulterated pride was on his face. Joyce's brother, sport's icon, Chuck Montgomery and his wife, Gold Medalist and Supreme Court Justice, Vivian Alexander, and their twenty-five children were in attendance. Vivian hugged her younger brother, Gregory, while holding onto her oldest child, teenager Linda's hand.

The state-of-art, hybrid-power-and-propulsion sea craft was a sailing pleasure. A windmill sat at the top of the mast and the solar panels generated power for propellers when engaged and for the batteries when not.

"She's awesome," said Kristen Catherine in a near-reverent voice. She and Tina interlocked arms with Cheryl.

"She's a big girl," said Cheryl grinning as she rubbed the smooth surface. "She'll run true and fast."

"That she will," said Diaz, his eyes shining as he inspected her undercarriage.

Everyone had to touch the beauty while waiting to christen her before her maiden voyage from New York City to Buenos Aires, Argentina.

In lieu of the champagne bottle broken across her bow, Reverend Justice offered a prayer, shook up a bottle of champagne, and held it out so that his wife, Anna Lettie, could pop the cork. The effervescent liquid shot out onto the bow of the boat as all cheered. Everyone toasted with champagne while the ropes were removed that had held the newly christened **Outlaw Justice II** as she slid into the waters of the Hudson.

That night they stowed supplies and food aboard and got a good night's sleep and a hearty breakfast in the early morning hours. Leaving at the crack of dawn under full sail, they were accompanied by **The Vivian Lynn**, the yacht so named by Vivian's first husband years before his death. With Diaz as captain and Peter Calloway as helmsman, things went smoothly on the open waters of the Atlantic Ocean. They were joined by **The Navajo Princess**, at the mouth of the Chesapeake Bay and put into port at the deep-water, beachfront home of J. Roderick and JaiHonnah Baylor who, in their yacht had sailed south from Washington, DC, on the Chesapeake Bay. The vessels made it to Sandbridge just south of Norfolk, Virginia, by late afternoon; a testament to the fact they knew their assignments and did them well.

The beach house was a round structure like a grain silo several levels high with balconies around the circumference. They pitched tents on the beach and Bouchard with helpers cooked a massive amount of food on outdoor grills. They had done some deep-sea fishing off **The Navajo Princess** and **The Vivian Lynn** and were eager for the fresh grilled fish fare. The children swam in the ocean or the in-ground pool, flew kites, and threw Frisbees until sunset. With dips in the pool and showers complete, everyone turned in early in preparation for a daybreak departure. The next leg of the journey would take them to a small private island in Bimini Vivian owned that only had a few native inhabitants. It was the westernmost area of the Bahamas, comprised of a chain of islands over fifty miles due east of Miami. It promised to bring more challenging winds, perhaps as much as thirty knots.

The scheduled breaks were necessary for the sailing party to regroup. Diaz praised their progress as did Peter Callaway and adjusted where necessary to ensure the best fit of a person to a task. Nico was assigned to the mainsail; a crucial role when hoisting and dropping the spinnaker along with Big Red and Tina's brothers. George Bryant and Peter Brock were part of the pit crew with Kristen. Cheryl and Thomas were on the foredeck responsible for calling the line and repacking the spinnaker. Joyce, Anna Lettie, and Marguerite kept eyes on the children making the voyage a teachable experience for the little ones. There was a camera displaying the undersea world they traveled above. It kept the children enthralled with the schools of fish and other sea creatures and underwater landscape.

Nico was pleasantly weary at the end of each day, but as a team, he liked their chances of making a credible showing at this leg of the contest for the America's Cup. He was getting his first taste of salt air and life at sea. Porpoises raced ahead and beside the yachts like daredevils to the delight of the children onboard all three yachts. He developed a respect for the elements of sea and rain and the ship that challenged and tested them often to limits of their endurance. Working with a group of seasoned sailors, both men and women, young and older, proved to be an invaluable asset.

The Outlaw Justice II readily took to the tasks for which she was designed, thought Tina. Her hull was built of steel with teak overlaying. With the good winds between fifteen to twenty knots, both boat speed and handling were tested. Daily, they were improving their racing talents. None, other than Diaz, had prior experience or necessary skill to manage the one-hundred-fifty-footer. They had participated as a family in races, like the three-hundred-mile one from Chicago to Mackinac Island, a freshwater race, but according to the videos shot from the decks of *The Vivian Lynn* and *The Navajo Princess*, they were doing better than a credible job against the times recorded for classic open sea races of three-thousand miles or more.

It was difficult to grab a little privacy with more than seventy other men, women, and children around, thought Tina. Sleeping in tents on air-filled mattresses did not shield against the transference of noise. Most times she fell into sleep in Nicholas' arms eager for the next day's voyage.

"Land ho!" someone enthusiastically yelled as the crew battled the strong winds and currents off the coast of one of the small islands in the Bahamas which was Vivian and her family's retreat. They maneuvered into the cove of gentler waters sheltered by higher ridges against the winds. Some stripped down and jumped into the warm, clear water to frolic and swim to shore.

Everyone laughed exhausted at the strenuous journey. Those still on board secured the sails, dropped anchor offshore, battened down the hatches, and then transferred to **The Vivian Lynn** or **The Navaho Princess** with supplies and duffels for the trip to the docks on shore. A seaplane drifted gently in the tidewaters that lapsed against the sand. Vivian's brother, Benny, his wife, and their seven children had flown in to join the group.

Because it was such a grueling voyage from Sandbridge, they were shutting down early rather than putting in more practice time that day. The kites, balls, and other breach games came out while sand castles began to take shape. It was a child's wonderland more exciting than any amusement park. The adults delighted in watching the children and teens having fun while they relaxed.

The round house similar to the Baylor's Sandbridge home, but much larger, stood out on a hill several levels high. A glide rose on rails up the craggy hillside and carried duffels, supplies, and those not willing to scale the hundred or so steps up from the beach. Joyce opted for the ride along with Reverend Justice and Anna Lettie, while Peter carried a sleepy Alex up the steps on his shoulder.

The children were like banshees having the time of their lives on the beach and swimming in the crystal-clear waters of the cove. Some of the adults stayed and played, too.

With ample room indoors, the meal was prepared by available hands and set up buffet style. Nicholas and Tina stretched out on a wide chaise lounge awaiting the call to dine. Tina had been one to strip down to a bikini and jump overboard to swim to shore. She, Cheryl, KC, JaiHonnah and her sister LaiLoni, all Spelman grads, had been to Vivian's island paradise several times for a women's retreat. LaiLoni and her husband, Jefferson Logan, former US Ambassador, now resided in Summer County, South Carolina, Vivian's birthplace. Jefferson took over as Dean of Summer County Academy from Vivian's father. The Logans were aboard The Navaho Princess with their five children, though the older boys were now in their teens. They helped to crew *The Outlaw Justice II* from Sandbridge and enjoyed having pictures taken of their efforts by their father.

The next few days when they would have started out for Miami and points south, they were forced to stay put as a hurricane with an unpredictable route caused torrential rains and high seas. Even bigger ships, like oil tankers and cargo vessels, heeded the weather warnings and stayed in port.

On the third day of the constant rain squalls, Joyce was helping in the kitchen area to make soup and hoagie sandwiches for lunch when suddenly her water broke. She was several weeks early, but with two doctors and a nurse in the group, the baby girl, Joy Ann Calloway, came into the world to the jubilant applause of seventy plus people.

"That was nice," said Tina as she and Nicholas sat outside on one of the sheltered decks watching the rain fall.

"Do you ever think about becoming a parent?" Nico asked.

"I have thought about it from time to time, but then I just take a nap and the thought just goes away."

Nico laughed.

"However, I see how much joy children add to KC's and Cheryl's lives and sometimes I wonder."

"I've never had a sense of family, but then I look at your friends, Vivian and Chuck. They have over twenty-five children, the majority of whom were abandoned, health-challenged orphans they adopted. They have natural born children as well, but for the most part, I can't distinguish which are adopted and which aren't."

"They don't make those distinctions. All of the children they have adopted have been abandoned at birth or as a result of the child's health challenges. Vivian and Chuck also help to get other families to adopt abandoned children. Chuck and Joyce are the babies of their other twelve siblings. Their family lives on farms in the Pennsylvania Poconos and many have adopted at least one child and, in some cases, more than one. Vivian has been successful in placing orphans with members of her first husband's family in Pennsylvania and members of her family in South Carolina. If I were to have children, I believe that's the route I would take. "

"Adoption," Nico said nodding. "I can see that. After all, Chuck is an Emergency Room doctor with his own Physicians' Hospital and a private practice in a rural area outside of Washington, DC. He also has privileges at Georgetown

Medical Center where he teaches. Vivian is a Supreme Court Justice and former Gold Medalist in basketball. She writes books, lectures at Georgetown Law, and manages her multibillion-dollar conglomerate. Oh, yeah, I can see how they have ample time on their hands to have, adopt, and raise twenty-five or more toddlers, children, and teens."

Tina laughed. "For them it's seamless. They never let their careers interfere with their family life. Chuck and Vivian even have date night several times a week. The two of them are raising a wholesome family with adventures such as this.

"Look around," she continued meaning the yacht and the family retreat. "From the time Vivian married Derrick Jackson, who was also a Gold Medal Olympian in basketball, and later an established pediatrician and pediatric surgeon; they made time to adopt many of Derrick's patients. They had one son who was born on the day Derrick died, April Fool's Day, but they had established a wholesome life Vivian continued by adopting orphans with health challenges. The ones who were not likely to be adopted.

"Derrick and Chuck were best friends and five years after Derrick's death, when Vivian and Chuck married, they continued the practice. Vivian adopted nine children after Derrick's death and before she married Chuck. We, her pals, were there for each and every party held to welcome a new addition into their lives. Like me, Vivian is in her mid-thirties. Chuck is nine years her senior, but they are nowhere near cutting back. They live on a working farm with plenty of space in the household and have boundless love to share. They don't take their children for granted and are actively involved parents in every aspect of their lives.

"That's the type of parent I would want to be," she finished.

Nico nodded. "I can see that, and you'd be good at it because that's the type of environment you grew up in. Your brothers would be in every aspect of their nieces and nephews' lives, too."

"They would, yes. I wouldn't be able to stop them. Just as we gather up Cheryl's and KC's children every chance we get when they come home for a visit or like now."

"I noticed. So, it's adoption rather than having your own?"

"No, not instead of, in addition to. However, the clock is ticking on my reproductive life," she said grinning.

When they were called to lunch, they entered the chaos that was family enjoying it thoroughly.

On the fourth day, the hurricane passed into the history books and *The Outlaw Justice II*, *The Vivian Lynn*, and *The Navajo Princess* sailed from the Bahamas through much calmer seas to Miami where they stocked up on food and supplies and had the large fish they caught cleaned, scaled, and cut into large roast size pieces for the more than thirty-eight-thousand nautical miles it would take to reach Buenos Aires, Argentina.

The storm had eaten precious days they needed to make the journey with the children, but schools would be opening the following week. It was with sad smiles that the school-aged children and teens waved goodbye as they boarded an Adventurer Executive Airline jet bound for Washington, DC. Grandparents and other relatives would meet the flight on the other end at the airport. Without the school-age children and teens, the sailing party was cut nearly in half. However, every one of the children would fly to Argentina for the three-day race for the America's Cup. Their parents felt a few missed school days were well worth the valuable life experience they would gain from seeing the race. Grandparents and other relatives and friends would join the festivities, too.

When they left Miami, they sailed across the Gulf of Mexico where they were joined by JaiHonnah's brother, Adam Hawkins, in the hundred-forty-foot yacht *The SkaiHawk* on the way to Caracas, Venezuela; a location on the Guairá River for an overnight stay in a McCoy Grand Hotel. The next day they crossed the Equator into the South Atlantic Ocean headed for Rio De Janeiro, Brazil. Everyone was glad to see The Christ statue on the hilltop with arms open wide to greet them as they sailed into the harbor. This would be the last stop before reaching Buenos Aires, Argentina, late on the next day.

Raphael and Alicia Alonza Dela Vega met the four sailing yachts at a large dock with deep water slips in boathouses. It was more than a week before the race, hosted by the prestigious Semana de Buenos Aires Yachting Club, would begin. However, as they came into port, they saw sailing vessels flying flags from Ecuador, Chile, Uruguay, the US Virgin Islands, Italy, and Spain. More countries with boats in the J-Class were expected to arrive during the week to participate. The weather was perfect and predicted to remain so throughout the event.

The daily schedule consisted of a morning briefing followed by on-the-water practice. They ran the route the contest would take several times a day; fifty miles one way. Once back on shore they viewed the videos recorded and analyzed them during debriefing. They worked on their technique in order to get *The Outlaw Justice II* faster in the choppy water conditions of Buenos Aires. More than a few

240 | Ann Jeffries

times the crew had to ride the gunwale to keep the yacht on a more even keel and to keep her from tipping over in the strong winds. The yacht, with its custom-designed sails, was giving them everything demanded of her, but to make a decent showing during the race it was the crews' skill and ability which would determine their fate. The fully-crewed, thirty-plus positions learned quickly the tactics needed to work as a team.

After each hard day's work, they relished the after-hours camaraderie they shared together and with teams from other boats and countries in the bars, restaurants, and nightclubs around the city.

One night in a bar, Tina noticed Kristen Catherine was craning her neck to peer over the crowd. Then she got her husband's attention beside her and had Thomas search the crowd, too.

"What is it?" asked Tina of Kristen.

Without shifting her eyes from the crowd, she whispered across the table to Tina, "Believe it or not, I think I saw Webster in the crowd."

Tina immediately stood up and turned, but even her superior height couldn't easily pick out individuals in the packed nightclub with low lighting. Although the club was large, the dance floor was jam packed and the walls were lined six deep. She spotted two of her brothers dancing energetically with very attractive young women from various other countries, but she had no idea where the rest of her brothers were. They had broken out one of *The Outlaw Justice II* sailing uniforms as had all of the other yachters in the race. Tonight, they wore the blue shorts, white shirts with red *Outlaw Justice II* lettering scrolled on the back and the American flag over the breast pocket.

"I could have sworn it was him," said Kristen as she, too, stood searching the crowd.

"Let's dance," suggested Thomas when a slower tune was struck up by the band. "Maybe we can get a better look that way."

Kristen and Thomas passed Cheryl and Peter Brock as they left the dance floor.

"Let's circulate," suggested Nicholas to Tina, who readily agreed, relinquishing their seats at a table to Cheryl and Peter. They managed to squeeze past the energetic crowd and people speaking different languages. Once they circumnavigated the interior of the club, they stepped outside where people sat on the club's veranda chatting and enjoying the crowds passing in the streets. Nicholas pointed out Miguel who had a woman against the wall in a lip lock. When Tina would have interrupted her brother, Nico placed his hand over her mouth and goose-stepped her away.

"Looks like he'll get lucky tonight," teased Tina.

"After all that time at sea, he's not the only one who wants to get lucky tonight," Nicholas deadpanned.

"I think that's doable," Tina parried slinging an arm around Nicholas' waist and squeezing him to her.

He swung her into his arms and leaned her back against the railing between others standing on the veranda. He leaned down and nibbled on her lips. "The man in question is directly behind you, but he may have spotted us so don't turn around to look and don't move. I have my arm over our insignia on your back and I'm keeping my face hidden in your hair, so he doesn't get a good look at us."

"Good moves. You're not just a handsome face and great body."

"He's not looking in this direction right now. Ease away from me and head inside to get Thomas and KC. I'll stay here and try to keep an eye on him."

Tina did as suggested and returned with both of her friends. As they arranged themselves along the railing intermingled with others to be less conspicuous, both Kristen and Thomas nodded.

"Well, hell, who would have thought it," commented Kristen. "He's someone I would never have expected to see again in my lifetime."

"You never expected to see me again in your lifetime," commented Thomas. "Look at us now; married with three children."

"What are you thinking, Tina?" asked Nico.

"It's not proof positive that he's involved in human trafficking. If he has a yacht nearby, I'd like to get a look at it."

"Uh, no," said Thomas and Nico, simultaneously.

"If you mean getting aboard to look around, fuhgeddaboutit," said Kristen in a Jersey accent. "I don't know what the laws are in Argentina for breaking and entering, but your grandparents would be mortified if you were caught."

"The sticking point is not getting caught," said Tina.

"I do know the laws here," said Thomas, "and they aren't pretty, particularly for an American and a member of the US Bar Association. You could put your ability to practice law in jeopardy."

Tina said no more, but they continued to surreptitiously watch the man they knew as Webster.

Tina waited until Nicholas was sleeping soundly to slip out of bed and onto the deck of *The Outlaw Justice II* before she wiggled into her wetsuit. Her security team was walking the deck and dock. She could hear them talking. They tended not to shadow her as closely when she and Nicholas were together allowing a modicum of privacy. She sat on the gunwale and slipped into her flippers. Her air tanks were secured to her back before she pulled on her face mast and slipped silently into the water.

Earlier that night they followed Webster to a yacht named *The III Ws*. It had a Panamanian registry, but the owner was none other than the English conglomerate, Wayne Agra Industries.

Thomas confirmed he had once represented the company in one of the best and most complicated court cases of his career. It was the only case he handled where Jillian Harris had been his second chair. Before making the leap to the Marshall and Marshall Law firm owned by Thomas and his mother, Sheila, Jillian was Wayne Agra Industries' chief in-house legal counsel. She obviously would have known the head of Wayne Agra Industries and likely his son, too.

Kristen had been slated to sit in judgment of the case when she recognized Thomas Marshall as the man she had an affair with on an island in the Pacific Ocean; a man she never expected to see again. It was possible, that being the son of the Wayne Agra Industry's owner, he may have known who Kristen was and that she would potentially be one of the federal court judges who would adjudicate the trial his father was facing. There may have been any number of reasons why he may have wanted to seek her out. Some form of blackmail being the first thought coming to mind.

Tina remembered the circumstances of the case because she and Cheryl were clerking for Kristen at the time and Peter Brock was KC's chief of staff and senior legal counsel. Shortly before the verdict was released, Jillian disappeared. Thomas confirmed Jillian seemed to have a "special" relationship with the owner, Wallace Wayne, head of Wayne Agra Industries. Special because Wayne insisted Jillian be given an active role on Thomas' legal team. However, Thomas had no idea whether the relationship between Wallace Wayne and Jillian Harris was intimate. As with most clients, Thomas had Slade's Investigations and Security company probe whether there were any red flags before Thomas took on Wayne as a client. What Thomas had forgotten was that Wallace Wayne had a son, Wallace Webster Wayne, III.

That's what made things fall into place for Tina. She didn't hold much stock in coincidences. It was entirely possible that if Jillian didn't have an intimate relationship with the father, it was quite possible she may have had one with the son. Having a relationship with both seemed to fit Jillian's *modus operandi*.

She had quite a reputation for using sex in her toolkit to get what she wanted. Rumor had it that was what propelled her over more qualified lawyers to the top legal position in Wayne Agra Industries; one of the top fifty companies in the world.

What was a little daunting was the sparsity of information on Wallace Webster Wayne, III. He was descended from an English and French dynasty. His mother was a French aristocracy baroness who was noted for the extravagant parties she held at several of the castles she or her family owned. She and Wallace, II married young and only had the one child whom they indulged with every advantage. Beyond that bit of history, not much was known about how the savant made his money and lived on a fleet of yachts year-round.

Tina was determined to learn more as she surfaced at the stern of *The III Ws*. Securing her flipper, she stole silently aboard and made her way below deck. Once she identified where the Master Stateroom was located, she moved in that direction. She wasn't sure who was aboard ship, but her reconnaissance was strictly to determine what she could find out about Webster, as he apparently preferred to be called, and his relationship to Jillian Harris.

A laptop sat open on a desk in plain view. She slipped a jump drive out of a plastic bag in her wetsuit and inserted it in a port. Within moments she had hacked into the system without tripping any alarms. While the data downloaded, she searched for other information among his personal effects. Just as she completed her search and the data dump finished, she heard voices and footsteps above her head. She couldn't squeeze through a porthole, but she knew it was past time for her to be on her way. She stowed the jump drive in a zipper part of her wetsuit and stepped into a closet partially closing the door.

Suddenly a hand clamped over her mouth and an arm pinned her arms to her body. When she would have fought to free herself, a voice whispered a name in her ear just as the door to the Master Cabin opened and Webster walked in.

He was talking on a cellphone in an annoyed voice as one-handed he stripped off his clothes. "I want to know who else is on the crew of that Justice yacht!" he demanded.

Tina's blood ran to ice at the thought of this man's interest in her family and friends. Nicholas was asleep on the yacht. She needed to gather everyone to warn them of possible danger, particularly KC. The crew had rooms on the same floor of the McCoy Hotel, Resort and Conference Center in the up-scaled section of Buenos Aires. Her grandparents, Ellis and Anna Lettie, were staying at the home of Raphael and Alicia. Her parents and the parents of Cheryl, Peter, Thomas, and Kristen were also at her grandparents' estate. Though they were protected there, they still needed to be aware of potential danger. She and Nicholas opted to stay on board the yacht at her instigation. While her mind worked at warp speed, the cabin door opened again and two women with their arms bound behind their backs, blindfolded and gagged were brought in. When Webster pulled a riding crop from a drawer, it was clear to Tina what was about to happen. She wanted to surge forward but was held back. She was forced to endure the S&M sights and sounds for nearly an hour until Webster wore himself out and fell asleep with the two women in his bed. That's when she and her unexpected partner were able to make a clean escape from *The III Ws*.

"What the hell did you think you were doing?" asked Slade Richardson, his voice calm, but strident.

"*Me?* What were *you* doing?" demanded Tina. "You scared the life out of me."

"I was doing my job trying to keep you from blowing a covert operation to hell that's been ongoing for several years and simultaneously trying to keep you from being snatched."

Tina had been marching back and forth, but that bit of intelligence brought her up short. "What are you talking about?" she asked.

"You made yourself a target at The Hamptons Yacht Club gala and unknowingly put yourself on the market. Bidding has been brisk and if Nico hadn't bid higher and higher amounts to protect you and, in the meantime, had you under constant surveillance, you may have already been on your way to a higher bidder; a sheikh from a Middle Eastern country without a care about your rights as an American citizen or as a woman."

Tina turned sharply to look at Nicholas who stood feet apart, back straight, head up with his arms folded across his chest. Incongruent anger seemed to leap off of him in the midst of the yachts' luxury salon with custom mahogany raised paneling and sublime art-deco walls. None of that registered with her as she stared angrily. "You bid on me like I was a slave on an auction block and had me under surveillance?" she demanded.

"You're damn right I did!" he said through gritted teeth, his fury radiating off of him.

"After all the time we've spent together, you didn't trust me?" she asked, her voice harsh.

"It's precisely because I know you so well that I took the extra precaution to protect you. Do you think for one damn moment I'd let anything happen to you if I could prevent it?"

"It wasn't your call to make!" she thundered.

"Oh, yeah, that's rich considering what these bastards have in store for you. Do you want to know how much you were worth on the open market for celebrities?"

"No," she said morosely.

"Arguing isn't going to get us anywhere," said a female voice.

Everyone turned to the woman still wearing a wetsuit.

"The fact remains, Tina, if we hadn't gotten you out of there, you would have been in serious trouble," said Admiral Stacy Greene. "Slade is right, you were about to screw up big time. As it is, we have to rework the security video on the yacht to erase your presence before his security people see it.

"Look, Tina," she continued. I know it's not about television ratings for you or the celebrity of the big story. You care about the welfare of people you see as victims and you go to the mat to help no matter what it takes. I get that and your motivation, but you took it too far this time."

"What I got will put criminals behind bars where they belong and free women who are being abused."

"You're right, but Webster is one among many. We believe we've identified every player in the trafficking scheme that has been in operation for years. Many of them are here in Argentina, but not all."

"If you know who they are and what they've done, why haven't they been arrested?"

For a pregnant moment, no one said anything as Tina looked between Slade and Stacy.

"You've got a mole inside the organization, don't you?" asked Nico.

Slade nodded. "Two moles and we have undercover yachters. We were taking no chances. These people hold the evidence we need to take this matter before the World Court in The Hague. These are all heavy hitters with unlimited resources at their disposal. Our case has to be airtight or we could end up with nothing but a few low-level criminals."

"We want them all. That includes those members of the Boko Haram who routinely abduct women, children, and teens to sell into slavery and to the highest bidders in this exclusive society ring. That's not to say this practice won't go on, but it will take time for them to organize again. By then, we'll be on to them again."

"Stacy, something tells me that you're not just an Admiral in the US Navy," said Nico.

"I don't know who 'something' is, but don't listen to him or her. I'm in Buenos Aires to participate in a regatta with my family and friends."

"We need your word, Tina, that you will stand down or else," threatened Slade.

"Or else, what?"

"We'll be forced to put you in protective custody. That will involve telling your family and friends what you've been up to."

Oh, hell, no, she thought, as she began to pace again. *If her family found out any of this, she'd be sequestered so deep daylight would only be a fond memory.*

"You're a damn good attorney, Tina, a helluva researcher, and you have great instincts, but you're not a cop. If you give your word, I know you'll keep it without finding a way around it. You've got friends with children and teens just like the ones who have gone missing. I can make this very clear for you, but I hate putting that image in your head. So, I'm waiting, Tina, what's it going to be?" asked Slade.

Begrudgingly she nodded. "You have my word, but I want an exclusive on the perp walk."

"Maybe that can be arranged, but no promises," agreed Stacy.

Slade and Stacy left among a hanging silence between Tina and Nicholas.

Without a word between them, Nico turned his back on her and went into one of the other ship's cabins closing the door behind him.

That suited her just right, thought Tina as she went into the Master stateroom. She was in no mood to be conciliatory.

They each went about their normal routines, but everyone sensed something amiss between Tina and Nico.

The night before the start of the race, Tina got the call. The net would be sprung on all of the suspects worldwide in the early morning hours in each time zone. She organized all of her camera personnel and journalists dispatching them to the various countries to await the go orders, but she was torn between seeing the arrests take place or participating in the race. Ultimately, being with her family and friends won out over being on board to orchestrate the filming of a major law enforcement story.

They ran a valiant race on *The Outlaw Justice II* coming in third by a nose, edged out of second place by the US Virgin Island team.

Wasting no time after the celebration of their victory and news interviews about the novice crew's accomplishments, Tina flew back to Chicago to get back to work. Her family would spend more time in Argentina vacationing. As she viewed the raw footage submitted by one of the film crews at the perp walk, the name Lana Norton snapped her back ramrod straight. *Well,* she thought, *good riddance to bad rubbish.* The woman had molested a teenager and misused his father. Apparently, Nicholas wasn't her only victim. Tina had no sympathy for the woman who would stand trial before The World Court in The Hague for kidnapping, sexual molestation of male minors and men, and other heinous crimes. Tina's crews would be there to film the entire trial of some of the world's most notable high-society people. The Nuremberg trials would pale by comparison.

Though her journalists weren't there for every liberation of abducted victims, she managed to have Strickland Briggs on site when Jillian Harris was found on a yacht owned by the person who had her abducted, Wallace Webster Wayne, III. Strickland sent a text message to her expressing his appreciation.

It had been over a month since she last saw Nicholas in Argentina. However, he was in the news quite a bit. The media managed to catch pictures of him on his yacht, **Nico's Pride** on the New York waterway sailing early in the morning. Then there were those shots of him in Europe, Asia, and Africa in one high-level meeting, event or another.

After their return from Argentina, her family and friends were walking on eggshells around her and not mentioning him by name. Although she was out and about in public when necessary, particularly when she won awards for the exposés, she went unescorted to each event. Though she thought about Nicholas a little too often for her own comfort, she still believed it best they parted without rancor. If she happened to Google her brothers, his name popped up, too, only because he was seen as one of the top whatever most eligible bachelors in the United States as were her brothers. She ignored it all as best she could. However, sometimes she didn't manage that very well.

23

The blasted woman had been on his mind for the last month he'd been in Europe, Asia, and Africa. He knew she was still pissed with him for having Slade's security people shadow her without telling her. She wasn't at all happy he won bids to keep her out of the clutches of criminals. Every day he checked the media outlets, his own and others, for tidbits of information concerning her whereabouts and who she was with.

It pleased him that, after Argentina, no man was paired with her in the news media. What he didn't know was who, if anyone, had taken up her time. For the time being, social media had not picked up gossip about Tina and any other man. That fact buoyed his flagging spirits. So, he was particularly surprised and pleased when his clear glass elevator crested his penthouse floor. He saw, through the glass-paneled walls, a distinctive female figure. She was standing in the dim light looking out at the nighttime New York City skyline.

He walked into his penthouse and directly to his security panel to lock down all exits from or access to his home. Then he loosed his tie, unbuttoned his shirt, and took off his jacket flinging it into a chair. She hadn't moved or spoken when he went to his wet bar, poured a straight shot, and downed it. Placing his hands on the bar and leaning on his outstretched arms, he looked at the void between himself and the floor.

"How long are we going to do this?" he asked.

"I have no clue."

"Let's start with the fact you're in my house without my knowledge or consent. How you gained access is a mystery. You want me, you tell me when and where. I'll be there. You want unfettered access to me, ignoring me stops right here, right now."

"I don't telegraph my moves."

"Neither do I. That means we're too much alike and unpredictable."

"We both get what we want, when we want it. However, this would be much easier if you just let me have my way."

"Yeah, uh, no, that's not how this is going to work, Tina. There will only be one man and one woman in his relationship."

"I know most people find you, your strength intimidating, but I regret I find you . . . interesting."

"I'm a lot to handle, so I will not permit you to reduce me to the status of the flavor of the moment or a boy toy. You seriously want me for more than a moment; you come and get me but only for the long haul. Let me make myself perfectly clear, I mean for the rest of our lives."

"I can't keep doing this. It's exhausting. Yet, it's obvious we have something here. I just don't know what it is or why we can't get over this hump."

"I don't know what the hell it is, either, but no one else has ever done this to me. I'm telling you now, Tina. This isn't going to work for me unless you open up to me completely. You can't come into my house and expect to not end up in my bed."

"Is that what you tell all the women you bring here? That their exit has to be through your bedroom?"

"Stop fishing for information about my life. I didn't bring you here and I have never had another woman here."

"You expect me to believe that?"

"I don't give a rat's ass whether you believe me or not. I don't repeat myself. I'm tired and I'm going to shower and go to bed. Either leave the same way you got in or be in my bed when I get out of the shower."

"You locked down the penthouse. If you wanted me out, you would not have done that. That tells me you want me here."

"You're damn right I do. You came to me. You obviously have been tracking my movements just as I have been tracking yours. Otherwise, you would not have known I was going to be here tonight and arranged to be here ahead of my arrival. So, come and get me, Tina."

"No. I'm frustrated by this relationship because it seems to be causing more tension than relaxation."

"No one said love was easy, but it doesn't have to be miserable."

She sharply turned to look at him in the murky dimness. A scary little sensation skittered up her spine. "Who said anything about that word?"

"What word? Love?" He stood feet apart, shirt open to his bare chest, arms crossed, muscles bulging in stark relief.

She could see the place where the bullet had pierced his skin and filled her with regret. She looked her fill from the bottom up. He was certainly a magnificently, well-built piece of manhood. "Yeah, that one."

He laughed at the sheer panic on her face and in her voice. "I did. Didn't you hear me?"

"You just need a thesaurus," she dismissed with a flick of her hand and turned her back to him again.

He snickered. "The key is to not get too stressed out about the little things now and expect some things aren't going to match your expectations. You simply have no control over some aspects of a relationship; the other person, for example. Namely me."

"We don't need to talk about that word," she insisted looking at him over her right shoulder again.

His smile was lethal; a toothy grin that showed signs of male arrogance. The never-ending struggle for supremacy. She saw the gleam in his eyes and realized too late he was right. Damn it! She was in love ... with him.

She got him, all right! All the damn night long, he mentally groaned as he rolled over in his now empty bed and stared out his expansive, floor-to-ceiling, bedroom window. The sky was turning an interesting shade of golden orange and yellow. So where was she now? he wondered. She hit it and quit it! He closed his eyes for a few damn moments and she was gone leaving her scent on his sheets to torment him. Well, he wasn't going to take it lying down. Tina Justice was about to have a come to Nicholas Collins moment.

***

A rather upsetting dream disturbed her sleep. When she woke up and focused on the real world, sixty thousand feet in the air, it could seem so bizarre as to not be worthy of serious consideration. Nonetheless, she wrote it down. After some time had passed, she went over the symbols to see what they suggested to her. The dream is trying to tell her something about a specific situation in her life, albeit in a weird way. It was not the first time she had sleeping premonitions of events to come. This one was more vivid than others.

Nicholas Collins was a patient man, reminiscent of her father, but like her father when he acted, he did so decisively. She and Nicholas were compatible on so many levels; physically, emotionally, and intellectually. He didn't take for granted that because she was a woman she was expected to bow down and become subservient. Rather, he thought outside the box and creative thinker that he was, he found ways to out-think her. He proved time and time again that his hands weren't put on backward. He gave as good as he got, and he was open to learning new things; regardless of who taught the lesson. He was by no means a pushover. He had a healthy amount of machismo and ego, but he wasn't arrogant. No, he was everything she had been searching for in a man. He was the complete package.

She picked up the phone and called the pilot. "Maurice, turn the plane around, please. I need to go back to New York City."

A car was waiting for her when she deplaned. She didn't know what the hell made her do such a crazy thing. She could have given it more thought, but it was without question necessary. When she got to the elevator, she took a deep breath and keyed in the code Tyson had obtained for her. As she rode up in the clear box, she watched the gears and mechanism until they were replaced by a man standing just outside the elevator doors. She stepped out and faced him.

"I just spoke with your father. He said, yes, I have his permission to marry you. Your mother wants you to call her about your wedding gown. She says she wants to do this sooner rather than later. Your grandfather says this is one wedding ceremony he's been waiting for a long time to perform. He's reserving the church for the occasion and you shouldn't be late. My father said he's looking forward to being my best man and a grandfather."

"How did you know I would come back?"

"I knew because you couldn't make love with me the way you did last night and not be in love with me. Sooner or later you would realize all the signs were there proving we are right for each other. I was betting on sooner."

"Have you already figured out where we're going for our honeymoon?"

"I have, yes. I called Geo and asked him to round up your wild horses. Benny Alexander says he can get his hands on a decommissioned C-17 Globemaster seaplane. Your grand-aunt said she can give the horses a sedative that should hold them until we can fly them to Argentina. Your maternal grandfather and grandmother said the land, farm, and hacienda are ours as a wedding gift if we want them. There is more than enough land for the horses for the next hundred years. We can bring your grand-aunt and uncles down twice a year to see to the horses' health. I figured we could take a year or two in Argentina, raise wild horses, have babies, and sail. I happen to own a satellite with transponder space, so we can communicate with the outside world if we want to. It gives new meaning to the term telecommuting."

"You've been busy."

"I'm going to be Constantina Anna Alanza Justice's husband. I might as well learn to keep up."

With her eyes on his, she moved in, stood on her toes, and kissed him. "First, you're going to have to take me back to bed. I'm not quite finished with you yet, that's why I came back for you."

"As my wife, you can have me when and where ever you want. I won't accept anything less."

"That's the plan, pal. We'll take care of that detail next week. That's all the time I need to plan our wedding. For now, I'm going to be late for a meeting in Albuquerque, New Mexico, if you don't hurry. You're going to join the mile-high club. My flight is waiting. Ready to go?"

He grinned at her and picked up his already packed duffle bag.

"You packed light."

He shrugged. "I figure where we're going, I won't need a lot of clothes and neither will you," he said guiding her back into the elevator and up against the wall with her thighs up around his hips. The glass doors closed on them locked in a passionate kiss.

About the Author

Ann Jeffries, the critically acclaimed author of the Family Reunion—Wisdom of the Ancestors Series, is a native of Washington, DC. As an only child, she enjoyed the benefits of a private school education at Allen in Asheville, North Carolina, and a public education at the University of Maryland. Ann began writing fiction for her own amusement.

Ms. Jeffries is the recipient of many awards for leadership and public service. A keynote speaker at colleges, universities, conferences, and conventions, she has extensively traveled the North American continent, Asia, and Europe. Among other endeavors, she is an entrepreneur, an avid supporter of public television, a genealogist, and a voracious reader.

Her pride and joy are her family, particularly her Fabulous Four grands. She lives in Maryland and South Carolina.

Follow Ann on her website: www.annjeffries.net, Facebook @Ann Jeffries, on Twitter @Ann Jeffries and her publishing house site: www.newviewliterature.com. Her novels are available in both e-book and paperback. Her autographed copies can be found through annjeffries.net and also un-autographed on Amazon.com and barnesandnoble.com.